D0049523

HIGH FIDELITY

ALSO BY NICK HORNBY

FEVER PITCH

RIVERHEAD BOOKS
NEW YORK 1995

HIGH FIDELITY

NICK HORNBY

RIVERHEAD BOOKS
a division of G. P. Putnam's Sons
Publishers Since 1838
200 Madison Avenue
New York, NY 10016

Published simultaneously in Canada
First American edition published in 1995

Library of Congress Catalog-in-Publication Data
Hornby, Nick.
High fidelity / Nick Hornby.
p. cm
ISBN 1-57322-016-7
I. Title.
PR6058.0689H54 1995 95-8469 CIP
813'.54—dc20

Printed in the United States of America
10 9 8 7 6 5 4 3 2 1

This book is printed on acid-free paper. ♾

BOOK DESIGN BY CLAIRE VACCARO

FOR VIRGINIA

HIGH FIDELITY

THEN . . .

desert-island, all-time, top five most memorable split-ups, in chronological order:

1. Alison Ashworth
2. Penny Hardwick
3. Jackie Allen
4. Charlie Nicholson
5. Sarah Kendrew.

These were the ones that really hurt. Can you see your name in that lot, Laura? I reckon you'd sneak into the top ten, but there's no place for you in the top five; those places are reserved for the kind of humiliations and heartbreaks that you're just not capable of delivering. That probably sounds crueler than it is meant to, but the fact is that we're too old to make each other miserable, and that's a good thing, not a bad thing, so don't take your failure to make the list personally. Those days are gone, and good fucking riddance to them; unhappiness really meant something back then. Now it's just a drag, like a cold or having no money. If you really wanted to mess me up, you should have got to me earlier.

1. Alison Ashworth (1972)

Most nights we used to mess around in the park around the corner from my house. I lived in Hertfordshire, but I might just as well have lived in any suburb in England: it was that sort of suburb, and that sort of park—three minutes away from home, right across the road from a little row of shops (a VG supermarket, a newsagent, an off-license). There was nothing around that could help you get your geographical bearings; if the shops were open (and they closed at five-thirty, and one o'clock on Thursdays, and all day Sunday), you could go into the newsagent's and look for a local newspaper, but even that might not give you much of a clue.

We were twelve or thirteen, and had recently discovered irony—or at least, what I later understood to be irony: we only allowed ourselves to play on the swings and the roundabout and the other kids' stuff rusting away in there if we could do it with a sort of self-conscious ironic detachment. This involved either an imitation of absentmindedness (whistling, or chatting, or fiddling with a cigarette stub or a box of matches usually did the trick) or a flirtation with danger, so we jumped off the swings when they could go no higher, jumped on to the roundabout when it would go no faster, hung on to the end of the swingboat until it reached an almost vertical position. If you could somehow prove that these childish entertainments had the potential to dash your brains out, then playing on them became OK somehow.

We had no irony when it came to girls, though. There was just no time to develop it. One moment they weren't there, not in any form that interested us, anyway, and the next you couldn't miss them; they were everywhere, all over the place. One moment you wanted to clonk them on the head for being your sister, or someone else's sister, and the next you wanted to . . . actually, we didn't know what we wanted next, but it was something, something. Almost overnight, all these sisters (there was no other kind of girl, not yet) had become interesting, *disturbing,* even.

See, what did we have that was any different from what we'd had before? Squeaky voices, but a squeaky voice doesn't do much for you, really—it makes you preposterous, not desirable. And the sprouting pubic hairs were our secret, strictly between us and our Y-fronts, and it would be years before a member of the opposite sex could verify that they were where they should be. Girls, on the other hand, quite clearly had breasts, and, to accompany them, a new way of walking: arms folded over the chest, a posture which simultaneously disguised and drew attention to what had just happened. And then there was makeup and perfume, invariably cheap, and inexpertly, sometimes even comically, applied, but still a quite terrifying sign that things had progressed without us, beyond us, behind our backs.

I started going out with one of them . . . no, that's not right, because I had absolutely no input into the decision-making process. And I can't say that she started going out with me, either: it's that phrase "going out with" that's the problem, because it suggests some sort of parity and equality. What happened was that David Ashworth's sister Alison peeled off from the female pack that gathered every night by the bench and adopted me, tucked me under her arm, and led me away from the swingboat.

I can't remember now how she did this. I don't think I was even aware of it at the time, because halfway through our first kiss, my first kiss, I can recall feeling utterly bewildered, totally unable to explain how Alison Ashworth and I had become so intimate. I wasn't even sure how I'd ended up on her side of the park, away from her brother and Mark Godfrey and the rest, nor how we had separated from her crowd, nor why she tipped her face toward me so that I knew I was supposed to put my mouth on hers. The whole episode defies any rational explanation. But all these things happened, and they happened again, most of them, the following evening, and the evening after that.

What did I think I was doing? What did she think she was doing? When I want to kiss people in that way now, with mouths and tongues and all that, it's because I want other things too: sex, Friday nights at the cinema, company and conversation, fused networks of family and friends, Lemsips brought to me in bed when I am ill, a new pair of ears for my records and CDs, maybe a little boy called Jack and a little girl called Holly or Maisie, I haven't decided yet. But I didn't want any of those things from Alison Ashworth. Not children, because we were children, and not Friday nights at the pictures, because we went Saturday mornings, and not

Lemsips, because my mum did that, not even sex, especially not sex, please God not sex, the filthiest and most terrifying invention of the early seventies.

So what was the significance of the snog? The truth is that there was no significance; we were just lost in the dark. One part imitation (people I had seen kissing by 1972: James Bond, Simon Templar, Napoleon Solo, Barbara Windsor and Sid James or maybe Jim Dale, Elsie Tanner, Omar Sharif and Julie Christie, Elvis, and lots of black-and-white people my mum wanted to watch, although they never waggled their heads from side to side) to one part hormonal slavery to one part peer group pressure (Kevin Bannister and Elizabeth Barnes had been at it for a couple of weeks) to one part blind panic . . . there was no consciousness, no desire and no pleasure, beyond an unfamiliar and moderately pleasant warmth in the gut. We were little animals, which is not to imply that by the end of the week we were tearing our tank tops off; just that, metaphorically speaking, we had begun to sniff each other's bottoms, and we did not find the odor entirely repellent.

But listen, Laura. On the fourth night of our relationship I turned up in the park and Alison was sitting on the bench with her arm around Kevin Bannister, with Elizabeth Barnes nowhere in sight. Nobody—not Alison, or Kevin, or me, or the sexually uninitiated retards hanging off the end of the swingboat said anything at all. I stung, and I blushed, and I suddenly forgot how to walk without being aware of every single part of my body. What to do? Where to go? I didn't want to fight; I didn't want to sit there with the two of them; I didn't want to go home. So, concentrating very hard on the empty packs of cheap cigarettes that marked out the path between the girls and the boys, and not looking up or behind me or to either side, I headed back toward the massed ranks of the single males hanging off the swing-boat. Halfway home, I made my only error of judgment: I stopped and looked at my watch, although for the life of me I don't know what I was attempting to convey, or whom I was trying to kid. What sort of time, after all, could make a thirteen-year-old boy spin away from a girl and toward a playground, palms sweating, heart racing, trying desperately not to cry? Certainly not four o'clock on a late September afternoon.

I scrounged a fag off Mark Godfrey and went and sat on my own on the roundabout.

"Scrubber," spat Alison's brother David, and I smiled gratefully at him.

And that was that. Where had I gone wrong? First night: park, fag, snog. Second night: ditto. Third night: ditto. Fourth night: chucked. OK, OK. Maybe I should have seen the signs. Maybe I was asking for it. Round about that second ditto I should have spotted that we were in a rut, that I had allowed things to fester to the extent that she was on the lookout for someone else. But she could have tried to tell me! She could at least have given me another couple of days to put things right!

My relationship with Alison Ashworth had lasted six hours (the two-hour gap between school and *Nationwide,* times three), so I could hardly claim that I'd got used to having her around, that I didn't know what to do with myself. In fact, I can hardly recall anything about her at all, now.

Long black hair? Maybe. Small? Smaller than me, certainly. Slanted, almost oriental eyes and a dark complexion? That could have been her, or it could have been someone else. Whatever. But if we were doing this list in grief order, rather than chronological order, I'd put it right up there at number two. It would be nice to think that as I've got older times have changed, relationships have become more sophisticated, females less cruel, skins thicker, reactions sharper, instincts more developed. But there still seems to be an element of that evening in everything that has happened to me since; all my other romantic stories seem to be a scrambled version of that first one. Of course, I have never had to take that long walk again, and my ears have not burned with quite the same fury, and I have never had to count the packs of cheap cigarettes in order to avoid mocking eyes and floods of tears . . . not really, not actually, not as such. It just feels that way, sometimes.

2. Penny Hardwick (1973)

Penny Hardwick was a nice girl, and, nowadays, I'm all for nice girls, although then I wasn't so sure. She had a nice mum and dad, and a nice house, detached, with a garden and a tree and a fishpond, and a nice girl's haircut (she was blond, and she kept her hair a sort of sporty, clean, wholesome, form-captain midlength), and nice, smiling eyes, and a nice younger sister, who smiled politely when I rang the doorbell and kept out of the way when we wanted her to. She had nice manners—my mum loved her—and she always got nice school reports. Penny was nice-looking, and her top five recording artists were Carly Simon, Carole King, James Taylor, Cat Stevens, and Elton John. Lots of people liked her. She was so nice, in fact, that she wouldn't let me put my hand underneath or even on top of her bra, and so I was finished with her, although obviously I didn't tell her why. She cried, and I hated her for it, because she made me feel bad.

I can imagine what sort of person Penny Hardwick became: a nice person. I know that she went to college, did well, and landed a job as a radio producer for the BBC. I would guess that she is bright, and serious-minded, maybe too much so, sometimes, and ambitious, but not in a way that makes you want to vomit; she was a version of all these things when we went out, and at another stage in my life I would have found all these virtues attractive. Then, however, I wasn't interested in qualities, just breasts, and she was therefore no good to me.

I would like to be able to tell you that we had long, interesting conversations, and that we remained firm friends throughout our teenage years—she would have made someone a lovely friend—but I don't think we ever talked. We went to the pictures, to parties and to discos, and we wrestled. We wrestled in her bedroom, and my bedroom, and her living room, and my living room, and in bedrooms at parties, and in living rooms at parties, and in the summer we wrestled on various plots of grass. We were wrestling over the same old issue. Sometimes I got so bored of trying to touch her breasts that I would try to touch her between her legs, a gesture that had a sort of self-parodying wit about it: it was like trying to borrow a fiver, getting turned down, and asking to borrow fifty quid instead.

These were the questions boys asked other boys at my school (a school that contained only boys): "Are you getting any?"; "Does she let you have any?"; "How much does she let you have?"; and so on. Sometimes the questions were derisory, and expected the answer "No": "You're not getting anything, are you?"; "You haven't even had a bit of tit, have you?" Girls, meanwhile, had to be content with the passive voice. Penny used the expression "broken into": "I don't want to be broken into yet," she would explain patiently and maybe a little sadly (she seemed to understand that one day—but not now—she would have to give in, and when it happened she wouldn't like it) when she removed my hand from her chest for the one hundred thousandth time. Attack and defense, invasion and repulsion . . . it was as if breasts were little pieces of property that had been unlawfully annexed by the opposite sex—they were rightfully ours and we wanted them back.

Luckily, however, there were traitors, fifth columnists, in the opposing camp. Some boys knew of other boys whose girlfriends would "let" them do anything; sometimes these girls were supposed to have actively assisted in their own molestation. Nobody had ever heard of a girl who had gone as far as undressing, or even removing or loosening undergarments, of course. That would have been taking collaboration too far. As I understood it, these girls had simply positioned themselves in a way that encouraged access. "She tucks her stomach in and everything," Clive Stevens remarked approvingly of his brother's girlfriend; it took me nearly a year to work out the import of this maneuver. No wonder I still remember the stomach-tucker's first name (Judith); there's a part of me that still wants to meet her.

. . .

Read any women's magazine and you'll see the same complaint over and over again: men—those little boys ten or twenty or thirty years on—are hopeless in bed. They are not interested in "foreplay"; they have no desire to stimulate the erogenous zones of the opposite sex; they are selfish, greedy, clumsy, unsophisticated. These complaints, you can't help feeling, are kind of ironic. Back then, all we wanted was foreplay, and girls weren't interested. They didn't want to be touched, caressed, stimulated, aroused; in fact, they used to thump us if we tried. It's not really very surprising, then, that we're not much good at all that. We spent two or three long and extremely formative years being told very forcibly not even to think about it. Between the ages of fourteen and twenty-four, foreplay changes from being something that boys want to do and girls don't, to something that women want and men can't be bothered with. (Or so they say. Me, I like foreplay—mostly because the times when all I wanted to do was touch are alarmingly fresh in my mind.) The perfect match, if you ask me, is between the *Cosmo* woman and the fourteen-year-old boy.

If somebody had asked me why I was so hell-bent on grabbing a piece of Penny Hardwick's chest, I wouldn't have known what to say. And if somebody were to ask Penny why she was so hell-bent on stopping me, I'll bet she'd be stumped for an answer too. What was in it for me? I wasn't asking for any sort of reciprocation, after all. Why didn't she want her erogenous zones stimulated? I have no idea. All I know is that you could, if you wanted to, find the answers to all sorts of difficult questions buried in that terrible war-torn interregnum between the first pubic hair and the first soiled Trojan.

And in any case, maybe I didn't want to put my hand under Penny's bra as much as I thought. Maybe other people wanted me to touch her more than I did. After a couple of months of fighting on sofas all over town with Penny, I'd had enough: I had admitted, unwisely in retrospect, to a friend that I wasn't getting anywhere, and my friend had told some other friends, and I was the butt of a number of cruel and unpleasant jokes. I gave Penny one last try, in my bedroom while my mum and dad were at the town hall watching a local dramatic society interpretation of *Toad of Toad Hall;* I used a degree of force that would have outraged and terrified an adult female, but got nowhere, and when I walked her home we hardly spoke.

I was offhand with her the next time we went out, and when she went to kiss me at the end of the evening, I shrugged her off. "What's the point?" I asked her. "It never goes anywhere." The time after that she asked whether I still wanted to see her, and I looked the other way. We had been going out for three months, which was as near to a permanent relationship as you could get in the fourth year. (Her mum and dad had even met my mum and dad. They liked each other.) She cried, then, and I loathed her for making me feel guilty, and for making me finish with her.

I went out with a girl called Kim, who I knew for a fact had already been invaded, and who (I was correct in assuming) wouldn't object to being invaded again. Penny went out with Chris Thomson from my class, a boy who had had more girlfriends than all the rest of us put together. I was out of my depth, and so was she. One morning, maybe three weeks after my last grapple with Penny, Thomson came roaring into our form room. "Oi, Fleming, you spastic. Guess who I knobbed last night?"

I felt the room spin round.

"You never got so much as a bit of tit in three months, and I shagged her the first week!"

I believed him; everyone knew that he got whatever he wanted from whomever he saw. I had been humiliated, beaten, outperformed; I felt stupid, and small, and much, much younger than this unpleasant, oversized, big-mouthed moron. It shouldn't have mattered so much. Thomson was in a league of his own when it came to matters of the lower body, and there were plenty of little jerky creeps in 4b who had never so much as put their arm around a girl. Even my side of the debate, inaudible though it was, must have appeared impossibly sophisticated to them. I wasn't losing that much face. But I still couldn't understand what had happened. How had this transformation in Penny been effected? How had Penny gone from being a girl who wouldn't do anything to a girl who would do everything there was to do? Maybe it was best not to think about it too hard; I didn't want to feel sorry for anybody else except me.

I expect Penny turned out all right, and I know I turned out all right, and I would suspect that even Chris Thomson isn't the world's worst person. At least, it's hard to imagine him skidding into his place of work, his bank or his insurance office or car showroom, chucking his briefcase down and informing a colleague with raucous glee that he has "knobbed" said colleague's wife. (It is easy enough to imagine him knobbing the wife, however. He looked like a wife-knobber, even then.) Women who disapprove of men—and there's plenty to disapprove of—should remember how we started out, and how far we have had to travel.

3. Jackie Allen (1975)

Jackie Allen was my friend Phil's girlfriend, and I pinched her off him, slowly, patiently, over a period of months. It wasn't easy. It required a great deal of time, application, and deception. Phil and Jackie started going out together around the same time as Penny and I did, except they went on and on: through the giggly, hormonal fourth form, and the end-of-the-world "O"-level and school-leaving fifth, and on into the mock-adult sobriety of the lower sixth. They were our golden couple, our Paul and Linda, our Newman and Woodward, living proof that in a faithless, fickle world, it was possible to grow old, or at least older, without chopping and changing every few weeks.

I'm not too sure why I wanted to fuck it all up for them, and for everyone who needed them to go out together. You know when you see T-shirts piled up in a clothes shop, beautifully folded and color-coded, and you buy one? It never looks the same when you take it home. It only looked good in the shop, you realize too late, because it had its mates around it. Well, it was kind of like that. I had hoped that if I went out with Jackie, then some of that elder-stateswoman dignity would rub off on me, but of course without Phil, she didn't have any. (If that's what I wanted, I should perhaps have looked for a way to go out with both of them, but that sort of thing is hard enough to pull off when you're an adult; at seventeen it could be enough to get you stoned to death.)

Phil started working in a men's boutique on Saturdays, and I moved in. Those of us who didn't work, or who, like me, worked after school but not on weekends, met on Saturday afternoons to walk up and down High Street, spend too much time and too much money in Harlequin Records, and "treat ourselves" (we had somehow picked up our mothers' vocabulary of postwar abstention) to a filter coffee, which we regarded as the last word in French cool. Sometimes we called in to see Phil; sometimes he let me use his staff discount. It didn't stop me from screwing his girlfriend behind his back.

I knew, because both Alison and Penny had taught me, that busting up with someone could be miserable, but I didn't know that getting off with someone could be miserable too. But Jackie and I were miserable in a thrilling, grown-up way. We met in secret and phoned each other in secret and had sex in secret and said things like "What are we going to do?" in secret and talked about how nice it would be when we didn't have to do things in secret anymore. I never really thought about whether that was true or not. There wasn't time.

I tried not to run Phil down too much—I felt bad enough as it was, what with screwing his girlfriend and all. But it became unavoidable, because when Jackie expressed doubts about him, I had to nurture those doubts as if they were tiny, sickly kittens, until eventually they became sturdy, healthy grievances, with their own cat doors, which allowed them to wander in and out of our conversation at will.

And then one night at a party I saw Phil and Jackie huddled together in a corner, and Phil was obviously distressed, pale and near to tears, and then he went home, and the next morning she phoned up and asked if I wanted to go out for a walk, and we were away, and we weren't doing things in secret anymore; and we lasted about three weeks.

You'd say that this was childish, Laura. You'd say that it is stupid of me to compare Rob and Jackie with Rob and Laura, who are in their mid-thirties, established, living together. You'd say that adult adultery beats teenage adultery hands down, but you'd be wrong. I have been one point of a triangle several times since then, but that first point was the sharpest. Phil never spoke to me again; our Saturday shopping crowd wouldn't have much to do with us either. My mum had a phone call from Phil's mum. School was, for a few weeks, uncomfortable.

Compare and contrast with what happens if I make that sort of mess now: I can go to different pubs and clubs, leave the answering machine on, go out more, stay in more, fiddle around with my social compasses and draw a new circle of friends (and anyway, my friends are never her friends, whoever she might be), avoid all contact with disapproving parents. That sort of anonymity was unavailable then, though. You had to stand there and take it, whatever it was.

What perplexed me most of all was the feeling of flat disappointment that overtook me when Jackie called me that Sunday morning. I couldn't understand it. I had been plotting this capture for months, and when capitulation came I felt nothing—less than nothing, even. I couldn't tell Jackie this, obviously, but on the other hand, I was quite unable to show the enthusiasm I felt she needed, so I decided to have her name tattooed down my right arm.

I don't know. Scarring myself for life seemed much easier than having to tell Jackie that it had all been a grotesque mistake, that I'd just been messing about; if I could show her the tattoo, my peculiar logic ran, I wouldn't have to bother straining after words that were beyond me. I should explain that I am not a tattoo kind of guy; I am, and was, neither rock'n'roll go-to-hell decadent or wrestling-team muscular. But there was a disastrous fashion for them at our school around that time, and I know for a fact that several men now in their mid-thirties, accountants and schoolteachers, personnel managers and computer programmers, have terrible messages ("MUFC KICK TO KILL," "LYNYRD SKYNYRD") from that era burned into their flesh.

I was just going to have a discreet "J ♡ R" done on my upper arm, but Victor the tattooist wasn't having any of it.

"Which one is she? 'J' or 'R'?"

" 'J.' "

"And how long have you been seeing this 'J' bird, then?"

I was frightened by the aggressive masculinity of the parlor—the other customers (who were all firmly wrestling-team muscular, and seemed inexplicably amused to see me), the nude women on the walls, the lurid examples of services offered, most of which were conveniently located on Victor's forearms, even Victor's mildly offensive language.

"Long enough."

"I'll fucking be the judge of that, not you."

This struck me as an odd way to do business, but I decided to save this observation for another time.

"A couple of months."

"And you're going to marry her, are you? Or have you knocked her up?"

"No. Neither."

"So you're just going out? You're not stuck with her?"

"Yeah."

"And how did you meet her?"

"She used to go out with a friend of mine."

"Did she now. And when did they break up?"

"Saturday."

"Saturday." He laughed like a drain. "I don't want your mum in here moaning at me. Fuck off out of it."

I fucked off out of it.

Victor was spot on, of course; in fact, I have often been tempted to seek him out when I have been plagued by diseases of the heart. He'd be able to tell me in ten seconds whether someone was worth a tattoo or not. But even after Phil and Jackie were ecstatically and tearfully reunited, things didn't go back to the way they had been. Some of the girls at her school, and some of the boys at ours, presumed that Jackie had been using me to renegotiate the terms of her relationship with Phil, and the Saturday shopping afternoons were never the same again. And we no longer admired people who had gone out together for a long time; we were sarcastic about them, and they were even sarcastic about themselves. In a few short weeks, mock-marital status had ceased to be something to aspire to, and had become a cause for scorn. At seventeen, we were becoming as embittered and as unromantic as our parents.

See, Laura? You won't change everything around like Jackie could. It's happened too many times, to both of us; we'll just go back to the friends and the pubs and the life we had before, and leave it at that, and nobody will notice the difference, probably.

4. Charlie Nicholson (1977–1979)

I met Charlie at tech: I was doing a media studies course, and she was studying design, and when I first saw her I realized she was the sort of girl I had wanted to meet ever since I'd been old enough to want to meet girls. She was tall, with blond cropped hair (she said she knew some people who were at St. Martin's with some friends of Johnny Rotten, but I was never introduced to them), and she looked different and dramatic and exotic. Even her name seemed to me dramatic and different and exotic, because up until then I had lived in a world where girls had girls' names, and not very interesting ones at that. She talked a lot, so that you didn't have those terrible, strained silences that seemed to characterize most of my sixth-form dates, and when she talked she said remarkably interesting things—about her course, about my course, about music, about films and books and politics.

And she liked me. She liked *me. She* liked me. She *liked* me. Or at least, I think she did. I *think* she did. Etc. I have never been entirely sure what it is women like about me, but I know that ardor helps (even I know how difficult it is to resist someone who finds you irresistible), and I was certainly ardent: I didn't make a nuisance of myself, not until the end, anyway, and I never outstayed my welcome, not while there was still a welcome to be outstayed; but I was kind and sincere and thoughtful and devoted and I remembered things about her and I told her she was beautiful and bought her little presents that usually referred to a conversation we had had recently. None of this was an effort, of course, and none of it was done with any sense of calculation: I found it easy to remember things about her, because I didn't think about anything else, and I really did think she was beautiful, and I would not have been able to prevent myself from buying her little presents, and I did not have to feign devotion. There was no effort involved. So when one of Charlie's friends, a girl called Kate, said wistfully one lunchtime that she wished she could find somebody like me, I was surprised and thrilled. Thrilled because Charlie was listening, and it didn't do me any harm, but surprised because all I had done was act out of self-interest. And yet this was enough, it seemed, to turn me into someone desirable. Weird.

And, anyway, by moving to London I had made it easier to be liked by girls. At home, most people had known me, or my mum and dad—or had known somebody who knew me, or my mum and dad—when I was little, and consequently I'd always had the uncomfortable feeling that my boyhood was about to be exposed to the world. How could you take a girl out for an underage drink in a pub when you knew you had a scout uniform still hanging in your closet? Why would a girl want to kiss you if she knew (or knew somebody who knew) that just a few years before, you had insisted on sewing souvenir patches from the Norfolk Broads and Exmoor on your anorak? There were pictures all over my parents' house of me with big ears and disastrous clothes, sitting on tractors, clapping with glee as miniature trains drew into miniature stations; and though later on, distressingly, girlfriends found these pictures cute, it all seemed too close for comfort then. It had only taken me six years to change from a ten-year-old to a sixteen-year-old; surely six years wasn't long enough for a transformation of that magnitude? When I was sixteen, that anorak with the patches on was just a couple of sizes too small.

Charlie hadn't known me as a ten-year-old, however, and she didn't know anybody who knew me, either. She knew me only as a young adult. I was already old enough to vote when I met her; I was old enough to spend the night with her, the whole night, in her hall of residence, and have opinions, and buy her a drink in a pub, secure in the knowledge that my driving license with its scrambled proof of age was in my pocket . . . and I was old enough to have a history. At home I didn't have a history, just stuff that everybody already knew, and that, therefore, wasn't worth repeating.

But I still felt a fraud. I was like all those people who suddenly shaved their heads and said they'd *always* been punks, they'd been punks before punk was even thought of: I felt as though I was going to be found out at any moment, that somebody was going to burst into the college bar brandishing one of the anorak photos and yelling, "Rob used to be a *boy!* A little *lad!*," and Charlie would see it and pack me in. It never occurred to me that she probably had a whole pile of books about ponies and some ridiculous party dresses hidden away at her parents' place in St. Albans. As far as I was concerned, she had been born with enormous earrings, drainpipe jeans, and an incredibly sophisticated enthusiasm for the works of some guy who used to splodge orange paint around.

We went out for two years, and for every single minute I felt as though I was standing on a dangerously narrow ledge. I couldn't ever get comfortable, if you know what I mean; there was no room to stretch out and relax. I was depressed by the lack of flamboyance in my wardrobe. I was fretful about my abilities as a lover. I couldn't understand what she saw in the orange-paint guy, however many times she explained. I worried that I was never ever going to be able to say anything interesting or amusing to her about anything at all. I was intimidated by the other men in her design course, and became convinced that she was going to go off with one of them. She went off with one of them.

I lost the plot for a while then. And I lost the subplot, the script, the soundtrack, the intermission, my popcorn, the credits, and the exit sign. I hung around Charlie's hall of residence until some friends of hers caught me and threatened to give me a good kicking. I decided to kill Marco (Marco!), the guy she went off with, and spent long hours in the middle of the night working out how to do it, although whenever I bumped into him I just muttered a greeting and sloped off. I did a spot of shoplifting, the precise motivation for which escapes me now. I took an overdose of Valium, and stuck a finger down my throat within a minute. I wrote endless letters to her, some of which I posted, and scripted endless conversations, none of which we had. And when I came around, after a couple of months of darkness, I found to my surprise that I had flunked my course and was working in Record and Tape Exchange in Camden.

Everything happened so fast. I had kind of hoped that my adulthood would be long and meaty and instructive, but it all took place in those two years; sometimes it seems as though everything and everyone that have happened to me since were just minor distractions. Some people never got over the sixties, or the war, or the night their band opened for the Rolling Stones at the Marquee, and spend the rest of their days walking backwards; I never really got over Charlie. That was when the important stuff, the stuff that defines me, went on.

Some of my favorite songs: "Only Love Can Break Your Heart" by Neil Young; "Last Night I Dreamed That Somebody Loved Me" by the Smiths; "Call Me" by Aretha Franklin; "I Don't Want to Talk About It" by anybody. And then there's "Love Hurts" and "When Love Breaks Down" and "How Can You Mend a Broken Heart" and "The Speed of the Sound of Loneliness" and "She's Gone" and "I Just Don't Know What to Do with Myself" and . . . some of these songs I have listened to around once a week, on average (three hundred times in the first month, every now and again thereafter), since I was sixteen or nineteen or twenty-one. How can that not leave you bruised somewhere? How can that not turn you into the sort of person liable to break into little bits when your first love goes all wrong? What came first—the music or the misery? Did I listen to music because I was miserable? Or was I miserable because I listened to music? Do all those records turn you into a melancholy person?

People worry about kids playing with guns, and teenagers watching violent videos; we are scared that some sort of culture of violence will take them over. Nobody worries about kids listening to thousands—literally thousands—of songs about broken hearts and rejection and pain and misery and loss. The unhappiest people I know, romantically speaking, are the ones who like pop music the most; and I don't know whether pop music has caused this unhappiness, but I do know that they've been listening to the sad songs longer than they've been living the unhappy lives.

Anyway. Here's how not to plan a career: (a) split up with girlfriend; (b) junk college; (c) go to work in record shop; (d) stay in record shops for rest of life. You see those pictures of people in Pompeii and you think, how weird: one quick game of dice after your tea and you're frozen, and that's how people remember you for the next few thousand years. Suppose it was the first game of dice you've ever played? Suppose you were only doing it to keep your friend Augustus company? Suppose you'd just at that moment finished a brilliant poem or something? Wouldn't it be annoying to be commemorated as a dice player? Sometimes I look at my shop (because I haven't let the grass grow under my feet the last fourteen years! About ten years ago I borrowed the money to start my own!), and at my regular Saturday punters, and I know exactly how those inhabitants of Pompeii must feel, if they could feel anything (although the fact that they can't is kind of the point of them). I'm stuck in this pose, this shop-managing pose, forever, because of a few short weeks in 1979 when I went a bit potty for a while. It could be worse, I guess; I could have walked into an army recruiting office, or the nearest Slaughterhouse. But even so, I feel as though I made a face and the wind changed, and now I have to go through life grimacing in this horrible way.

Eventually I stopped posting the letters; a few months after that I stopped writing them, too. I still fantasized about killing Marco, although the imagined deaths became swifter (I allow him a brief moment to register, and then BLAM!)—I didn't go in quite so much for the sicko slow stuff. I started sleeping with people again, although every one of these affairs I regarded as a fluke, a one-off, nothing likely to alter my dismal self-perception. (And, like James Stewart in *Vertigo,* I had developed a "type": cropped blond hair, arty, dizzy, garrulous, which led to some disastrous mistakes.) I stopped drinking so much, I stopped listening to song lyrics with quite the same morbid fascination (for a while, I regarded just about any song in which somebody had lost somebody else as spookily relevant, which, as that covers the whole of pop music, and as I worked in a record shop, meant I felt pretty spooked more or less the whole time), I stopped constructing the killer one-liners that left Charlie writhing on the floor with regret and self-loathing.

I made sure, however, that I was never in anything, work or relationships, too deep: I convinced myself that I might get the call from Charlie at any moment, and would therefore have to leap into action. I was even unsure about opening my own shop, just in case Charlie wanted me to go abroad with her and I wasn't able to move quickly enough; marriage, mortgages, and fatherhood were out of the question. I was realistic too: every now and again I updated Charlie's life, imagining a whole series of disastrous events (She's living with Marco! They've bought a place together! She's married him! She's pregnant! She's had a little girl!), just to keep myself on my toes, events which required a whole series of readjustments and conversions to keep my fantasies alive. (She'll have nowhere to go when they split! She'll *really* have nowhere to go when they split, and I'll have to support her financially! Marriage'll wake her up! Taking on another man's kid will show her what a great guy I am!) There was no news I couldn't handle; there was nothing she and Marco could do that would convince me that it wasn't all just a stage we were going through. They are together still, for all I know, and, as of today, I am unattached again.

5. Sarah Kendrew (1984–1986)

The lesson I learned from the Charlie débâcle is that you've got to punch your weight. Charlie was out of my class: too pretty, too smart, too witty, too much. What am I? Average. A middleweight. Not the brightest bloke in the world, but certainly not the dimmest: I have read books like *The Unbearable Lightness of Being* and *Love in the Time of Cholera,* and understood them, I think (they were about girls, right?), but I don't like them very much; my all-time top five favorite books are *The Big Sleep* by Raymond Chandler, *Red Dragon* by Thomas Harris, *Sweet Soul Music* by Peter Guralnick, *The Hitchhiker's Guide to the Galaxy* by Douglas Adams, and, I don't know, something by William Gibson, or Kurt Vonnegut. I read the *Guardian* and the *Observer,* as well as the *New Musical Express* and music glossies; I am not averse to going down to Camden to watch subtitled films (top five subtitled films: *Betty Blue, Subway, Tie Me Up! Tie Me Down!, The Vanishing, Diva*), although on the whole I prefer American films. (Top five American films, and therefore the best films ever made: *The Godfather, The Godfather Part II, Taxi Driver, Goodfellas,* and *Reservoir Dogs.*)

I'm OK-looking; in fact, if you put, say, Mel Gibson on one end of the looks spectrum and, say, Berky Edmonds from school, whose grotesque ugliness was legendary, on the other, then I reckon I'd be on Mel's side, just. A girlfriend once told me that I looked a bit like Peter Gabriel, and he's not too bad, is he? I'm average height, not slim, not fat, no unsightly facial hair. I keep myself clean, wear jeans and T-shirts and a leather jacket more or less all the time apart from in the summer, when I leave the leather jacket at home. I vote Labour. I have a pile of classic comedy videos—*Monty Python, Fawlty Towers, Cheers,* and so on. I can see what feminists are on about, most of the time, but not the radical ones.

My genius, if I can call it that, is to combine a whole load of averageness into one compact frame. I'd say that there were millions like me, but there aren't, really: lots of blokes have impeccable music taste but don't read, lots of blokes read but are really fat, lots of blokes are sympathetic to feminism but have stupid beards, lots of blokes have a Woody Allen sense of humor but look like Woody Allen. Lots of blokes drink too much, lots of blokes behave stupidly when they drive cars, lots of blokes get into fights, or show off about money, or take drugs. I don't do any of these things, really; if I do OK with women, it's not because of the virtues I have, but because of the shadows I don't have.

Even so, you've got to know when you're out of your depth. I was out of my depth with Charlie; after her, I was determined never to get out of my depth again, and so for five years, until I met Sarah, I just paddled around in the shallow end. Charlie and I didn't *match.* Marco and Charlie matched; Sarah and I matched. Sarah was average-attractive (smallish, slim, nice big brown eyes, crooked teeth, shoulder-length dark hair that always seemed to need a cut no matter how often she went to the hairdresser's), and she wore clothes that were the same as mine, more or less. All-time top five favorite recording artists: Madness, Eurythmics, Bob Dylan, Joni Mitchell, Bob Marley. All-time top five favorite films: *National Velvet, Diva* (hey!), *Gandhi, Missing, Wuthering Heights.*

And she was sad, in the original sense of the word. She had been dumped a couple of years before by a sort of male equivalent to Charlie, a guy called Michael who wanted to be something at the BBC. (He never made it, the wanker, and each day we never saw him on TV or heard him on the radio, something inside us rejoiced.) He was her moment, just as Charlie was mine, and when they split, Sarah had sworn off men for a while, just as I had sworn off women. It made sense to swear off together, to pool our loathing of the opposite sex and get to share a bed with someone at the same time. Our friends were all paired off, our careers seemed to have hardened into permanence, we were frightened of being left alone for the rest of our lives. Only people of a certain disposition are frightened of being alone for the rest of their lives at twenty-six; we were of that disposition. Everything seemed much later than it was, and after a few months she moved in with me.

We couldn't fill a room. I don't mean that we didn't have enough stuff: she had loads of books (she was an English teacher), and I had thousands of records, and the flat is pretty poky anyway—I've lived here for over ten years, and most days I feel like a cartoon dog in a kennel. I mean that neither of us seemed loud enough, or powerful enough, so that when we were together, I was conscious of how the only space we occupied was that taken up by our bodies. We couldn't *project* the way some couples can.

Sometimes we tried, when we were out with people even quieter than we; we never talked about why we suddenly became shriller and louder, but I'm sure we both knew that it happened. We did it to compensate for the fact that life was going on elsewhere, that somewhere Michael and Charlie were together, having a better time than we with people more glamorous than us, and making a noise was a sort of defiant gesture, a futile but necessary last stand. (You can see this everywhere you go: young, middle-class people whose lives are beginning to disappoint them making too much noise in restaurants and clubs and wine bars. "Look at me! I'm not as boring as you think I am! I know how to have fun!" Tragic. I'm glad I learned to stay home and sulk.) Ours was a marriage of convenience as cynical and as mutually advantageous as any, and I really thought that I might spend my life with her. I wouldn't have minded. She was OK.

There's a joke I saw in a sitcom once—*Man About the House,* maybe?—a terribly unsound joke, wherein a guy takes a really fat girl with specs out for the evening, gets her drunk, and makes a move on her when he takes her home. "I'm not that kind of girl!" she shrieks. He looks at her aghast. "But . . . but you *must* be," the bloke says. It made me laugh when I was sixteen, but I didn't think about it again until Sarah told me she had met someone else. "But . . . but you *can't* have," I wanted to splutter. I don't mean that Sarah was unfanciable—she wasn't, by any means, and anyway, this other guy must have fancied her. I just mean that her meeting someone else was contrary to the whole spirit of our arrangement. All we really had in common (our shared admiration of *Diva* did not, if truth be told, last us much beyond the first few months) was that we had been dumped by people, and that on the whole we were against dumping—we were fervent antidumpers. So how come I got dumped?

I was being unrealistic, of course. You run the risk of losing anyone who is worth spending time with, unless you are so paranoid about loss that you choose someone unlosable, somebody who could not possibly appeal to anybody else at all. If you're going to go in for this stuff at all, you have to live with the possibility that it won't work out, that somebody called Marco, say, or in this case, Tom, is going to come along and upset you. But I didn't see it like that at the time. All I saw then was that I'd moved down a division and that it still hadn't worked out, and this seemed a cause for a great deal of misery and self-pity.

And then I met you, Laura, and we lived together, and now you've moved out. But, you know, you're not offering me anything *new* here; if you want to force your way onto the list, you'll have to do better than this. I'm not as vulnerable as I was when Alison or Charlie dumped me, you haven't changed the whole structure of my daily life like Jackie did, you haven't made me feel bad about myself like Penny did (and there's no way you can humiliate me, like Chris Thomson did), and I'm more robust than I was when Sarah went—I know, despite all the gloom and self-doubt that bubbles up from the deep when you get dumped, that you did not represent my last and best chance of a relationship. So, you know. Nice try. Close, but no cigar. See you around.

N O W ...

ONE

LAURA

leaves first thing Monday morning with a hold-all and a carrier bag. It's sobering, really, to see how little she is taking with her, this woman who loves her things, her teapots and her books and her prints and the little sculpture she bought in India: I look at the bag and think, Jesus, this is how much she doesn't want to live with me.

We hug at the front door, and she's crying a little.

"I don't really know what I'm doing," she says.

"I can see that," I say, which is sort of a joke and sort of not. "You don't have to go now. You can stay until whenever."

"Thanks. But we've done the hard part now. I might as well, you know . . ."

"Well, stay for tonight, then."

But she just grimaces, and reaches for the door handle.

It's a clumsy exit. She hasn't got a free hand, but she tries to open the door anyway and can't, so I do it for her, but I'm in the way, so I have to go through on to the landing to let her out, and she has to prop the door open because I haven't got a key, and I have to squeeze back past her to catch the door before it shuts behind her. And that's it.

I regret to say that this great feeling, part liberation and part nervous excitement, enters me somewhere around my toes and sweeps through me in a great wave. I have felt this before, and I know it doesn't mean that much—confusingly, for example, it doesn't mean that I'm going to feel ecstatically happy for the next few weeks. But I do know that I should work with it, enjoy it while it lasts.

This is how I commemorate my return to the Kingdom of the Single: I sit down in my chair, the one that will stay here with me, and pick bits of the stuffing out of the arm; I light a cigarette, even though it is still early and I don't really feel like one, simply because I am now free to smoke in the flat whenever I want, without rows; I wonder whether I have already met the next person I will sleep with, or whether it will be someone currently unknown to me; I wonder what she looks like, and whether we'll do it here, or at her place, and what that place will be like; I decide to have a Chess Records logo painted on the sitting room wall. (There was a shop in Camden that had them all—Chess, Stax, Motown, Trojan—stenciled onto the brickwork beside the entrance, and it looked brilliant. Maybe I could get hold of the guy who did that and ask him to do smaller versions here.) I feel OK. I feel good. I go to work.

. . .

My shop is called Championship Vinyl. I sell punk, blues, soul, and R&B, a bit of ska, some indie stuff, some sixties pop—everything for the serious record collector, as the ironically old-fashioned writing in the window says. We're in a quiet street in Holloway, carefully placed to attract the bare minimum of window-shoppers; there's no reason to come here at all, unless you live here, and the people that live here don't seem terribly interested in my Stiff Little Fingers white label (twenty-five quid to you—I paid seventeen for it in 1986) or my mono copy of *Blonde on Blonde.*

I get by because of the people who make a special effort to shop here Saturdays—young men, always young men, with John Lennon specs and leather jackets and armfuls of square carrier bags—and because of the mail order: I advertise in the back of the glossy rock magazines, and get letters from young men, always young men, in Manchester and Glasgow and Ottowa, young men who seem to spend a disproportionate amount of their time looking for deleted Smiths singles and "ORIGINAL NOT RERELEASED" underlined Frank Zappa albums. They're as close to being mad as makes no difference.

I'm late to work, and when I get there Dick is already leaning against the door reading a book. He's thirty-one years old, with long, greasy black hair; he's wearing a Sonic Youth T-shirt, a black leather jacket that is trying manfully to suggest that it has seen better days, even though he only bought it a year ago, and a Walkman with a pair of ludicrously large headphones which obscure not only his ears but half his face. The book is a paperback biography of Lou Reed. The carrier bag by his feet—which really has seen better days—advertises a violently fashionable American independent record label; he went to a great deal of trouble to get hold of it, and he gets very nervous when we go anywhere near it. He uses it to carry tapes around; he has heard most of the music in the shop, and would rather bring new stuff to work—tapes from friends, bootlegs he has ordered through the post—than waste his time listening to anything for a second time. ("Want to come to the pub for lunch, Dick?" Barry or I ask him a couple of times a week. He looks mournfully at his little stack of cassettes and sighs. "I'd love to, but I've got all these to get through.")

"Good morning, Richard."

He fumbles nervously with the giant headphones, gets one side stuck around his ear, and the other side falls over one eye.

"Oh, hi. Hi, Rob."

"Sorry I'm late."

"No, no problem."

"Good weekend?"

I unlock the shop as he scrabbles around for his stuff.

"All right, yeah, OK. I found the first Liquorice Comfits album in Camden. The one on Testament of Youth. It was never released here. Japanese import only."

"Great." I don't know what the fuck he's talking about.

"I'll tape it for you."

"Thanks."

" 'Cos you liked their second one, you said. *Pop, girls, etc.* The one with Hattie Jacques on the cover. You didn't see the cover, though. You just had the tape I did for you."

I'm sure he did tape a Liquorice Comfits album for me, and I'm sure I said I liked it, too. My flat is full of tapes Dick has made me, most of which I've never played.

"How about you, anyway? Your weekend? Any good? No good?"

I cannot imagine what kind of conversation we'd have if I were to tell Dick about my weekend. He'd probably just crumble to dust if I explained that Laura had left. Dick's not big on that sort of thing; in fact, if I were ever to confess anything of a remotely personal nature—that I had a mother and father, say, or that I'd been to school when I was younger—I reckon he'd just blush, and stammer, and ask if I'd heard the new Lemonheads album.

"Somewhere in between. Good bits and bad bits."

He nods. This is obviously the right answer.

The shop smells of stale smoke, damp, and plastic dust-covers, and it's narrow and dingy and dirty and overcrowded, partly because that's what I wanted—this is what record shops should look like, and only Phil Collins's fans bother with those that look as clean and wholesome as a suburban Habitat—and partly because I can't get it together to clean or redecorate it.

There are browser racks on each side, and a couple more in the window, and CDs and cassettes on the walls in glass cases, and that's more or less the size of it; it's just about big enough, provided we don't get any customers, so most days it's just about big enough. The stockroom at the back is bigger than the shop part in the front, but we have no stock, really, just a few piles of secondhand records that nobody can be bothered to price up, so the stockroom is mostly for messing about in. I'm sick of the sight of the place, to be honest.

Some days I'm afraid I'll go berserk, rip the Elvis Costello mobile down from the ceiling, throw the "Country Artists (Male) A–K" rack out into the street, go off to work in a Virgin Megastore, and never come back.

Dick puts a record on, some West Coast psychedelic thing, and makes us some coffee while I go through the post; and then we drink the coffee; and then he tries to stuff some records into the bulging, creaking browser racks while I parcel up a couple of mail orders; and then I have a look at the *Guardian* quick crossword while he reads some American import rock magazine; then he has a look at the *Guardian* quick crossword while I read the American import magazine; and before we know it, it's my turn to make the coffee.

At about half-past eleven, an Irish drunk called Johnny stumbles in. He comes to see us about three times a week, and his visits have become choreographed and scripted routines that neither he nor I would want to change. In a hostile and unpredictable world, we rely on each other to provide something to count on.

"Fuck off, Johnny," I tell him.

"So my money's no good to you?" he says.

"You haven't got any money. And we haven't got anything that you want to buy."

This is his cue to launch into an enthusiastic rendition of Dana's "All Kinds of Everything," which is my cue to come out from behind the counter and lead him back toward the door, which is his cue to hurl himself at one of the browser racks, which is my cue to open the door with one hand, loosen his grip on the rack with the other, and push him out.

We devised these moves a couple of years ago, so we've got them off pat now.

Johnny is our only prelunch customer. This isn't a job for the wildly ambitious.

Barry doesn't show up until after lunch, which isn't unusual. Both Dick and Barry were employed to work part-time, three days each, but shortly after I'd taken them on they both started turning up every day, including Saturdays. I didn't know what to do about it—if they really had nowhere else to go and nothing else to do, I didn't want to, you know, draw attention to it, in case it prompted some sort of spiritual crisis—so I upped their money a bit and left it at that. Barry interpreted the pay rise as a signal to cut his hours back, so I haven't given him one since. That was four years ago, and he's never said anything about it.

He comes into the shop humming a Clash riff. Actually, "humming" is the wrong word: he's making that guitar noise that all little boys make, the one where you stick your lips out, clench your teeth and go "DA-DA!" Barry is thirty-three years old.

"Awlright boys? Hey, Dick, what's this music, man? It stinks." He makes a face and holds his nose. "Phwooar."

Barry intimidates Dick, to the extent that Dick rarely says a word when Barry is in the shop. I only get involved when Barry is being really offensive, so I just watch Dick reach for the hi-fi on the shelf above the counter and turn the cassette off.

"Thank fuck for that. You're like a child, Dick. You

need watching all the time. I don't know why I should have to do it all, though. Rob, didn't you notice what he was putting on? What are you playing at, man?"

He talks relentlessly, and more or less everything he says is gibberish. He talks a lot about music, but also a lot about books (Terry Pratchett and anything else which features monsters, planets, and so on), and films, and women. Pop, girls, etc., as the Liquorice Comfits said. But his conversation is simply enumeration: if he has seen a good film, he will not describe the plot, or how it made him feel, but where it ranks in his best-of-year list, his best-of-all-time list, his best-of-decade list—he thinks and talks in tens and fives, and as a consequence, Dick and I do too. And he makes us write lists as well, all the time: "OK, guys. Top five Dustin Hoffman films." Or guitar solos, or records made by blind musicians, or Gerry and Sylvia Anderson shows ("I don't believe you've got Captain Scarlet at number one, Dick. The guy was immortal! What's fun about that?"), or sweets that come in jars ("If either of you have got Rhubarb and Custard in the top five, I'm resigning now.").

Barry puts his hand into his leather jacket pocket, produces a tape, puts it in the machine, and jacks up the volume. Within seconds the shop is shaking to the bass line of "Walking on Sunshine," by Katrina and the Waves. It's February. It's cold. It's wet. Laura has gone. I don't want to hear "Walking on Sunshine." Somehow it doesn't fit my mood.

"Turn it off, Barry." I have to shout, like a lifeboat captain in a gale.

"It won't go up any more."

"I didn't say 'up,' you fuckwit. I said 'off.' "

He laughs, and walks through into the stockroom, shouting out the horn parts: "Da DA! da da da da da-da da-da-da-da." I turn it off myself, and Barry comes back into the shop.

"What are you doing?"

"I don't want to hear 'Walking on Sunshine'!"

"That's my new tape. My Monday morning tape. I made it last night, specially."

"Yeah, well, it's fucking Monday afternoon. You should get out of bed earlier."

"And you'd have let me play it this morning, would you?"

"No. But at least this way I've got an excuse."

"Don't you want something to cheer you up? Bring a bit of warmth to your miserable middle-aged bones?"

"Nope."

"What do you want to hear when you're pissed off then?"

"I don't know. Not 'Walking on Sunshine,' for a start."

"OK, I'll wind it on."

"What's next?"

" 'Little Latin Lupe Lu.' "

I groan.

"Mitch Ryder and the Detroit Wheels?" Dick asks.

"No. The Righteous Brothers." You can hear the defensiveness in Barry's voice. He has obviously never heard the Mitch Ryder version.

"Oh. Oh well. Never mind." Dick would never go so far as to tell Barry that he's messed up, but the implication is clear.

"What?" says Barry, bristling.

"Nothing."

"No, come on. What's wrong with the Righteous Brothers?"

"Nothing. I just prefer the other one," says Dick mildly.

"Bollocks."

"How can it be bollocks to state a preference?" I ask.

"If it's the wrong preference, it's bollocks."

Dick shrugs and smiles.

"What? What? What's that smug smile for?"

"Leave him alone, Barry. It doesn't matter. We're not listening to fucking 'Little Latin Lupe Lu' anyway, so give it a rest."

"Since when did this shop become a fascist regime?"

"Since you brought that terrible tape in."

"All I'm trying to do is cheer us up. That's all. Very sorry. Go and put some old sad bastard music on, see if I care."

"I don't want old sad bastard music on either. I just want something I can ignore."

"Great. That's the fun thing about working in a record shop, isn't it? Playing things that you don't want to listen to. I thought this tape was going to be, you know, a talking point. I was going to ask you for your top five records to play on a wet Monday morning and all that, and you've gone and ruined it."

"We'll do it next Monday."

"What's the point of that?"

And so on, and on, probably for the rest of my working life.

I'd like to do a top five records that make you feel nothing at all; that way, Dick and Barry would be doing me a favor. Me, I'll be playing the Beatles when I get home. *Abbey Road,* probably, although I'll program the CD to skip over "Something." The Beatles were bubblegum cards and *Help* at the Saturday morning cinema and toy plastic guitars and singing "Yellow Submarine" at the top of my voice in the back row of the coach on school trips. They belong to me, not to me and Laura, or me and Charlie, or me and Alison Ashworth, and though they'll make me feel something, they won't make me feel anything bad.

TWO

I WAS worried about what it would be like, coming back to the flat tonight, but it's fine: the unreliable sense of well-being I've had since this morning is still with me. And, anyway, it won't always be like this, with all her things around. She'll clear it out soon, and the Marie Celestial air about the place—the half-read Julian Barnes paperback on the bedside table and the knickers in the dirty clothes basket—will vanish. (Women's knickers were a terrible disappointment to me when I embarked on my cohabiting career. I never really recovered from the shock of discovering that women do what we do: they save their best pairs for the nights when they know they are going to sleep with somebody. When you live with a woman, these faded, shrunken tatty scraps suddenly appear on radiators all over the house; your lascivious schoolboy dreams of adulthood as a time when you are surrounded by exotic lingerie for ever and ever amen . . . those dreams crumble to dust.)

I clear away the evidence of last night's traumas—the spare duvet on the sofa, the balled-up paper hankies, the coffee mugs with dog-ends floating in the cold, oily-looking dregs, and then I put the Beatles on, and then when I've listened to *Abbey Road* and the first few tracks of *Revolver,* I open the bottle of white wine that Laura brought home last week, sit down and watch the *Brookside* omnibus that I taped.

In the same way that nuns end up having their periods at the same time, Laura's mum and my mum have mysteriously ended up synchronizing their weekly phone calls. Mine rings first.

"Hello, love, it's me."

"Hi."

"Everything all right?"

"Not bad."

"What sort of week have you had?"

"Oh, you know."

"How's the shop doing?"

"So-so. Up and down." Up and down would be great. Up and down would imply that some days are better than others, that customers came and went. This has not been the case, frankly.

"Your dad and I are very worried about this recession."

"Yeah. You said."

"You're lucky Laura's doing so well. If it wasn't for her, I don't think either of us would ever get off to sleep."

She's gone, Mum. She's thrown me to the wolves. The bitch has fucked off and left me . . . Nope. Can't do it. This does not seem to be the right time for bad news.

"Heaven knows she's got enough on her plate without having to worry about a shop full of bloomin' old pop records . . ."

How can one describe the way people born before 1940 say the word "pop"? I have been listening to my parents' sneering one-syllable explosion—heads forward, idiotic look on their faces (because pop fans are idiots) for the time it takes them to spit the word out—for well over two decades.

". . . I'm surprised she doesn't make you sell up and get a proper job. It's a wonder she's hung on as long as she has. I would have left you to get on with it years ago."

Hold on, Rob. Don't let her get to you. Don't rise to the bait. Don't . . . ah, fuck it.

"Well, she has left me to get on with it now, so that should cheer you up."

"Where's she gone?"

"I don't bloody know. Just . . . gone. Moved out. Disappeared."

There is a long, long silence. The silence is so long, in fact, that I can watch the whole of a row between Jimmy and Jackie Corkhill without hearing so much as a long-suffering sigh down the receiver.

"Hullo? Anybody there?"

And now I *can* hear something—the sound of my mother crying softly. What is it with mothers? What's happening here? As an adult, you know that as life goes on, you're going to spend more and more time looking after the person who started out looking after you, that's par for the course; but my mum and I swapped roles when I was about nine. Anything bad that has happened to me in the last couple of decades—detentions, bad exam marks, getting thumped, getting bunged from college, splitting up with girlfriends—has ended up like this, with Mum visibly or audibly upset. It would have been better for both of us if I had moved to Australia when I was fifteen, phoned home once a week and reported a sequence of fictitious major triumphs. Most fifteen-year-olds would find it tough, living on their own, on the other side of the world, with no money and no friends and no family and no job and no qualifications, but not me. It would have been a piece of piss compared to listening to this stuff week after week.

It's . . . well, it's *not fair.* 'Snot fair. It's never been fair. Since I left home, all she's done is moan, worry, and send cuttings from the local newspaper describing the minor successes of old school friends. Is that good parenting? Not in my book. I want sympathy, understanding, advice, and money, and not necessarily in that order, but these are alien concepts in Canning Close.

"I'm all right, if that's what's upsetting you."

I know that's not what's upsetting her.

"You know that's not what's upsetting me."

"Well, it bloody well should be, shouldn't it? Shouldn't it? Mum, I've just been dumped. I'm not feeling so good." And not so bad, either—the Beatles, half a bottle of Chardonnay, and *Brookside* have all done their stuff—but I'm not telling her that. "I can't deal with me, let alone you."

"I knew this would happen."

"Well, if you knew it would happen, what are you so cut up about?"

"What are you going to *do,* Rob?"

"I'm going to drink the rest of a bottle of wine in front of the box. Then I'm going to bed. Then I'll get up and go to work."

"And after that?"

"Meet a nice girl, and have children."

This is the right answer.

"If only it was that easy."

"It is, I promise. Next time I speak to you, I'll have it sorted."

She's almost smiling. I can hear it. I'm beginning to see some light at the end of the long, dark telephonic tunnel.

"But what did Laura say? Do you know why she's gone?"

"Not really."

"Well, I do."

This is momentarily alarming until I understand what she's on about.

"It's nothing to do with marriage, Mum, if that's what you mean."

"So *you* say. I'd like to hear her side of it."

Cool it. Don't let her . . . Don't rise . . . ah, fuck it.

"Mum, how many more times, for Christ's sake? Laura didn't *want* to get married. She's not that sort of girl. To coin a phrase. That's not what happens now."

"I don't know what does happen now. Apart from you meet someone, you move in together, she goes. You meet someone, you move in together, she goes."

Fair point, I guess.

"Shut up, Mum."

. . .

Mrs. Lydon rings a few minutes later.

"Hello, Rob. It's Janet."

"Hello, Mrs. L."

"How are you?"

"Fine. You?"

"Fine, thanks."

"And Ken?"

Laura's dad isn't too clever—he has angina, and had to retire from work early.

"Not too bad. Up and down. You know. Is Laura there?"

Interesting. She hasn't phoned home. Some indication of guilt, maybe?

"She's not, I'm afraid. She's round at Liz's. Shall I get her to give you a ring?"

"If she's not too late back."

"No problem."

And that's the last time we will ever speak, probably. "No problem": the last words I ever say to somebody I have been reasonably close to before our lives take different directions. Weird, eh? You spend Christmas at somebody's house, you worry about their operations, you give them hugs and kisses and flowers, you see them in their dressing gown . . . and then, bang, that's it. Gone forever. And sooner or later there will be another mum, another Christmas, more varicose veins. They're all the same. Only the addresses, and the colors of the dressing gown, change.

THREE

I'M in the back of the shop, trying to tidy it up a bit, when I overhear a conversation between Barry and a customer—male, middle-aged, from the sound of him, and certainly not hip in any way whatsoever.

"I'm looking for a record for my daughter. For her birthday. 'I Just Called to Say I Love You.' Have you got it?"

"Oh, yeah," says Barry. "Course we've got it."

I know for a fact that the only Stevie Wonder single we have at the moment is "Don't Drive Drunk"; we've had it for donkey's years and have never managed to get rid of it, even at sixty pence. What's he playing at?

I go out the front to see what's going on. Barry is standing there, smiling at him; the guy looks a bit flustered.

"Could I have it then?" He half smiles with relief,

as if he were a little boy who has remembered to say "please" at the very last minute.

"No, I'm sorry, but you can't."

The customer, older than I first thought and wearing a cloth cap and a dirty beige raincoat, stands rooted to the spot; I didn't want to come into this noisy dark hell-hole in the first place, you can see him thinking, and now I'm being messed about.

"Why not?"

"Sorry?" Barry's playing Neil Young, and Neil has just this second gone electric.

"Why not?"

"Because it's sentimental, tacky crap, that's why not. Do we look like the sort of shop that sells fucking 'I Just Called to Say I Love You,' eh? Now, be off with you, and don't waste our time."

The old guy turns round and walks out, and Barry chuckles merrily.

"Thanks a lot, Barry."

"What's up?"

"You just drove a fucking customer away, that's what's up."

"We didn't have what he wanted. I was just having some fun, and I never cost you a penny."

"That's not the point."

"Oh, so what's the point, then?"

"The point is, I don't want you talking to anyone who comes in here like that ever again."

"Why not? You think that silly old duffer was going to become a regular?"

"No, but . . . listen Barry, the shop isn't doing so well. I know we used to take the piss out of anyone who asked for anything we didn't like, but it's got to stop."

"Bollocks. If we'd had the record, I would have sold it to him, and you'd be fifty pee or a quid better off, and you'd never have seen him again. Big fucking deal."

"What harm has he ever done you?"

"You know what harm he's done me. He offended me with his terrible taste."

"It wasn't even his terrible taste. It was his daughter's."

"You're going soft in your old age, Rob. There was a time when you'd have chased him out of the shop and up the road."

He's right; there was. It feels like a long time ago now. I just can't muster that sort of anger any more.

Tuesday night I reorganize my record collection; I often do this at periods of emotional stress. There are some people who would find this a pretty dull way to spend an evening, but I'm not one of them. This is my life, and it's nice to be able to wade in it, immerse your arms in it, touch it.

When Laura was here I had the records arranged alphabetically; before that I had them filed in chronological order, beginning with Robert Johnson, and ending with, I don't know, Wham!, or somebody African, or whatever else I was listening to when Laura and I met. Tonight, though, I fancy something different, so I try to remember the order I bought them in: that way I hope to write my own autobiography, without having to do anything like pick up a pen. I pull the records off the shelves, put them in piles all over the sitting room floor, look for *Revolver,* and go on from there; and when I've finished, I'm flushed with a sense of self, because this, after all, is who I am. I like being able to see how I got from Deep Purple to Howlin' Wolf in twenty-five moves; I am no longer pained by the memory of listening to "Sexual Healing" all the way through a period of enforced celibacy, or embarrassed by the reminder of forming a rock club at school, so that I and my fellow fifth-formers could get together and talk about Ziggy Stardust and *Tommy.*

But what I really like is the feeling of security I get from my new filing system; I have made myself more complicated than I really am. I have a couple of thousand records, and you have to be me—or, at the very least, a doctor of Flemingology—to know how to find any of them. If I want to play, say, *Blue* by Joni Mitchell, I have to remember that I bought it for someone in the autumn of 1983, and thought better of giving it to her, for reasons I don't really want to go into. Well, you don't know any of that, so you're knackered, really, aren't you? You'd have to ask me to dig it out for you, and for some reason I find this enormously comforting.

A weird thing happens on Wednesday. Johnny comes in, sings "All Kinds of Everything," tries to grab a handful of album covers. And we're doing our little dance out of the shop when he twists away from me, looks up and says, "Are you married?"

"I'm not, Johnny, no. You?"

He laughs into my armpit, a terrifying, maniacal chuckle that smells of drink and tobacco and vomit and ends in an explosion of phlegm.

"You think I'd be in this fucking state if I had a wife?"

I don't say anything—I just concentrate on tangoing him toward the door—but Johnny's blunt, sad self-appraisal has attracted Barry's attention—maybe he's still cross because I told him off yesterday—and he leans over the counter. "It doesn't help, Johnny. Rob's got a lovely woman at home, and look at him. He's in a terrible way. Bad haircut. Zits. Terrible sweater. Awful socks. The only difference between you and him, Johnny, is that you don't have to pay rent on a shop every week."

I get this sort of stuff from Barry all the time. Today, though, I can't take it and I give him a look that is supposed to shut him up, but which he interprets as an invitation to abuse me further.

"Rob, I'm doing this for your own good. That's the worst sweater I've ever seen. I have never seen a sweater that bad worn by anybody I'm on speaking terms with. It's a disgrace to the human race."

I hurl Johnny out onto the pavement, slam the door shut, race across the shop floor, pick Barry up by the lapels of his brown suede jacket, and tell him that if I have to listen to one more word of his useless, pathetic, meaningless babble again in my entire life I will kill him. When I let him go I'm shaking with anger.

Dick comes out from the stockroom and hops up and down.

"Hey, guys," he whispers. "Hey."

"What are you, some kind of fucking idiot?" Barry asks me. "If this jacket's torn, pal, you're gonna pay big." That's what he says, "pay big." Jesus. And then he stomps out of the shop.

I go and sit down on the stepladder in the stockroom, and Dick hovers in the doorway.

"Are you all right?"

"Yeah. I'm sorry." I take the easy way out. "Look, Dick, I haven't got a lovely woman at home. She's gone. And if we ever see Barry again, perhaps you could tell him that."

"Of course I will, Rob. No problem. No problem at all. I'll tell him next time I see him," Dick says.

I don't say anything. I just nod.

"I've . . . I've got some other stuff to tell him, anyway, so it's no problem. I'll just tell him about, you know, Laura, when I tell him the other stuff," Dick says.

"Fine."

"I'll start with your news before I tell him mine, obviously. Mine isn't much, really, just about someone playing at the Harry Lauder tomorrow night. So I'll tell him before that. Good news and bad news, kind of thing," Dick says.

He laughs nervously. "Or rather, bad news and good news, because he likes this person playing at the Harry Lauder." A look of horror crosses his face. "I mean, he liked Laura too, I didn't mean that. And he likes you. It's just that . . ."

I tell him that I know what he meant, and ask him to make me a cup of coffee.

"Sure. Course. Rob, look. Do you want to . . . have a chat about it, kind of thing?"

For a moment, I'm almost tempted: a heart-to-heart with Dick would be a once-in-a-lifetime experience. But I tell him there's nothing to say, and for a moment I thought he was going to hug me.

FOUR

THE three of us go to the Harry Lauder. Things are cool with Barry now; Dick filled him in when he came back to the shop, and the two of them are doing their best to look after me. Barry has made me an elaborately annotated compilation tape, and Dick now rephrases his questions four or five times instead of the usual two or three. And they more or less insisted that I came to this gig with them.

It's an enormous pub, the Lauder, with ceilings so high that the cigarette smoke gathers above your head like a cartoon cloud. It's tatty, and drafty, and the benches have had the stuffing slashed out of them, and the staff are surly, and the regular clientele are either terrifying or unconscious, and the toilets are wet and smelly, and there's nothing to eat in the evening, and the wine is hilariously bad, and the bitter is fizzy and much too cold; in other words, it's a run-of-the-mill north London pub. We don't come here that often, even though it's only up the road, because the bands that usually play here are the kind of abysmal second-division punk group you'd pay half your wages not to listen to. Occasionally, though, like tonight, they stick on some obscure American folk/country artist, someone with a cult following which could arrive together in the same car. The pub's nearly a third full, which is pretty good, and when we walk in Barry points out Andy Kershaw and a guy who writes for *Time Out.* This is as buzzy as the Lauder ever gets.

The woman we have come to see is called Marie LaSalle; she's got a couple of solo records out on an independent label, and once had one of her songs covered by Nanci Griffith. Dick says Marie lives here now; he read somewhere that she finds England more open to the kind of music she makes, which means, presumably, that we're cheerfully indifferent rather than actively hostile. There are a lot of single men here—not single as in unmarried, but single as in no friends. In this sort of company the three of us—me morose and monosyllabic, Dick nervy and shy, Barry solicitously self-censoring—constitute a wild and massive office outing.

There's no support, just a crappy PA system squelching out tasteful country-rock, and people stand around cradling their pints and reading the handbills that were thrust at them on the way in. Marie LaSalle comes onstage (as it were—there is a little platform and a couple of microphones a few yards in front of us) at nine; by five past nine, to my intense irritation and embarrassment, I'm in tears, and the feel-nothing world that I've been living in for the last few days has vanished.

There are many songs that I've been trying to avoid since Laura went, but the song that Marie LaSalle opens with, the song that makes me cry, is not one of them. The song that makes me cry has never made me cry before; in fact, the song that makes me cry used to make me puke. When it was a hit, I was at college, and Charlie and I used to roll our eyes and stick our fingers down our throats when somebody—invariably a geography student, or a girl training to be a primary school teacher (and I don't see how you can be accused of snobbishness if all you are doing is stating the plain, simple truth)—put it on the jukebox in the bar. The song that makes me cry is Marie LaSalle's version of Peter Frampton's "Baby, I Love Your Way."

Imagine standing with Barry, and Dick, in his Lemonheads T-shirt, and listening to a cover version of a Peter Frampton song, and blubbering! Peter Frampton! "Show Me the Way"! That perm! That stupid bag thing he used to blow into, which made his guitar sound like Donald Duck! *Frampton Comes Alive,* top of the American rock charts for something like seven hundred and twenty years, and bought, presumably, by every brain-dead, coke-addled airhead in L.A.! I understand that I was in dire need of symptoms to help me understand that I have been deeply traumatized by recent events, but did they have to be this extreme? Couldn't God have settled for something just mildly awful—an old Diana Ross hit, say, or an Elton John original?

And it doesn't stop there. As a result of Marie LaSalle's cover version of "Baby, I Love Your Way" ("I know I'm not supposed to like that song, but I do," she says with a cheeky smile when she's finished), I find myself in two apparently contradictory states: a) I suddenly miss Laura with a passion that has been entirely absent for the last four days, and b) I fall in love with Marie LaSalle.

These things happen. They happen to men, at any rate. Or to this particular man. Sometimes. It's difficult to explain why or how you can find yourself pulled in two different directions at once, and obviously a certain amount of dreamy irrationality is a prerequisite. But there's a logic to it, too. Marie is pretty, in that nearly cross-eyed American way—she looks like a slightly plumper, post–*Partridge Family,* pre–*L.A. Law* Susan Dey—and if you were going to develop a spontaneous and pointless crush on somebody, you could do a lot worse. (One Saturday morning, I woke up, switched on the TV, and found myself smitten with Sarah Greene from *Going Live,* a devotion I kept very quiet about at the time.) And she's charming, as far as I can tell, and not without talent: once she has got Peter Frampton out of her system, she sticks to her own songs, and they're good, affecting and funny and delicate. All my life I have wanted to go to bed with—no, have a relationship with—a musician: I'd want her to write songs at home, and ask me what I thought of them, and maybe include one of our private jokes in the lyrics, and thank me in the sleeve notes, maybe even include a picture of me on the inside cover, in the background somewhere, and I could watch her play live from the back, in the wings (although I'd look a bit of a berk at the Lauder, where there are no wings: I'd be standing on my own, in full view of everybody).

The Marie bit is easy enough to understand, then. The Laura thing takes a bit more explaining, but what it is, I think, is this: sentimental music has this great way of taking you back somewhere at the same time that it takes you forward, so you feel nostalgic and hopeful all at the same time. Marie's the hopeful, forward part of it—maybe not her, necessarily, but somebody like her, somebody who can turn things around for me. (Exactly that: I always think that women are going to save me, lead me through to a better life, that they can change and redeem me.) And Laura's the backward part, the last person I loved, and when I hear those sweet, sticky acoustic guitar chords, I reinvent our time together, and, before I know it, we're in the car trying to sing the harmonies on "Love Hurts" and getting it wrong and laughing. We never did that in real life. We never sang in the car, and we certainly never laughed when we got something wrong. This is why I shouldn't be listening to pop music at the moment.

Tonight, it really doesn't matter either way. Marie could come up to me as I was leaving and ask if I wanted to go for something to eat; or I could get home, and Laura would be sitting there, sipping tea and waiting nervously for absolution. Both of these daydreams sound equally attractive, and either would make me very happy.

Marie takes a break after an hour or so. She sits on the stage and swigs from a bottle of Budweiser, and some guy comes out with a box of cassettes and puts them on the stage beside her. They're £5.99, but they haven't got any pennies, so really they're six quid. We all buy one from her, and to our horror she speaks to us.

"You enjoying yourselves?"

We nod.

"Good, 'cause I'm enjoying myself."

"Good," I say, and that seems to be the best I can do for the moment.

I've only got a tenner, so I stand there twiddling my thumbs while the guy fishes around for four-pound coins.

"You live in London now, is that right?" I ask her.

"Yup. Not far from here, actually."

"You like it?" Barry asks. Good one. I wouldn't have thought of that.

"It's OK. Hey, you guys might be the sort to know. Are there any good record shops up around here, or do I have to go into the West End?"

What's the use of taking offense? We are the sort of guys who would know about record shops. That's what we look like, and that's what we are.

Barry and Dick almost fall over in their haste to explain.

"He's got one!"

"He's got one!"

"In Holloway!"

"Just up the Seven Sisters' Road!"

"Championship Vinyl!"

"We work there!"

"You'd love it!"

"Come in!"

She laughs at the onslaught of enthusiasm.

"What d'you sell?"

"Bit of everything good. Blues, country, vintage soul, new wave . . ."

"Sounds great."

Somebody else wants to talk to her, so she smiles nicely at us and turns round. We go back to where we were standing.

"What did you tell her about the shop for?" I ask the others.

"I didn't know it was classified information," says Barry. "I mean, I know we don't have any customers, but I thought that was a bad thing, not, like, a business strategy."

"She won't spend any money."

"No, course not. That's why she was asking if we knew any good record shops. She just wants to come in and waste our time."

I know I'm being stupid, but I don't want her coming to my shop. If she came into my shop, I might really get to like her, and then I'd be waiting for her to come in all the time, and then when she did come in I'd be nervous and stupid, and probably end up asking her out for a drink in some cack-handed roundabout way, and either she wouldn't catch my drift, and I'd feel like an idiot, or she'd turn me down flat, and I'd feel like an idiot. And on the way home after the gig, I'm already wondering whether she'll come tomorrow, and whether it will mean anything if she does, and if it does mean something, then which one of us it will mean something to, although Barry is probably a nonstarter.

Fuck. I hate all this stuff. How old do you have to get before it stops?

When I get home there are two answering machine messages, one from Laura's friend Liz and one from Laura. They go like this:

1. Rob, it's Liz. Just phoning up to see, well, to see if you're OK. Give us a ring sometime. Um... I'm not taking sides. Yet. Lots of love, bye.
2. Hi, it's me. There are a couple of things I need. Can you call me at work in the morning? Thanks.

Mad people could read all sorts of things into either of these calls; sane people would come to the conclusion that the first caller is warm and affectionate, and that the second doesn't give a shit. I'm not mad.

FIVE

I CALL Laura first thing. I feel sick, dialing the number, and even sicker when the receptionist puts me through. She used to know who I am, but now there's nothing in her voice at all. Laura wants to come around on Saturday afternoon, when I'm at work, to pick up some more underwear, and that's fine by me; we should have stopped there, but I try to have a different sort of conversation, and she doesn't like it because she's at work, but I persist, and she hangs up on me in tears. And I feel like a jerk, but I couldn't stop myself. I never can.

I wonder what she'd say, if she knew that I was simultaneously uptight about Marie coming into the shop? Laura and I have just had a phone call in which I suggested that she'd fucked up my life and, for the duration of the call, I believed it. But now—and I can do this with no trace of bemusement or self-dissatisfaction—I'm worrying about what to wear, and whether I look better stubbly or clean-shaven, and about what music I should play in the shop today.

Sometimes it seems as though the only way a man can judge his own niceness, his own *decency,* is by looking at his relationships with women—or rather, with prospective or current sexual partners. It's easy enough to be nice to your mates. You can buy them a drink, make them a tape, ring them up to see if they're OK . . . there are any number of quick and painless methods of turning yourself into a Good Bloke. When it comes to girlfriends, though, it's much trickier to be consistently honorable. One moment you're ticking along, cleaning the toilet bowl, and expressing your feelings and doing all the other things that a modern chap is supposed to do; the next, you're manipulating and sulking and double-dealing and fibbing with the best of them. I can't work it out.

I phone Liz early afternoon. She's nice to me. She says how sorry she is, what a good couple she thought we made, that I have done Laura good, given her a center, brought her out of herself, allowed her to have fun, turned her into a nicer, calmer, more relaxed person, given her an interest in something other than work. Liz doesn't use these words, as such—I'm interpreting. But this is what she means, I think, when she says we made a good couple. She asks how I am, and whether I'm looking after myself; she tells me that she doesn't think much of this Ian guy. We arrange to meet for a drink sometime next week. I hang up.

Which fucking Ian guy?

Marie comes into the shop shortly afterward. All three of us are there. I'm playing her tape, and when I see her walk in

I try to turn it off before she notices, but I'm not quick enough, so I end up turning it off just as she begins to say something about it, and then turning it back on again, then blushing. She laughs. I go to the stockroom and don't come out. Barry and Dick sell her seventy quid's worth of cassettes.

Which fucking Ian guy?

Barry explodes into the stockroom. "We're only on the guest list for Marie's gig at the White Lion, that's all. All three of us."

In the last half-hour, I have humiliated myself in front of somebody I'm interested in, and found out, I think, that my ex was having an affair. I don't want to know about the guest list at the White Lion.

"That's really, really great, Barry. The guest list at the White Lion! All we've got to do is get to Putney and back and we've saved ourselves a fiver each. What it is to have influential friends, eh?"

"We can go in your car."

"It's not my car, is it? It's Laura's. Laura's got it. So we're two hours on the tube, or we get a minicab, which'll cost us, ooh, a fiver each. Fucking great."

Barry gives a what-can-you-do-with-this-guy shrug and walks out. I feel bad, but I don't say anything to him.

I don't know anybody called Ian. Laura doesn't know anybody called Ian. We've been together three years and I've never heard her mention an Ian. There's no Ian at her office. She hasn't got any friends called Ian, and she hasn't got any girlfriends with boyfriends called Ian. I won't say that she has never met anyone called Ian in the whole of her life—there must have been one at college, although she went to an all-girls school—but I am almost certain that since 1989 she has been living in an Ianless universe.

And this certitude, this Ian-atheism, lasts until I get home. On the windowsill where we put the post, just inside the communal front door, there are three letters amidst the takeout menus and the minicab cards: a bill for me, a bank statement for Laura . . . and a TV license reminder for Mr. I. Raymond (Ray to his friends and, more pertinently, to his neighbors), the guy who until about six weeks ago lived upstairs.

I'm shaking when I get into the flat, and I feel sick. I know it's him; I knew it was him the moment I saw the letter. I remember Laura going up to see him a couple of times; I remember Laura . . . not *flirting,* exactly, but certainly flicking her hair more often, and grinning more inanely, than seemed to be strictly necessary when he came down for a drink last Christmas. He would be just her type—little-boy-lost, right-on, caring, just enough melancholy in his soul to make him appear interesting. I never liked him much then, and I fucking hate him now.

How long? How often? The last time I spoke to Ray—Ian—the night before he moved . . . was something going on then? Did she sneak upstairs on nights when I was out? Do John and Melanie, the couple in the ground-floor flat, know anything about this? I spend a long time looking for the change-of-address card he gave us, but it's gone, ominously and significantly—unless I chucked it, in which case strike the ominous significance. (What would I do if I found it? Give him a ring? Drop round, and see if he's got company?)

I'm starting to remember things now: his dungarees; his music (African, Latin, Bulgarian, whatever fucking world music fad was trendy that week); his hysterical, nervous, nerve-jangling laugh; the terrible cooking smells that used to pollute the stairway; the visitors that used to stay too late and drink too much and leave too noisily. I can't remember anything good about him at all.

I manage to block out the worst, most painful, most disturbing memory until I go to bed, when I hear the woman who lives up there now stomping around and banging wardrobe doors. This is the very worst thing, the thing that would bring anybody (any man?) in my position out in the coldest and clammiest of sweats: *we used to listen to him having sex.* We could hear the noises he made; we could hear the noises she made (and there were two or three different partners in the time the three of us—the four of us, if you count whoever was in Ray's bed—were separated by a few square meters of creaking floorboard and flaking plaster).

"He goes on long enough," I said one night, when we were both lying awake, staring at the ceiling. "I should be so lucky," said Laura. This was a joke. We laughed. Ha, ha, we went. Ha, ha, ha. I'm not laughing now. Never has a joke filled me with such nausea and paranoia and insecurity and self-pity and dread and doubt.

When a woman leaves a man, and the man is unhappy (and yes, finally, after all the numbness and the silly optimism and the who-cares shrug of the shoulders, I am unhappy—although I would still like to be included somewhere in the cover shot of Marie's next album) . . . is this what it's all about? Sometimes I think so, and sometimes I don't. I went through this period, after the Charlie and Marco thing, of imagining them together, *at it,* and Charlie's face contorted with a passion that I was never able to provoke.

I should say, even though I do not feel like saying it (I want to run myself down, feel sorry for myself, celebrate my inadequacies—that's what you do at times like these), that I think things were OK in That Department. I think. But in my fearful imaginings Charlie was as abandoned and as noisy as any character in a porn film. She was Marco's plaything, she responded to his every touch with shrieks of orgasmic delight. No woman in the history of the world had better sex than the sex Charlie had with Marco in my head.

But that was nothing. That had no basis in reality at all. For all I know, Marco and Charlie never even consummated their relationship and Charlie has spent the intervening decade trying—but failing miserably—to recapture the quiet, undemonstrative ecstasy of the nights that we spent together. I know, however, that Ian was something of a demon lover; so does Laura. I could hear it all; so could Laura. In truth, it pissed me off; I thought it pissed her off, too. Now I'm not so sure. Is this why she went? Because she wanted a bit of what was happening upstairs?

I don't really know why it matters so much. Ian could be better at talking than me, or cooking, or working, or housework, or saving money, or earning money, or spending money, or understanding books or films; he could be nicer than me, better-looking, more intelligent, cleaner, more generous-spirited, more helpful, a better human being in any way you care to mention . . . and I wouldn't mind. Really. I accept and understand that you can't be good at everything, and I am tragically unskilled in some very important areas. But sex is different; knowing that a successor is better in bed is impossible to take, and I don't know why.

I know enough to know that this is daft. I know, for example, that the best sex I have ever had was not important; the best sex I have ever had was with a girl called Rosie, whom I slept with just four times. It wasn't enough (the good sex, I mean, not the four times, which were more than enough). She drove me mad, and I drove her mad, and the fact that we had the knack of being able to come at the same time (and this, it seems to me, is what people mean when they talk about good sex, no matter what Dr. Ruth tells you about sharing and consideration and pillow talk and variety and positions and handcuffs) counted for nothing.

So what is it that sickens me so much about "Ian" and Laura? Why do I care so much about how long he can go on for and how long I could go on for and what noises she made with me and what noises she makes with him? Just, I guess, this in the end: that I still hear Chris Thomson, the Neanderthal, testosterone-crazed, fourth-year adulterer, calling me a spastic and telling me he has knobbed my girlfriend. And that voice still makes me feel bad.

During the night, I have one of those dreams that aren't really dreams at all, just stuff about Laura fucking Ray, and Marco fucking Charlie, and I'm pleased to wake up in the middle of the night, because it means stopping the dream. But the pleasure only lasts a few seconds and then everything sinks in: that somewhere Laura really is fucking Ray (maybe not exactly now, because it's 3:56 A.M., although with his stamina—his *inability to climax,* ha ha—you never know), and I'm here, in this stupid little flat, on my own, and I'm thirty-five years old, and I own a tiny failing business, and my friends don't seem to be friends at all but people whose phone numbers I haven't lost. And if I went back to sleep and slept for forty years and woke up without any teeth to the sound of Melody Radio in an old people's home, I wouldn't worry that much, because the worst of life, i.e., the rest of it, would be over. And I wouldn't even have had to kill myself.

It's only just beginning to occur to me that it's important to have something going on somewhere, at work or at home, otherwise you're just clinging on. If I lived in Bosnia, then not having a girlfriend wouldn't seem like the most important thing in the world, but here in Crouch End it does. You need as much ballast as possible to stop you from floating away; you need people around you, things going on, otherwise life is like some film where the money ran out, and there are no sets, or locations, or supporting actors, and it's just one bloke on his own staring into the camera with nothing to do and nobody to speak to, and who'd believe in this character then? I've got to get more stuff, more clutter, more *detail* in here, because at the moment I'm in danger of falling off the edge.

. . .

"Have you got any soul?" a woman asks the next afternoon. That depends, I feel like saying; some days yes, some days no. A few days ago I was right out; now I've got loads, too much, more than I can handle. I wish I could spread it a bit more evenly, I want to tell her, get a better balance, but I can't seem to get it sorted. I can see she wouldn't be interested in my internal stock control problems though, so I simply point to where I keep the soul I have, right by the exit, just next to the blues.

SIX

EXACTLY one week after Laura has gone, I get a call from a woman in Wood Green who has some singles she thinks I might be interested in. I normally don't bother with house clearance, but this woman seems to know what she's talking about: she mutters about white labels and picture sleeves and all sorts of other things that suggest we're not just talking about half a dozen scratched Electric Light Orchestra records that her son left behind when he moved out.

Her house is enormous, the sort of place that seems to have meandered to Wood Green from another part of London, and she's not very nice. She's mid-to-late forties, with a dodgy tan and a suspiciously taut-looking face; and though she's wearing jeans and a T-shirt, the jeans have the name of an Italian where the name of Mr. Wrangler or Mr. Levi should be, and the T-shirt has a lot of jewelry stuck to the front of it, arranged in the shape of a peace sign.

She doesn't smile, or offer me a cup of coffee, or ask me whether I found the place OK despite the freezing, driving rain that prevented me from seeing the street map in front of my face. She just shows me into a study off the hall, turns the light on, and points out the singles—there are hundreds of them, all in custom-made wooden boxes—on the top shelf, and leaves me to get on with it.

There are no books on the shelves that line the walls, just albums, CDs, cassettes, and hi-fi equipment; the cassettes have little numbered stickers on them, always a sign of a serious person. There are a couple of guitars leaning against the walls, and some sort of computer that looks as though it might be able to do something musical if you were that way inclined.

I climb up on a chair and start pulling the singles boxes down. There are seven or eight in all, and, though I try not to look at what's in them as I put them on the floor, I catch a glimpse of the first one in the last box: it's a James Brown single on King, thirty years old, and I begin to prickle with anticipation.

When I start going through them properly, I can see straightaway that it's the haul I've always dreamed of finding, ever since I began collecting records. There are fan-club-only Beatles singles, and the first half-dozen Who singles, and Elvis originals from the early sixties, and loads of rare blues and soul singles, and . . . *there's a copy of* "God Save the Queen" *by the Sex Pistols on A&M!* I have never even seen one of these! I have never even seen anyone who's seen one! And oh no oh no oh God—"You Left the Water Running" by Otis Redding, released seven years after his death, withdrawn immediately by his widow because she didn't . . .

"What d'you reckon?" She's leaning against the door frame, arms folded, half smiling at whatever ridiculous face I'm making.

"It's the best collection I've ever seen." I have no idea what to offer her. This lot must be worth at least six or seven grand, and she knows it. Where am I going to get that kind of money from?

"Give me fifty quid and you can take every one away with you today."

I look at her. We're now officially in Joke Fantasy Land, where little old ladies pay good money to persuade you to cart off their Chippendale furniture. Except I am not dealing with a little old lady, and she knows perfectly well that what she has here is worth a lot more than fifty quid. What's going on?

"Are these stolen?"

She laughs. "Wouldn't really be worth my while, would it, lugging all this lot through someone's window for fifty quid? No, they belong to my husband."

"And you're not getting on too well with him at the moment?"

"He's in Spain with a twenty-three-year-old. A friend of my daughter's. He had the *fucking* cheek to phone up and ask to borrow some money and I refused, so he asked me to sell his singles collection and send him a check for whatever I got, minus ten percent commission. Which reminds me. Can you make sure you give me a five pound note? I want to frame it and put it on the wall."

"They must have taken him a long time to get together."

"Years. This collection is as close as he has ever come to an achievement."

"Does he work?"

"He calls himself a musician, but . . ." She scowls her disbelief and contempt. "He just sponges off me and sits around on his fat arse staring at record labels."

Imagine coming home and finding your Elvis singles and your James Brown singles and your Chuck Berry singles flogged off for nothing out of sheer spite. What would you do? What would you say?

"Look, can't I pay you properly? You don't have to tell him what you got. You could send the forty-five quid anyway, and blow the rest. Or give it to charity. Or something."

"That wasn't part of the deal. I want to be poisonous but fair."

"I'm sorry, but it's just . . . I don't want any part of this."

"Suit yourself. There are plenty of others who will."

"Yeah, I know. That's why I'm trying to find a compromise. What about fifteen hundred? They're probably worth four times that."

"Sixty."

"Thirteen."

"Seventy-five."

"Eleven. That's my lowest offer."

"And I won't take a penny more than ninety." We're both smiling now. It's hard to imagine another set of circumstances that could result in this kind of negotiation.

"He could afford to come home then, you see, and that's the last thing I want."

"I'm sorry, but I think you'd better talk to someone else." When I get back to the shop I'm going to burst into tears and cry like a baby for a month, but I can't bring myself to do it to this guy.

"Fine."

I stand up to go, and then get back on my knees: I just want one last, lingering look.

"Can I buy this Otis Redding single off you?"

"Sure. Ten pee."

"Oh, come on. Let me give you a tenner for this, and you can give the rest away for all I care."

"OK. Because you took the trouble to come up here. And because you've got principles. But that's it. I'm not selling them to you one by one."

So I go to Wood Green and I come back with a mint-condition "You Left the Water Running," which I pick up for a tenner. That's not a bad morning's work. Barry and Dick will be impressed. But if they ever find out about Elvis and James Brown and Jerry Lee Lewis and the Pistols and the Beatles and the rest, they will suffer immediate and possibly dangerous traumatic shock, and I will have to counsel them, and . . .

How come I ended up siding with the bad guy, the man who's left his wife and taken himself off to Spain with some nymphette? Why can't I bring myself to feel whatever it is his wife is feeling? Maybe I should go home and flog Laura's sculpture to someone who wants to smash it to pieces and use it for scrap; maybe that would do me some good. But I know I won't. All I can see is that guy's face when he gets his pathetic check through the mail, and I can't help but feel desperately, painfully sorry for him.

. . .

It would be nice to report that life is full of exotic incidents like this, but it isn't. Dick tapes me the first Liquorice Comfits album, as promised; Jimmy and Jackie Corkhill stop arguing, temporarily; Laura's mum doesn't ring, but my mum does. She thinks Laura might be more interested in me if I did some evening classes. We agree to differ or, at any rate, I hang up on her. And Dick, Barry, and I go by minicab to the White Lion to see Marie, and our names are indeed on the guest list. The ride costs exactly fifteen quid, but that doesn't include the tip, and bitter is two pounds a pint. The White Lion is smaller than the Harry Lauder, so it's half full rather than two-thirds empty, and it's much nicer, too, and there's even a support act, some terrible local singer-songwriter for whom the world ended just after "Tea for the Tillerman" by Cat Stevens, not with a bang but a wimp.

The good news: (1) I don't cry during "Baby, I Love Your Way," although I do feel slightly sick. (2) We get a mention: "Is that Barry and Dick and Rob I see down there? Nice to see you, fellas." And then she says to the audience, "Have you ever been to their shop? Championship Vinyl in north London? You really should." And people turn round to look at us, and we look at each other sheepishly, and Barry is on the verge of giggling with excitement, the idiot. (3) I still want to be on an album cover somewhere, despite the fact that I was violently sick when I got to work this morning because I'd been up half the night smoking roll-ups made with dog-ends and drinking banana liqueur and missing Laura. (Is that good news? Maybe it's bad news, definite, final proof that I'm mad, but it's good news in that I still have an ambition of sorts, and that Melody Radio is not my only vision of the future.)

The bad news: (1) Marie brings someone out to sing with her for her encore. A bloke. Someone who shares her microphone with her with an intimacy I don't like, and sings harmony on "Love Hurts," and looks at her while he's doing so in a way that suggests that he's ahead of me in the queue for the album shoot. Marie still looks like Susan Dey, and this guy—she introduces him as "T-Bone Taylor, the best-kept secret in Texas"—looks like a prettier version of Daryl Hall of Hall and Oates, if you can imagine such a creature. He's got long blond hair, and cheekbones, and he's well over nine feet tall, but he's got muscles too (he's wearing a denim waistcoat and no shirt) and a voice that makes that man who does the Guinness adverts sound soppy, a voice so deep that it seems to land with a thud on the stage and roll toward us like a cannonball.

I know my sexual confidence is not high at the moment, and I know that women are not necessarily interested in long blond hair, cheekbones, and height; that sometimes they are looking for shortish dark hair, no cheekbones and width, but even so! Look at them! Susan Dey and Daryl Hall! Entwining the naked melody lines from "Love Hurts"! Mingling their saliva, almost! Just as well I wore my favorite shirt when she came into the shop the other day, otherwise I wouldn't have stood a chance.

There is no other bad news. That's it.

When the gig finishes I pick my jacket up off the floor and start to go.

"It's only half-ten," Barry says. "Let's get another one in."

"You can if you want. I'm going back." I don't want to have a drink with someone called T-Bone, but I get the feeling that this is exactly what Barry would like to do. I get the feeling that having a drink with someone called T-Bone could be the high point of Barry's decade. "I don't want to muck your evening up. I just don't feel like staying."

"Not even for half an hour?"

"Not really."

"Hold on a minute, then. I've got to take a piss."

"Me too," Dick says.

When they're gone, I get out quickly, and hail a black cab. It's brilliant, being depressed; you can behave as badly as you like.

Is it so wrong, wanting to be at home with your record collection? It's not like collecting records is like collecting stamps, or beermats, or antique thimbles. There's a whole world in here, a nicer, dirtier, more violent, more peaceful, more colorful, sleazier, more dangerous, more loving world than the world I live in; there is history, and geography, and poetry, and countless other things I should have studied at school, including music.

When I get home (twenty quid, Putney to Crouch End, and no tip) I make myself a cup of tea, plug in the headphones, and plow through every angry song about women by Bob Dylan and Elvis Costello I own, and when I've got through those, I stick on a Neil Young live album until I have a head ringing with feedback, and when I've finished with Neil Young I go to bed and stare at the ceiling, which is no longer the dreamy, neutral activity it once was. It was a joke, wasn't it, all that Marie stuff? I was kidding myself that there was something I could go on to, an easy, seamless transition to be made. I can see that now. I can see everything once it's already happened—I'm very good at the past. It's the present I can't understand.

I get to work late, and Dick has already taken a message from Liz. I'm to ring her at work, urgently. I have no intention of ringing her at work. She wants to cancel our drink this evening, and I know why, and I'm not going to let her. She'll have to cancel to my face.

I get Dick to ring her back and tell her that he'd forgotten I wouldn't be in all day—I've gone to a record fair in Colchester and I'm coming back specially for a date this evening. No, Dick doesn't have a number. No, Dick doesn't think I'll be ringing the shop. I don't answer the phone for the rest of the day, just in case she tries to catch me out.

We've arranged to meet in Camden, in a quiet Youngs pub on Parkway. I'm early, but I've got a *Time Out* with me, so I sit in a corner with my pint and some cashews and work out which films I'd see if I had anyone to go with.

The date with Liz doesn't take long. I see her stomping toward my table—she's nice, Liz, but she's huge, and when she's angry, like she is now, she's pretty scary—and I try a smile, but I can see it's not going to work, because she's too far gone to be brought back like that.

"You're a fucking arsehole, Rob," she says, and then she turns around and walks out, and the people at the next table stare at me. I blush, stare at the *Time Out* and take a big pull on my pint in the hope that the glass will obscure my reddening face.

She's right, of course. I am a fucking arsehole.

SEVEN

FOR a couple of years, at the end of the eighties, I was a DJ at a club in Kentish Town, and it was there I met Laura. It wasn't much of a club, just a room above a pub, really, but for a six-month period it was popular with a certain London crowd—the almost fashionable, right-on, black 501s-and-DMs-crowd that used to move in herds from the market to the Town and Country to Dingwalls to the Electric Ballroom to the Camden Plaza. I was a good DJ, I think. At any rate, people seemed happy; they danced, stayed late, asked me where they could buy some of the records I played, and came back week after week. We called it the Groucho Club, because of Groucho Marx's thing about not wanting to join any club that would have him as a member; later on we found out that there was another Groucho Club somewhere in the West End, but nobody seemed to get confused about which was which. (Top five floor-fillers at the Groucho, incidentally: "It's a Good Feeling" by Smokey Robinson and the Miracles; "No Blow No Show" by Bobby Bland; "Mr. Big Stuff" by Jean Knight; "The Love You Save" by the Jackson Five; "The Ghetto" by Donny Hathaway.)

And I loved, loved doing it. To look down on a roomful of heads all bobbing away to the music you have chosen is an uplifting thing, and for that six-month period when the club was popular, I was as happy as I have ever been. It was the only time I have ever really had a sense of momentum, although later I could see that it was a false momentum, because it didn't belong to me at all, but to the music: anyone playing his favorite dance records very loud in a crowded place, to people who had paid to hear them, would have felt exactly the same thing. Dance music, after all, is supposed to have momentum—I just got confused.

Anyway, I met Laura right in the middle of that period, in the summer of '87. She reckons she had been to the club three or four times before I noticed her, and that could well be right—she's small, and skinny, and pretty, in a sort of Sheena Easton pre-Hollywood makeover way (although she looked tougher than Sheena Easton with her radical lawyer spiky hair and her boots and her scary pale blue eyes), but there were prettier women there, and when you're looking on in that idle kind of way, it's the prettiest ones you look at. So, on this third or fourth time, she came up to my little rostrum thing and spoke to me, and I liked her straightaway: she asked me to play a record that I really loved ("Got to Get You off My Mind" by Solomon Burke, if anyone cares), but which had cleared the floor whenever I'd tried it.

"Were you here when I played it before?"

"Yeah."

"Well, you saw what happened. They were all about to go home."

It's a three-minute single, and I'd had to take it off after about a minute and a half. I played "Holiday" by Madonna instead; I used modern stuff every now and again, at times of crisis, just like people who believe in homeopathy have to use conventional medicine sometimes, even though they disapprove of it.

"They won't this time."

"How do you know that?"

"Because I brought half of this lot here, and I'll make sure they dance."

So I played it, and sure enough Laura and her mates flooded the dance floor, but one by one they all drifted off again, shaking their heads and laughing. It is a hard song to dance to; it's a mid-tempo R&B thing, and the intro sort of stops and starts. Laura stuck with it, and though I wanted to see whether she'd struggle gamely through to the end, I got nervous when people weren't dancing, so I put "The Love You Save" on quick.

She wouldn't dance to the Jackson Five, and she marched over to me, but she was grinning and said she wouldn't ask again. She just wanted to know where she could buy the record. I said if she came next week I'd have a tape for her, and she looked really pleased.

I spent hours putting that cassette together. To me, making a tape is like writing a letter—there's a lot of erasing and rethinking and starting again, and I wanted it to be a good one, because . . . to be honest, because I hadn't met anyone as promising as Laura since I'd started the DJ-ing, and meeting promising women was partly what the DJ-ing was supposed to be about. A good compilation tape, like breaking up, is hard to do. You've got to kick off with a corker, to hold the attention (I started with "Got to Get You off My Mind," but then realized that she might not get any further than track one, side one if I delivered what she wanted straightaway, so I buried it in the middle of side two), and then you've got to up it a notch, or cool it a notch, and you can't have white music and black music together, unless the white music sounds like black music, and you can't have two tracks by the same artist side by side, unless you've done the whole thing in pairs, and . . . oh, there are loads of rules.

Anyway, I worked and worked at this one, and I've still got a couple of early demons knocking around the flat, prototype tapes I changed my mind about when I was checking them through. And on Friday night, club night, I produced it from my jacket pocket when she came over to me, and we went on from there. It was a good beginning.

Laura was, is, a lawyer, although when I met her she was a different kind of lawyer from the one she is now: then, she worked for a legal aid firm (hence, I guess, the clubbing and the black leather motorcycle jacket). Now, she works for a City law firm (hence, I guess, the restaurants and the expensive suits and the disappearance of the spiky haircut and a previously unrevealed taste for weary sarcasm) not because she underwent any kind of political conversion, but because she was made redundant and couldn't find any legal aid work. She had to take a job that paid about forty-five grand a year because she couldn't find one that paid under twenty; she said that this was all you need to know about Thatcherism, and I suppose she had a point. She changed when she got the new job. She was always intense, but, before, the intensity had somewhere to go: she could worry about tenants' rights, and slum landlords, and kids living in places without running water. Now she's just intense about *work*—how much she has, the pressure she's under, how she's doing, what the partners think of her, that kind of stuff. And when she's not being intense about work, she's being intense about why she shouldn't be intense about work, or this kind of work, anyway.

Sometimes—not so often recently—I could do something or say something that allowed her to escape from herself, and that's when we worked best; she complains frequently about my "relentless triviality," but it has its uses.

I never had any wild crush on her, and that used to worry me about the long-term future: I used to think—and given the way we ended up, maybe I still do—that all relationships need the kind of violent shove that a crush brings, just to get you started and to push you over the humps. And then, when the energy from that shove has gone and you come to something approaching a halt, you have a look around and see what you've got. It could be something completely different, it could be something roughly the same, but gentler and calmer, or it could be nothing at all.

With Laura, I changed my mind about that whole process for a while. There weren't any sleepless nights or losses of appetite or agonizing waits for the phone to ring for either of us. But we just carried on regardless, anyway, and, because there was no steam to lose, we never had to have that look around to see what we'd got, because what we'd got was the same as what we'd always had. She didn't make me miserable, or anxious, or ill at ease, and when we went to bed I didn't panic and let myself down, if you know what I mean, and I think you do.

We went out a lot, and she came to the club every week, and when she lost the lease on her flat in Archway she moved in, and everything was good, and stayed that way for years and years. If I was being obtuse, I'd say that money changed everything: when she switched jobs, she suddenly had loads, and when I lost the club work, and the recession seemed to make the shop suddenly invisible to passers-by, I had none. Of course things like that complicate life, and there are all kinds of readjustments to think about, battles to fight and lines to draw. But really, it wasn't the money. It was me. Like Liz said, I'm an arsehole.

The night before Liz and I were supposed to have a drink in Camden, Liz and Laura met up somewhere for something to eat, and Liz had a go at Laura about Ian, and Laura wasn't planning on saying anything in her own defense, because that would have meant assaulting me, and she has a powerful and sometimes ill-advised sense of loyalty. (I, for example, would not have been able to restrain myself.) But Liz pushed it too far, and Laura snapped, and all these things about me poured out in a torrent, and then they both cried, and Liz apologized between fifty and one hundred times for speaking out of turn. So the following day Liz snapped, tried to phone me and then marched into the pub and called me names. I don't know any of this for sure, of course. I have had no contact at all with Laura and only a brief and unhappy meeting with Liz. But, even so, one does not need a sophisticated understanding of the characters in question to guess this much.

I do not know what, precisely, Laura said, but she would have revealed at least two, maybe even all four, of the following pieces of information:

1. That I slept with somebody else while she was pregnant.
2. That my affair contributed directly to her terminating the pregnancy.
3. That, after her abortion, I borrowed a large sum of money from her and have not yet repaid any of it.
4. That, shortly before she left, I told her I was unhappy in the relationship, and I was kind of sort of maybe looking around for someone else.

Did I do and say these things? Yes, I did. Are there any mitigating circumstances? Not really, unless any circumstances (in other words, context) can be regarded as mitigating. And before you judge, although you have probably already done so, go away and write down the worst four things that you have done to your partner, even if—especially if—your partner doesn't know about them. Don't dress these things up, or try to explain them; just write them down, in a list, in the plainest language possible. Finished? OK, so who's the arsehole now?

EIGHT

WHERE the fuck have you been?" I ask Barry when he turns up for work on Saturday morning. I haven't seen him since we went to Marie's gig at the White Lion—no phone calls, no apologies, nothing.

"Where the fuck have I been? Where the fuck have *I* been? God, you're an arsehole," Barry says by way of an explanation. "I'm sorry, Rob. I know things aren't going so well for you and you have problems and stuff, but, you know. We spent fucking hours looking for you the other night."

"Hours? More than one hour? At least two? I left at half-ten, so you abandoned the search at half-twelve, right? You must have walked from Putney to Wapping."

"Don't be a smartarse."

One day, maybe not in the next few weeks, but certainly in the conceivable future, somebody will be able to refer to me without using the word *arse* somewhere in the sentence.

"OK, sorry. But I'll bet you looked for ten minutes, and then had a drink with Marie and thingy. T-Bone."

I hate calling him T-Bone. It sets my teeth on edge, like when you have to ask for a Big Heap Buffalo Billburger, when all you want is a quarter-pounder, or a Just Like Mom Used to Make, when all you want is a piece of apple pie.

"That's not the point."

"Did you have a good time?"

"It was great. T-Bone's played on two Guy Clark albums and a Jimmie Dale Gilmore album."

"Far out."

"Oh, fuck off."

I'm glad it's Saturday because we're reasonably busy, and Barry and I don't have to find much to say to each other. When Dick's making a cup of coffee and I'm looking for an old Shirley Brown single in the stockroom, he tells me that T-Bone's played on two Guy Clark albums and a Jimmie Dale Gilmore album.

"And do you know what? He's a really nice guy," he adds, astonished that someone who has reached these dizzying heights is capable of exchanging a few civil words in a pub. But that's about it as far as staff interaction goes. There are too many other people to talk to.

Even though we get a lot of people into the shop, only a small percentage of them buy anything. The best customers are the ones who just *have* to buy a record on a Saturday, even if there's nothing they really want; unless they go home clutching a flat, square carrier bag, they feel uncomfortable.

You can spot the vinyl addicts because after a while they get fed up with the rack they are flicking through, march over to a completely different section of the shop, pull a sleeve out from the middle somewhere, and come over to the counter; this is because they have been making a list of possible purchases in their head ("If I don't find anything in the next five minutes, that blues compilation I saw half an hour ago will have to do"), and suddenly sicken themselves with the amount of time they have wasted looking for something they don't really want. I know that feeling well (these are my people, and I understand them better than I understand anybody in the world): it is a prickly, clammy, panicky sensation, and you go out of the shop reeling. You walk much more quickly afterward, trying to recapture the part of the day that has escaped, and quite often you have the urge to read the international section of a newspaper, or go to see a Peter Greenaway film, to consume something solid and meaty which will lie on top of the cotton-candy worthlessness clogging up your head.

The other people I like are the ones who are being driven to find a tune that has been troubling them, distracting them, a tune that they can hear in their breath when they run for a bus, or in the rhythm of their windshield wipers when they're driving home from work. Sometimes something banal and obvious is responsible for the distraction: they have heard it on the radio, or at a club. But sometimes it has come to them as if by magic. Sometimes it has come to them because the sun was out, and they saw someone who looked nice, and they suddenly found themselves humming a snatch of a song they haven't heard for fifteen or twenty years; once, a guy came in because he had *dreamed* a record, the whole thing, melody, title, and artist. And when I found it for him (it was an old reggae thing, "Happy Go Lucky Girl" by the Paragons), and it was more or less exactly as it had appeared to him in his sleep, the look on his face made me feel as though I was not a man who ran a record shop, but a midwife, or a painter, someone whose life is routinely transcendental.

You can really see what Dick and Barry are for on Saturdays. Dick is as patient and as enthusiastic and as gentle as a primary-school teacher: he sells people records they didn't know they wanted because he knows intuitively what they should buy. He chats, then puts something on the record deck, and soon they're handing over fivers almost distractedly as if that's what they'd come in for in the first place. Barry, meanwhile, simply bulldozes customers into submission. He rubbishes them because they don't own the first Jesus and Mary Chain album, and they buy it, and he laughs at them because they don't own *Blonde on Blonde,* so they buy that, and he explodes in disbelief when they tell him that they have never heard of Ann Peebles, and then they buy something of hers, too. At around four o'clock most Saturday afternoons, just when I make us all a cup of tea, I have a little glow on, maybe because this is after all my work, and it's going OK, maybe because I'm proud of us, of the way that, though our talents are small and peculiar, we use them to their best advantage.

So when I come to close the shop, and we're getting ready to go out for a drink as we do every Saturday, we are all happy together again; we have a fund of goodwill which we will spend over the next few empty days, and which will have completely run out by Friday lunchtime. We are so happy, in fact, that between throwing the customers out and leaving for the day, we list our top five Elvis Costello songs (I go for "Alison," "Little Triggers," "Man Out of Time," "King Horse," and a bootleg Merseybeat-style version of "Everyday I Write the Book" I've got on a bootleg tape somewhere, the obscurity of the last cleverly counteracting the obviousness of the first, I thought, and thus preempting scorn from Barry) and, after the sulks and rows of the last week, it feels good to think about things like this again.

But when we walk out of the shop, Laura's waiting there for me, leaning against the strip of wall that separates us from the shoe shop next door, and I remember that it's not supposed to be a feel-good period of my life.

NINE

THE money is easy to explain: she had it, I didn't, and she wanted to give it to me. This was when she'd been in the new job a few months and her salary was starting to pile up in the bank a bit. She lent me five grand; if she hadn't, I would have gone under. I have never paid her back because I've never been able to, and the fact that she's moved out and is seeing somebody else doesn't make me five grand richer. The other day on the phone, when I gave her a hard time and told her she'd fucked my life up, she said something about the money, something about whether I'd start paying her back in installments, and I said I'd pay her back at a pound a week for the next hundred years. That's when she hung up.

So that's the money. The stuff I told her about being unhappy in the relationship, about half looking around for someone else: she pushed me into saying it. She *tricked* me into saying it. That sounds feeble, but she did. We were having a state-of-the-nation conversation and she said, quite matter-of-factly, that we were in a pretty unhappy phase at the moment, and I agreed; she asked whether I ever thought about meeting somebody else, and I denied it, and she laughed, and said that people in our position were always thinking about meeting somebody else. So I asked if she was always thinking about meeting somebody else, and she said of course, so I admitted that I did daydream about it sometimes. At the time I thought it was a let's-be-grown-up-about-life's-imperfectibility sort of conversation, an abstract, adult analysis; now I see that we were really talking about her and Ian, and that she suckered me into absolving her. It was a sneaky lawyer's trick, and I fell for it, because she's much smarter than me.

I didn't know she was pregnant, of course I didn't. She hadn't told me because she knew I was seeing somebody else. (She knew I was seeing somebody else because I'd told her. We thought we were being grown-up, but we were being preposterously naive, childish even, to think that one or the other of us could get up to no good, and own up to the misdemeanor, while we were living together.) I didn't find out until ages afterward: we were going through a good period and I made some joke about having kids and she burst into tears. So I made her tell me what it was all about, and she did, after which I had a brief and ill-advised bout of noisy self-righteousness (the usual stuff—my child, too, what right did she have, blah blah) before her disbelief and contempt shut me up.

"You didn't look a very good long-term bet at the time," she said. "I didn't like you very much, either. I didn't want to have a baby by you. I didn't want to think about some awful visiting-rights relationship that stretched way on into the future. And I didn't want to be a single mother. It wasn't a very hard decision to make. There wasn't any point in consulting you about it."

These were all fair points. In fact, if I'd got pregnant by me at the time, I would have had an abortion for exactly the same reasons. I couldn't think of anything to say.

Later on the same evening, after I'd rethought the whole pregnancy thing using the new information I had at my disposal, I asked her why she had stuck with it.

She thought for a long time.

"Because I'd never stuck at anything before, and I'd made a promise to myself when we started seeing each other that I'd make it through at least one bad patch, just to see what happened. So I did. And you were so pathetically sorry about that idiotic Rosie woman . . ."—Rosie, the four-bonk, simultaneous orgasm, pain-in-the-arse girl, the girl I was seeing when Laura was pregnant—" . . . that you were very nice to me for quite a long time, and that was just what I needed. We go quite deep, Rob, if only because we've been together a reasonable length of time. And I didn't want to knock it all over and start again unless I really had to. So."

And why had I stuck with it? Not for reasons as noble and as adult as that. (Is there anything more adult than sticking with a relationship that's falling apart in the hope that you can put it right? I've never done that in my life.) I stuck with it because, suddenly, right at the end of the Rosie thing, I found myself really attracted to Laura again; it was like I needed Rosie to spice Laura up a bit. And I thought I'd blown it (I didn't know then that she was experimenting with stoicism). I could see her losing interest in me, so I worked like mad to get that interest back, and when I got it back, I lost interest in her all over again. That sort of thing happens to me a lot, I find. I don't know how to sort it out. And that more or less brings us up to date. When the whole sorry tale comes out in a great big lump like that, even the most shortsighted jerk, even the most self-deluding and self-pitying of jilted, wounded lovers can see that there is some cause and effect going on here, that abortions and Rosie and Ian and money all belong to, *deserve* each other.

Dick and Barry ask us if we want to go with them to the pub for a quick one, but it's hard to imagine us all sitting round a table laughing about the customer who confused Albert King with Albert Collins ("He didn't even flinch when he was looking at the record for scratches and he saw the Stax label," Barry told us, shaking his head at the previously unsuspected depths of human ignorance), and I politely decline. I presume that we're going back to the flat, so I walk toward the bus stop, but Laura tugs me on the arm and wheels around to look for a cab.

"I'll pay. It wouldn't be much fun on the twenty-nine, would it?"

Fair point. The conversation we need to have is best conducted without a conductor—and without dogs, kids, and fat people with huge Marks and Spencer bags.

We're pretty quiet in the cab. It's only a ten-minute ride from the Seven Sisters' Road to Crouch End, but the journey is so uncomfortable and intense and unhappy that I feel I'll remember it for the rest of my life. It's raining, and the fluorescent lights make patterns on our faces; the taxi driver asks us if we've had a good day, and we grunt, and he slams the partition shut behind him. Laura stares out of the window, and I sneak the odd look at her, trying to see if the last week has made any difference in her face. She's had her hair cut, same as usual, very short, sixties short, like Mia Farrow, except—and I'm not just being creepy—she's better suited to this sort of cut than Mia. It's because her hair is so dark, nearly black, that when it's short her eyes seem to take up most of her face. She's not wearing any makeup, and I reckon this is for my benefit. It's an easy way of showing me that she's careworn, distracted, too miserable for fripperies. There's a nice symmetry here: when I gave her that tape with the Solomon Burke song on it, all those years ago, she was wearing loads of makeup, much more than she was used to wearing, and much more than she had worn the previous week, and I knew, or hoped, that this was for my benefit, too. So you get loads at the beginning, to show that things are good, positive, exciting, and none at the end, to show that things are desperate. Neat, eh?

(But later, just as we're turning the corner into my road, and I'm beginning to panic about the pain and difficulty of the impending conversation, I see a woman on her own, Saturday-night-smart, off to meet somebody somewhere, friends, or a lover. And when I was living with Laura, I missed . . . what? Maybe I missed somebody traveling on a bus or tube or cab, *going out of her way,* to meet me, maybe dressed up a little, maybe wearing more makeup than usual, maybe even slightly nervous; when I was younger, the knowledge that I was responsible for any of this, even the bus ride, made me feel pathetically grateful. When you're with someone permanently, you don't get that: if Laura wanted to see me, she only had to turn her head, or walk from the bathroom to the bedroom, and she never bothered to dress up for the trip. And when she came home, she came home because she lived in my flat, not because we were lovers, and when we went out, she sometimes dressed up and sometimes didn't, depending on where we were going, but again, it was nothing whatsoever to do with me. Anyway, all this is by way of saying that the woman I saw out of the cab window inspired me and consoled me, momentarily: maybe I am not too old to provoke a trip from one part of London to another, and if I ever do have another date, and I arrange to meet that date in, say, Islington, and she has to come all the way from Stoke Newington, a journey of some three to four miles, I will thank her from the bottom of my wretched thirty-five-year-old heart.)

Laura pays the cabbie and I unlock the front door, put the timer light on, and usher her inside. She stops and goes through the post on the windowsill, just through force of habit, I guess, but of course she gets herself in difficulties immediately: as she's shuffling through the envelopes, she comes across Ian's TV license reminder, and she hesitates, just for a second, but long enough to remove any last remaining trace of doubt from my mind, and I feel sick.

"You can take it with you if you want," I say, but I can't look at her, and she doesn't look at me. "Save me having to redirect it." But she just puts it back in the pile, and then puts the pile back among the takeaway menus and minicab cards on the windowsill, and starts walking up the stairs.

When we get into the flat, it's weird seeing her there. But what's particularly odd is how she tries to avoid doing the things that she used to do—you can see her checking herself. She takes her coat off; she used to chuck it over one of the chairs, but she doesn't want to do that tonight. She stands there holding it for a little while, and I take it off her and chuck it over one of the chairs. She starts to go into the kitchen, either to put the kettle on or to pour herself a glass of wine, so I ask her, politely, whether she'd like a cup of tea, and she asks me, politely, whether there's anything stronger, and when I say that there's a half-empty bottle of wine in the fridge, she manages not to say that there was a whole one when she left, and she bought it. Anyway, it's not hers any more, or it's not the same bottle, or something. And when she sits down, she chooses the chair nearest the stereo—my chair—rather than the one nearest the TV—her chair.

"Have you done them yet?" She nods toward the shelves full of albums.

"What?" I know what, of course.

"The Great Reorganization." I can hear the capital letters.

"Oh. Yes. The other night." I don't want to tell her that I did it the evening after she'd gone, but she gives an irritating little, well-fancy-that smile anyway.

"What?" I say. "What's that supposed to mean?"

"Nothing. Just, you know. Didn't take you long."

"Don't you think there are more important things to talk about than my record collection?"

"Yes, I do, Rob. I've always thought that."

I'm supposed to have the moral high ground here (she's the one who's been sleeping with the neighbors, after all), but I can't even get out of base camp.

"Where have you been staying for the last week?"

"I think you know that," she says quietly.

"Had to work it out for myself, though, didn't I?"

I feel sick again, really sick. I don't know how it shows on my face, but suddenly Laura loses it a little: she looks tired, and sad, and she stares hard straight ahead to stop herself from crying.

"I'm sorry. I made some bad decisions. I haven't been very fair to you. That's why I came to the shop this evening, because I thought it was time to be brave."

"Are you scared now?"

"Yes, of course I am. I feel terrible. This is really hard, you know."

"Good."

Silence. I don't know what to say. There are loads of things I want to ask, but they are all questions I don't really want answered: when did you start seeing Ian, and was it because of the, you know, the ceiling noise thing, and is it better (What? she'd ask; Everything, I'd say), and is this really definitely it, or just some sort of phase, and—this is how feeble I'm becoming—have you missed me at all even one bit, do you love me, do you love him, do you want to end up with him, do you want to have babies with him, and is it better, *is it better,* IS IT BETTER?

"Is it because of my job?"

Where did that one come from? Of course it's not because of my fucking job. Why did I ask that?

"Oh, Rob, of course it isn't."

That's why I asked that. Because I felt sorry for myself, and I wanted some sort of cheap consolation: I wanted to hear "Of course it isn't" said with a tender dismissiveness, whereas if I'd asked her the Big Question, I might have got an embarrassed denial, or an embarrassed silence, or an embarrassed confession, and I didn't want any of them.

"Is that what you think? That I've left you because you're not grand enough for me? Give me some credit, please." But again, she says it nicely, in a tone of voice I recognize from a long time ago.

"I don't know. It's one of the things I thought of."

"What were the others?"

"Just the obvious stuff."

"What's the obvious stuff?"

"I don't know."

"So it's not *that* obvious, then."

"No."

Silence again.

"Is it working out with Ian?"

"Oh, come on, Rob. Don't be childish."

"Why is that childish? You're living with the bloke. I just wanted to know how it was going."

"I'm not living with him. I've just been staying with him for a few days until I work out what I'm doing. Look, this has nothing to do with anyone else. You know that, don't you?"

They always say that. They always, always say that it's nothing to do with anyone else. I'll bet you any money that if Celia Johnson had run off with Trevor Howard at the end of *Brief Encounter,* she would have told her husband that it was nothing to do with anyone else. It's the first law of romantic trauma. I make a rather repulsive and inappropriately comic snorting noise to express my disbelief, and Laura nearly laughs, but thinks better of it.

"I left because we weren't really getting on, or even talking, very much, and I'm at an age where I want to sort myself out, and I couldn't see that ever happening with you, mostly because you seem incapable of sorting yourself out. And I was sort of interested in someone else, and then that went further than it should have done, so it seemed like a good time to go. But I've no idea what will happen with Ian in the long run. Probably nothing. Maybe you'll grow up a bit and we'll put things right. Maybe I'll never see either of you ever again. I don't know. All I do know is that it's not a good time to be living here."

More silence. Why are people—let's face it, women—like this? It doesn't pay to think this way, with all this mess and doubt and gray, smudged lines where there should be a crisp, sharp picture. I agree that you need to meet somebody new in order to dispense with the old—you have to be incredibly brave and adult to pack something in just because it isn't working very well. But you can't go about it all half-heartedly, like Laura is doing now. When I started seeing Rosie the simultaneous orgasm woman, I wasn't like this; as far as I was concerned, she was a serious prospect, the woman who was going to lead me painlessly out of one relationship and into another, and the fact that it didn't happen like that, that she was a disaster area, was just bad luck. At least there was a clear battle-plan in my head, and there was none of this irritating oh-Rob-I-need-time stuff.

"But you haven't definitely decided to pack me in? There's still a chance that we'll get back together?"

"I don't know."

"Well, if you don't know, that must mean there's a chance."

"I don't know if there's a chance."

Jesus.

"That's what I'm saying. That if you don't know there's a chance, there must be a chance, mustn't there? It's like, if someone was in hospital, and he was seriously ill, and the doctor said, I don't know if he's got a chance of survival or not, then that doesn't mean the patient's definitely going to die, does it? It means he might live. Even if it's only a remote possibility."

"I suppose so."

"So we have a chance of getting back together again."

"Oh, Rob, shut up."

"I just want to know where I stand. What chance I have."

"I don't bloody know what bloody fucking chance you have. I'm trying to tell you that I'm confused, that I haven't been happy for ages, that we got ourselves into a terrible mess, that I've been seeing someone else. These are the important things."

"I guess. But if you could just tell me roughly, it would help."

"OK, OK. We have a nine percent chance of getting back together. Does that clarify the situation?" She's so sick of this, so near to bursting, that her eyes are clenched tight shut and she's speaking in a furious, poisonous whisper.

"You're just being stupid now."

I know, somewhere in me, that it's not her that's being stupid. I understand, on one level, that she doesn't know, that everything's up in the air. But that's no use to me. You know the worst thing about being rejected? The lack of control. If I could only control the when and how of being dumped by somebody, then it wouldn't seem as bad. But then, of course, it wouldn't be rejection, would it? It would be by mutual consent. It would be musical differences. I would be leaving to pursue a solo career. I know how unbelievably and pathetically childish it is to push and push like this for some degree of probability, but it's the only thing I can do to grab any sort of control back from her.

When I saw Laura outside the shop I knew *absolutely,* without any question at all, that I wanted her again. But that's probably because she's the one doing the rejecting. If I can get her to concede that there is a chance we'll patch things up, that makes things easier for me: if I don't have to go around feeling hurt, and powerless, and miserable, I can cope without her. In other words, I'm unhappy because she doesn't want me; if I can convince myself that she does want me a bit, then I'll be OK again, because then I won't want her, and I can get on with looking for someone else.

Laura is wearing an expression I have come to know well

in recent months, a look that denotes both infinite patience and hopeless frustration. It doesn't feel good to know that she has invented this look just for me. She never needed it before. She sighs, and puts her head on her hand, and stares at the wall.

"OK, it could be that we sort things out. There may be a chance of that happening. I would say not a good chance, but a chance."

"Great."

"No, Rob, it's not great. Nothing's great. Everything's shit."

"But it won't be, you'll see."

She shakes her head, apparently in disbelief. "I'm too tired for this now. I know I'm asking a lot, but will you go back to the pub and have a drink with the others while I'm sorting some stuff out? I need to be able to think while I'm doing it, and I can't think with you here."

"No problem. If I can ask one question."

"OK. One."

"It sounds stupid."

"Never mind."

"You won't like it."

"Just . . . just ask it."

"Is it better?"

"Is what better? Is what better than what?"

"Well. Sex, I guess. Is sex with him better?"

"Jesus Christ, Rob. Is that really what's bothering you?"

"Of course it is."

"You really think it would make a difference either way?"

"I don't know." And I don't.

"Well, the answer is that I don't know either. We haven't done it yet."

Yes!

"Never?"

"No. I haven't felt like it."

"But not even before, when he was living upstairs?"

"Oh, thanks a lot. No. I was living with you then, remember?"

I feel a bit embarrassed and I don't say anything.

"We've slept together but we haven't made love. Not yet. But I'll tell you one thing. The sleeping together is better."

Yes! Yes! This is fantastic news! Mr. Sixty-Minute Man hasn't even clocked on yet! I kiss her on the cheek and go to the pub to meet Dick and Barry. I feel like a new man, although not very much like a New Man. I feel so much better, in fact, that I go straight out and sleep with Marie.

TEN

FACT:

Over three million men in this country have slept with ten or more women. And do they all look like Richard Gere? Are they all as rich as Croesus, as charming as Clark Gable, as preposterously endowed as Errol Flynn, as witty as Oscar Wilde? Nope. It's nothing to do with any of that. Maybe half a dozen or so of that three million have one or more of these attributes, but that still leaves . . . well, three million, give or take half a dozen. And they're just blokes. *We're* just blokes, because I, even I, am a member of the exclusive three million club. Ten is not so many if you're unmarried and in your mid-thirties. Ten partners in a couple of decades of sexual activity is actually pretty feeble, if you think about it: one partner every two years, and if any of those partners was a one-night stand, and that one-night stand came in the middle of a two-year drought, then you're not *in trouble* exactly, but you're hardly the

Number One Lover Man in your particular postal district. Ten isn't a lot, not for the thirtysomething bachelor. Twenty isn't a lot, if you look at it that way. Anything over thirty, I reckon, and you're entitled to appear on an Oprah about promiscuity.

Marie is my seventeenth lover. "How does he do it?" you ask yourselves. "He wears bad sweaters, he gives his ex-girlfriend a hard time, he's grumpy, he's broke, he hangs out with the Musical Moron Twins, and yet he gets to go to bed with an American recording artist who looks like Susan Dey. What's going on?"

First off, let's not get carried away here. Yes, she's a recording artist, but she records with the ironically titled Blackpool-based Hit Records, and it's the type of record contract where you sell your own tapes during the interval of your own show in London's prestigious Sir Harry Lauder nightspot. And if I know Susan Dey, and after a relationship that has endured for over twenty years I feel I do, I reckon she'd be the first to admit that looking like Susan Dey in *L.A. Law* is not the same as looking like, say, Vivien Leigh in *Gone With the Wind.*

But yes, even so, the night with Marie is my major sexual triumph, my *bonkus mirabilis.* And do you know how it comes about? Because I ask questions. That's it. That's my secret. If someone wanted to know how to get off with seventeen women, or more, no less, that's what I'd tell them: ask questions. It works precisely because that isn't how you're supposed to do it, if you listen to the collective male wisdom. There are still enough of the old-style, big-mouthed, self-opinionated egomaniacs around to make someone like me appear refreshingly different; Marie even says something like that to me halfway through the evening . . .

I had no idea that Marie and T-Bone were going to be in the pub with Dick and Barry, who had apparently promised them a real English Saturday night out—pub, curry, night bus, and all the trimmings. But I'm happy to see them, both of them; I'm really up after the triumph with Laura, and seeing as Marie has only ever seen me tongue-tied and grumpy, she must wonder what has happened. Let her wonder. It's not often that I get the chance to be enigmatic and perplexing.

They're sitting round a table, drinking pints of bitter. Marie shuffles along to let me sit down, and the moment she does that I'm lost, gone, away. It's the Saturday-night-date woman I saw through the window of the cab who has set me off, I think. I see Marie's shuffle along the seat as a miniature but meaningful romantic accommodation: hey, she's doing this for me! Pathetic, I know, but immediately I start to worry that Barry or Dick—let's face it, Barry—has told her about where I was and what I was doing. Because if she knows about Laura, and about the split, and about me getting uptight, then she'll lose interest and, as she had no interest in the first place, that would put me into a minus interest situation. I'd be in the red, interest-wise.

Barry and Dick are asking T-Bone about Guy Clark; Marie's listening, but then she turns to me and asks me, conspiratorially, if everything went all right. Bastard Barry bigmouth.

I shrug.

"She just wanted to pick some stuff up. No big deal."

"God, I hate that time. That picking-up-stuff time. I just went through that before I came here. You know that song called 'Patsy Cline Times Two' I play? That's about me and my ex dividing up our record collections."

"It's a great song."

"Thank you."

"And you wrote it just before you came here?"

"I wrote it on the way here. The words, anyway. I'd had the tune for a while, but I didn't know what to do with it until I thought of the title."

It begins to dawn on me that T-Bone, if I may Cuisinart my foodstuffs, is a red herring.

"Is that why you came to London in the first place? Because of, you know, dividing up your record collection and stuff?"

"Yup." She shrugs, then thinks, and then laughs, because the affirmative has told the entire story, and there's nothing else to say, but she tries anyway.

"Yup. He broke my heart, and suddenly I didn't want to be in Austin anymore, so I called T-Bone, and he fixed up a couple of gigs and an apartment for me, and here I am."

"You share a place with T-Bone?"

She laughs again, a big snorty laugh, right into her beer. "No *way!* T-Bone wouldn't want to share a place with me. I'd cramp his style. And I wouldn't want to listen to all that stuff happening on the other side of the bedroom wall. I'm way too unattached for that."

She's single. I'm single. I'm a single man talking to an attractive single woman who may or may not have just confessed to feelings of sexual frustration. Oh my God.

A while back, when Dick and Barry and I agreed that what really matters is what you like, not what you *are* like, Barry proposed the idea of a questionnaire for prospective partners, a two- or three-page multiple-choice document that covered all the music/film/TV/book bases. It was intended a) to dispense with awkward conversation, and b) to prevent a chap from leaping into bed with someone who might, at a later date, turn out to have every Julio Iglesias record ever made. It amused us at the time, although Barry, being Barry, went one stage further: he compiled the questionnaire and presented it to some poor woman he was interested in, and she hit him with it. But there was an important and essential truth contained in the idea, and the truth was that these things matter, and it's no good pretending that any relationship has a future if your record collections disagree violently, or if your favorite films wouldn't even speak to each other if they met at a party.

If I'd given Marie a questionnaire, she wouldn't have hit me with it. She would have understood the validity of the exercise. We have one of those conversations where everything clicks, meshes, corresponds, locks, where even our pauses, even our punctuation marks, seem to be nodding in agreement. Nanci Griffith and Kurt Vonnegut, the Cowboy Junkies and hip-hop, *My Life as a Dog* and *A Fish Called Wanda,* Pee-Wee Herman and *Wayne's World,* sports and Mexican food (yes, yes, yes, no, yes, no, no, yes, no, yes) . . . You remember that kid's game, Mousetrap? That ludicrous machine you had to build, where silver balls went down chutes, and little men went up ladders, and one thing knocked into another to set off something else, until in the end the cage fell onto the mouse and trapped it? The evening goes with that sort of breathtaking joke precision, where you can kind of see what's supposed to happen but you can't believe it's ever going to get there, even though afterwards it seems obvious.

When I begin to get the feeling that we're having a good time, I give her chances to get away: when there's a silence I start to listen to T-Bone telling Barry what Guy Clark is really like in real life as a human being, but Marie sets us back down a private road each time. And when we move from the pub to the curry house, I slow down to the back of the group, so that she can leave me behind if she wants, but she slows down with me. And in the curry house I sit down first, so she can choose where she wants to be, and she chooses the place next to me. It's only at the end of the evening that I make anything that could be interpreted as a move: I tell Marie that it makes sense for the two of us to share a cab. It's more or less true anyway, because T-Bone is staying in Camden and both Dick and Barry live in the East End, so it's not like I've remapped the entire city for my own purposes. And it's not like I've told her that it makes sense for me to stay the night at her place, either—if she doesn't want any further company, all she has to do is get out of the cab, try to shove a fiver at me, and wave me on my way. But when we get to her place, she asks me if I want to break into her duty free, and I find that I do. So.

So. Her place is very much like my place, a boxy first-floor flat in a north London three-story house. In fact, it's so much like my place that it's depressing. Is it really as easy as this to approximate my life? One quick phone call to a friend and that's it? It's taken me a decade or more to put down roots even as shallow as these. The acoustics are all wrong, though; there are no books, there's no wall of records, and there's very little furniture, just a sofa and an armchair. There's no hi-fi, just a little audiocassette and a few tapes, some of which she bought from us. And, thrillingly, there are two guitars leaning against the wall.

She goes into the kitchen, which is actually in the living room but distinguishable because the carpet stops and the lino begins, and gets some ice and a couple of glasses (she doesn't ask me if I want ice, but this is the first bum note she's played all evening, so I don't feel like complaining) and sits down next to me on the sofa. I ask her questions about Austin, about the clubs and the people there; I also ask her loads of questions about her ex, and she talks *well* about him. She describes the set-up and her knock-back with wisdom and honesty and a dry, self-deprecating humor, and I can see why her songs are as good as they are. I don't talk well about Laura, or, at least, I don't talk with the same sort of depth. I cut corners and trim edges and widen the margins and speak in big letters to make it all look a bit more detailed than it really is, so she gets to hear a bit about Ian (although she doesn't get to hear the noises I heard), and a bit about Laura's work, but nothing about abortions or money or pain-in-the-arse simultaneous orgasm women. It feels, even to me, like I'm being intimate: I speak quietly, slowly, thoughtfully, I express regret, I say nice things about Laura, I hint at a deep ocean of melancholy just below the surface. But it's all bollocks, really, a cartoon sketch of a decent, sensitive guy which does the trick because I am in a position to invent my own reality and because—I think—Marie has already decided she likes me.

I have completely forgotten how to do the next bit, even though I'm never sure whether there's going to be a next bit. I remember the juvenile stuff, where you put your arm along the sofa and let it drop onto her shoulder, or press your leg against hers; I remember the mock-tough adult stuff I used to try when I was in my mid-twenties, where I looked someone in the eye and asked if they wanted to stay the night. But none of that seems appropriate anymore. What do you do when you're old enough to know better? In the end—and if you'd wanted to place a bet, you would have got pretty short odds on this one—it's a clumsy collision standing up in the middle of the living room. I get up to go to the loo, she says she'll show me, we bump into each other, I grab, we kiss, and I'm back in the land of sexual neurosis.

Why is failure the first thing I think of when I find myself in this sort of situation? Why can't I just enjoy myself? But if you have to ask the question, then you know you're lost: self-consciousness is a man's worst enemy. Already I'm wondering whether she's as aware of my erection as I am, and if she is, what she feels about it; but I can't even maintain that worry, let alone anything else, because so many other worries are crowding it out, and the next stage looks intimidatingly difficult, unfathomably terrifying, absolutely impossible.

Look at all the things that can go wrong for men. There's the nothing-happening-at-all problem, the too-much-happening-too-soon problem, the dismal-droop-after-a-promising-beginning problem; there's the size-doesn't-matter-except-in-my-case problem, the failing-to-deliver-the-goods problem . . . and what do women have to worry about? A handful of cellulite? Join the club. A spot of I-wonder-how-I-rank? Ditto.

I'm happy to be a bloke, I think, but sometimes I'm not happy being a bloke in the late-twentieth century. Sometimes I'd rather be my dad. He never had to worry about delivering the goods, because he never knew that there were any goods to deliver; he never had to worry about how he ranked in my mother's all-time hot one hundred, because he was first and last on the list. Wouldn't it be great if you could talk about this sort of thing to your father?

One day, maybe, I'll try. "Dad, did you ever have to worry about the female orgasm in either its clitoral or its (possibly mythical) vaginal form? Do you, in fact, know what the female orgasm is? What about the G-spot? What did 'good in bed' mean in 1955, if it meant anything at all? When was oral sex imported to Britain? Do you envy me my sex life, or does it all look like terribly hard work to you? Did you ever fret about how long you could keep going for, or didn't you think about that sort of thing then? Aren't you glad that you've never had to buy vegetarian cookery books as the first small step on the road to getting inside someone's knickers? Aren't you glad that you've never had the 'You might be right-on but do you clean the toilet?' conversation? Aren't you relieved that you've been spared the perils of childbirth that all modern men have to face?" (And what would he say, I wonder, if he were not tongue-tied by his class and his sex and his diffidence? Probably something like,

"Son, stop whining. The good fuck wasn't even *invented* in my day, and however many toilets you clean and vegetarian recipes you have to read, you still have more fun than we were ever allowed." And he'd be right, too.)

This is the sort of sex education I never had—the one that deals in G-spots and the like. No one ever told me about anything that mattered, about how to take your trousers off with dignity or what to say to someone when you can't get an erection or what "good in bed" meant in 1975 or 1985, never mind 1955. Get this: no one ever told me about *semen* even, just sperm, and there's a crucial difference. As far as I could tell, these microscopic tadpole things just leaped invisibly out of the end of your whatsit, and so when, on the occasion of my first . . . well, never you mind. But this disastrously partial grasp of the male sex organs caused distress and embarrassment and shame until one afternoon in a Wimpy Bar, a school friend, apropos of nothing, remarked that the saliva he had left in his glass of Wimpy cola "looked like spunk," an enigmatic observation that had me puzzling feverishly for an entire weekend, although at the time, of course, I tittered knowingly. It is difficult to stare at foreign matter floating on the top of a glass of cola and from this minimal information work out the miracle of life itself, but that is what I had to do, and I did it, too.

Anyway. We stand up and kiss, and then we sit down and kiss, and half of me is telling myself not to worry, and the other half is feeling pleased with myself, and these two halves make a whole and leave no room for the here and now, for any pleasure or lust, so then I start wondering whether I have *ever* enjoyed this stuff, the physical sensation rather than the fact of it, or whether it's just something I feel I ought to do, and when this reverie is over I find that we're no longer kissing but hugging, and I'm staring at the back of the sofa. Marie pushes me away so that she can have a look at me and, rather than let her see me gazing blankly into space, I squeeze my eyes tight shut, which gets me out of the immediate hole but which in the long run is probably a mistake, because it makes it look as though I have spent most of my life waiting for this moment, and that will either scare her rigid or make her assume some things that she shouldn't.

"You OK?" she says.

I nod. "You?"

"For now. But I wouldn't be if I thought this was the end of the evening."

When I was seventeen, I used to lie awake at night hoping that women would say things like that to me; now, it just brings back the panic.

"I'm sure it isn't."

"Good. In that case, I'll fix us something else to drink. You sticking to the whiskey, or you want a coffee?"

I stick to the whiskey, so I'll have an excuse if nothing happens, or if things happen too quickly, or if blah blah blah.

"You know, I really thought you hated me," she says. "You'd never said more than two words to me before this evening, and they were real crotchety words."

"Is that why you were interested?"

"Yeah, kind of, I guess."

"That's not the right answer."

"No, but . . . if a guy's kind of weird with me, I want to find out what's going on, you know?"

"And you know now?"

"Nope. Do you?"

Yep.

"Nope."

We laugh merrily; maybe if I just keep laughing, I'll be able to postpone the moment. She tells me that she thought I was cute, a word that no one has ever previously used in connection with me, and soulful, by which I think she means that I don't say much and I always look vaguely pissed off. I tell her that I think she's beautiful, which I sort of do, and talented, which I definitely do. And we talk like this for a while, congratulating ourselves on our good fortune and each other for our good taste, which is the way these post-kiss pre-sex conversations always go, in my experience; and I'm grateful for every stupid word of it, because it buys me time.

I've never had the sexual heebie-jeebies this bad before. I used to get nervous, sure, but I was never in any doubt that I wanted to go through with it; now, it seems more than enough to know that I can if I want to, and if there was a way of cheating, of circumnavigating the next bit—getting Marie to sign some sort of affidavit which said I'd spent the night, for example—I'd take it. It's hard to imagine, in fact, that the thrill of actually doing it will be any greater than the thrill of finding myself in a *position* to do it, but then maybe sex has always been like that for me. Maybe I never really enjoyed the naked part of sex, just the dinner, coffee and get-away-that's-*my*-favorite-Hitchcock-film-*too* part of sex, as long as it's a sexual preamble, and not just a purposeless chat, and . . .

Who am I kidding? I'm just trying to make myself feel better. I used to love sex, all of it, the naked parts and the clothed parts and, on a good day, with a fair wind, when I hadn't had too much to drink and I wasn't too tired and I was just at the right stage of the relationship (not too soon, when I had the first-night nerves, and not too late, when I had the not-this-routine-again blues), I was OK at it. (By which I mean what exactly? Dunno. No complaints, I guess, but then there never are in polite company, are there?) The trouble is that it's been *years* since I've done anything like this. What if she laughs? What if I get my sweater stuck round my head? It does happen with this sweater. For some reason the neck hole has shrunk but nothing else—either that or my head has got fat at a faster rate than the rest of me—and if I'd known this morning that . . . anyway.

"I've got to go," I say. I have no idea that I'm going to say this, but when I hear the words they make perfect sense. But of course! What a fantastic idea! Just go home! You don't have to have sex if you don't want to! What a *grown-up!*

Marie looks at me. "When I said before that I hoped it wasn't the end of the evening, I was, you know . . . talking about breakfast and stuff. I wasn't talking about another whiskey and another ten minutes of shooting the shit. I'd like it if you could stay the night."

"Oh," I say lamely. "Oh. Right."

"Jesus, so much for delicacy. Next time I ask a guy to stay the night when I'm here, I'll do it the American way. I thought you English were supposed to be the masters of understatement, and beating around the bush, and all that jazz."

"We use it, but we don't understand it when other people use it."

"You understand me now? I'd rather stop there, before I have to say something really crude."

"No, that's fine. I just thought I should, you know, clear things up."

"So they're clear?"

"Yeah."

"And you'll stay?"

"Yeah."

"Good."

It takes genius to do what I have just done. I had the chance of going and I blew it; in the process I showed myself incapable of conducting a courtship with any kind of sophistication whatsoever. She uses a nice sexy line to ask me to stay the night, and I lead her to believe that it sailed right over my head, thus turning myself into the kind of person she wouldn't have wanted to sleep with in the first place. Brilliant.

But miraculously there are no more hiccups. We have the Trojan conversation, as in I tell her I haven't brought anything with me and she laughs and says that she'd be appalled if I had and anyway she has something in her bag. We both know what we're talking about and why, but we don't elaborate any further. (You don't need to, do you? If you ask someone for a loo-roll, you don't have to have a conversation about what you're going to do with it.) And then she picks up her drink, grabs me by the hand, and takes me into the bedroom.

Bad news: there's a bathroom interlude. I hate bathroom interludes, all that "You can use the green toothbrush and the pink towel" stuff. Don't get me wrong: personal hygiene is of the utmost importance, and people who don't clean their teeth are shortsighted and very silly, and I wouldn't let a child of mine, etc., and so on. But, you know, can't we take some time out every now and again? We're supposed to be in the grip of a passion that neither of us can control here, so how come she can find time to think about Neutrogena and carrot moisturizer and cotton balls and the rest of it? On the whole, I prefer women who are prepared to break the habit of half a lifetime in your honor, and, in any case, bathroom interludes do nothing for a chap's nerves, or for his enthusiasm, if you catch my drift. I'm particularly disappointed to learn that Marie is an interluder, because I thought she'd be a little more bohemian, what with the recording contract and all; I thought sex would be a little dirtier, literally and figuratively. Once we're in the bedroom she disappears straightaway, and I'm left cooling my heels and worrying about whether I'm supposed to get undressed or not.

See, if I get undressed and she then offers me the green toothbrush, I'm sunk: that means either the long nude walk to the bathroom, and I'm just not ready for that yet, or going fully clothed and getting your sweater stuck over your head afterwards. (To *refuse* the green toothbrush is simply not on, for obvious reasons.) It's all right for her, of course; she can avoid all this. She can come in wearing an extra-large Sting

T-shirt which she then slips off while I'm out of the room; she's given nothing away and I'm a humiliated wreck. But then I remember that I'm wearing a pair of reasonably snazzy boxers (a present from Laura) and a cleanish white T-shirt, so I can go for the underwear-in-bed option, a not unreasonable compromise. When Marie comes back I'm browsing through her John Irving paperback with as much cool as I can manage.

And then I go to the bathroom, and clean my teeth; and then I come back; and then we make love; and then we talk for a bit; and then we turn the light out, and that's it. I'm not going into all that other stuff, the who-did-what-to-whom stuff. You know "Behind Closed Doors" by Charlie Rich? That's one of my favorite songs.

You're entitled to know some things, I suppose. You're entitled to know that I didn't let myself down, that none of the major problems afflicted me, that I didn't deliver the goods but Marie said she had a nice time anyway, and I believed her; and you're entitled to know that I had a nice time, too, and that at some point or other along the way I remembered what it is I like about sex: what I like about sex is that I can lose myself in it entirely. Sex, in fact, is the most absorbing activity I have discovered in adulthood. When I was a child I used to feel this way about all sorts of things—Legos, *The Jungle Book, The Hardy Boys, The Man from U.N.C.L.E.,* Saturday morning cartoons . . . I could forget where I was, the time of day, who I was with. Sex is the only thing I've found like that as a grown-up, give or take the odd film: books are no longer like that once you're out of your teens, and I've certainly never found it in my work. All the horrible pre-sex self-consciousness drains out of me, and I forget where I am, the time of day . . . and yes, I forget who I'm with, for the time being. Sex is about the only grown-up thing I know how to do; it's weird, then, that it's the only thing that can make me feel like a ten-year-old.

I wake up around dawn, and I have the same feeling I had the other night, the night I caught on about Laura and Ray: that I've got no ballast, nothing to weigh me down, and if I don't hang on, I'll just float away. I like Marie a lot, she's funny and smart and pretty and talented, but who the hell is she? I don't mean that philosophically. I just mean, I don't know her from Eve, so what am I doing in her bed? Surely there's a better, safer, more friendly place for me than this? But I know there isn't, not at the moment, and that scares me rigid.

I get up, find my snazzy boxers and my T-shirt, go into the living room, fumble in my jacket pocket for my fags and sit in the dark smoking. After a little while Marie gets up, too, and sits down next to me.

"You sitting here wondering what you're doing?"

"No. I'm just, you know . . ."

" 'Cause that's why I'm sitting here, if it helps."

"I thought I'd woken you up."

"I ain't even been to sleep yet."

"So you've been wondering for a lot longer than me. Worked anything out?"

"Bits. I've worked out that I was real lonely, and I went and jumped into bed with the first person who'd have me.

And I've also worked out that I was lucky it was you, and not somebody mean, or boring, or crazy."

"I'm not mean, anyway. And you wouldn't have gone to bed with anyone who was any of those things."

"I'm not so sure about that. I've had a bad week."

"What's happened?"

"Nothing's happened. I've had a bad week in my head, is all."

Before we slept together, there was at least some pretense that it was something we both wanted to do, that it was the healthy, strong beginning of an exciting new relationship. Now all the pretense seems to have gone, and we're left to face the fact that we're sitting here because we don't know anybody else we could be sitting with.

"I don't care if you've got the blues," Marie says. "It's OK. And I wasn't fooled by you acting all cool about . . . what's her name?"

"Laura."

"Laura, right. But people are allowed to feel horny and fucked-up at the same time. You shouldn't feel embarrassed about it. I don't. Why should we be denied basic human rights just because we've messed up our relationships?"

I'm beginning to feel more embarrassed about the conversation than about anything we've just done. Horny? They really use that word? Jesus. All my life I've wanted to go to bed with an American, and now I have, and I'm beginning to see why people don't do it more often. Apart from Americans, that is, who probably go to bed with Americans all the time.

"You think sex is a basic human right?"

"You bet. And I'm not going to let that asshole stand between me and a fuck."

I try not to think about the peculiar anatomical diagram she has just drawn. And I also decide not to point out that though sex may well be a basic human right, it's kind of hard to insist on that right if you keep on busting up with the people you want to have sex with.

"Which arsehole?"

She spits out the name of a fairly well-known American singer-songwriter, someone you might have heard of.

"He's the one you had to split the Patsy Cline records with?"

She nods, and I can't control my enthusiasm.

"That's amazing!"

"What, that you've slept with someone who's slept with . . ." (Here she repeats the name of the fairly well-known American singer-songwriter, whom I shall hereafter refer to as Steve.)

She's right! Exactly that! Exactly that! I've slept with someone who's slept with . . . Steve! (That sentence sounds stupid without his real name in it. Like, I've danced with a man who danced with a girl who danced with . . . Bob. But just imagine the name of someone, not *really* famous, but quite famous—Lyle Lovett, say, although I should point out, for legal reasons, that it's not him—and you'll get the idea.)

"Don't be daft, Marie. I'm not that crass. I just meant, you know, it's amazing that someone who wrote—" (and here I name Steve's greatest hit, a drippy and revoltingly sensitive ballad) "should be such a bastard." I'm very pleased with this explanation for my amazement. Not only does it get me out of a hole, but it's both sharp and relevant.

"That song's about his ex, you know, the one before me. It felt real good listening to him sing that night after night, I can tell you."

This is great. This is how I imagined it would be, going out with someone who had a recording contract.

"And then I wrote 'Patsy Cline Times Two,' and he's probably writing something about me writing a song about all that, and she's probably writing a song about having a song written about her, and . . ."

"That's how it goes. We all do that."

"You all write songs about each other?"

"No, but . . ."

It would take too long to explain about Marco and Charlie, and how they wrote Sarah, in a way, because without Marco and Charlie there would have been no Sarah, and how Sarah and her ex, the one who wanted to be someone at the BBC, how they wrote me, and how Rosie the pain-in-the-arse simultaneous orgasm girl and I wrote Ian. It's just that none of us had the wit or the talent to make them into songs. We made them into life, which is much messier, and more time-consuming, and leaves nothing for anybody to whistle.

Marie stands up. "I'm about to do something terrible, so please forgive me." She walks over to her audiocassette, ejects one tape, rummages around, and then puts in another, and the two of us sit in the dark and listen to the songs of Marie LaSalle. I think I can understand why, too; I think if I were homesick and lost and unsure of what I was playing at, I'd do the same. Fulfilling work is a great thing at times like these. What am I supposed to do? Go and unlock the shop and walk around it?

"Is this gross or what?" she says after a little while. "It's kind of like masturbation or something, listening to myself for pleasure. How d'you feel about that, Rob? Three hours after we made love and I'm already jerking off."

I wish she hadn't said that. It kind of spoiled the moment.

We get back to sleep, in the end, and we wake up late, and I look and perhaps even smell a bit grottier than she might have wanted, in an ideal world, and she's friendly but distant; I get the feeling that last night is unlikely to be repeated. We go out for breakfast, to a place that is full of young couples who have spent the night together, and though we don't look out of place, I know we are: everybody else seems happy and comfortable and established, not nervy, and new and sad, and Marie and I read our newspapers with an intensity that is designed to cut out any further intimacy. It's only afterwards that we really set ourselves apart from the rest, though: a quick and rueful peck on the cheek, and I have the rest of Sunday to myself, whether I want it or not.

What went wrong? Nothing and everything. Nothing: we had a nice evening, we had sex that humiliated neither of us, we even had a predawn conversation that I and maybe she will remember for ages and ages. Everything: all that stupid business when I couldn't decide whether I was going home or not, and in the process giving her the impression that I was a halfwit; the way that we got on brilliantly and then had nothing much to say to each other; the manner of our parting; the fact that I'm no nearer to appearing in the record sleeve notes than I was before I met her. It's not a case of the glass being half full or half empty; more that we tipped a whole half-pint into an empty pint pot. I had to see how much was there, though, and now I know.

ELEVEN

ALL my life I've hated Sundays, for the obvious British reasons (*Songs of Praise,* closed shops, congealing gravy that you don't want to go near but no one's going to let you escape from) and the obvious international reasons as well, but this Sunday is a corker. There are loads of things I could do; I've got tapes to make and videos to watch and phone calls to return. But I don't want to do any of them. I get back to the flat at one; by two, things have got so bad that I decide to go home—*home* home, Mum and Dad home, congealing gravy and *Songs of Praise* home. It was waking up in the middle of the night and wondering where I belonged that did it: I don't belong at home, and I don't *want* to belong at home, but at least home is somewhere I know.

. . .

Home home is near Watford, a bus ride away from the Metropolitan Line station. It was a terrible place to grow up, I suppose, but I didn't really mind. Until I was thirteen or so, it was just a place where I could ride my bike; between thirteen and seventeen a place where I could meet girls. And I moved when I was eighteen, so I only spent a year seeing the place for what it was—a suburban shit hole—and hating it. My mum and dad moved about ten years ago, when my mum reluctantly accepted that I had gone and wasn't coming back, but they only moved around the corner, to a two-bedroom semi, and they kept their phone number and their friends and their life.

In Bruce Springsteen songs, you can either stay and rot, or you can escape and burn. That's OK; he's a songwriter, after all, and he needs simple choices like that in his songs. But nobody ever writes about how it is possible to escape and rot—how escapes can go off at half-cock, how you can leave the suburbs for the city but end up living a limp suburban life anyway. That's what happened to me; that's what happens to most people.

They're OK, if you like that sort of thing, which I don't. My dad is a bit dim but something of a know-all, which is a pretty fatal combination; you can tell from his silly, fussy beard that he's going to be the sort who doesn't talk much sense and won't listen to any reason. My mum is just a mum, which is an unforgivable thing to say in any circumstance, except this one. She worries, she gives me a hard time about the shop, she gives me a hard time about my childlessness. I wish I wanted to see them more, but I don't, and when I've got nothing else to feel bad about, I feel bad about that.

They'll be pleased to see me this afternoon, although my heart sinks when I see that fucking *Genevieve* is on TV this afternoon. (My dad's top five films: *Genevieve, The Cruel Sea, Zulu, Oh! Mr. Porter,* which he thinks is hilarious, and *The Guns of Navarone.* My mum's top five films: *Genevieve, Gone With the Wind, The Way We Were, Funny Girl,* and *Seven Brides for Seven Brothers.* You get the idea, anyway, and you'll get an even better idea when I tell you that going to the cinema is a waste of money, according to them, because sooner or later the films end up on television.)

When I get there, the joke's on me: they're not in. I've come a million stops on the Metropolitan Line on a Sunday afternoon, I've waited eight years for a bus, fucking *Genevieve* is on the fucking television, and they're not here. They didn't even call to let me know they wouldn't be here, not that I called to let them know I was coming. If I was at all prone to self-pity, which I am, I would feel bad about the terrible irony of finding your parents out when, finally, you need them.

But just as I'm about to head back to the bus stop, my mum opens the window of the house opposite and yells at me.

"Rob! Robert! Come in!"

I've never met the people across the road, but it soon becomes obvious that I'm in a minority of one: the house is packed.

"What's the occasion?"

"Wine tasting."

"Not Dad's homemade?"

"No. Proper wine. This afternoon, it's Australian. We all chip in and a man comes and explains it all."

"I didn't know you were interested in wine."

"Oh, yes. And your dad loves it."

Of course he does. He must be terrible to work with the morning after a wine-tasting session: not because of the reek of stale booze, or the bloodshot eyes, or the crabby behavior, but because of all the facts he has swallowed. He'd spend half the day telling people things they didn't want to know. He's over on the other side of the room, talking to a man in a suit—the visiting expert, presumably—who has a desperate look in his eye. Dad sees me, and mimes shock, but he won't break off the conversation.

The room is full of people I don't recognize. I've missed the part where the guy talks and hands out samples; I've arrived during the part where wine tasting becomes wine drinking and, though every now and again I spot someone swilling the wine around in their mouth and talking bollocks, mostly they're just pouring the stuff down their necks as fast as they can. I wasn't expecting this. I came for an afternoon of silent misery, not wild partying; the one thing I wanted from the afternoon was incontrovertible proof that my life may be grim and empty, but not as grim and empty as life in Watford. Wrong again. Life in Watford is grim, yes; but grim and full. What right do parents have to go to parties on Sunday afternoons for no reason at all?

"*Genevieve* is on the telly this afternoon, Mum."

"I know. We're taping it."

"When did you get a VCR?"

"Months ago."

"You never told me."

"You never asked."

"Is that what I'm supposed to do every week? Ask you whether you've bought any consumer durables?"

A huge lady wearing what appears to be a yellow kaftan glides towards us.

"You must be Robert."

"Rob, yeah. Hi."

"I'm Yvonne. Your host. Hostess." She laughs insanely, for no discernible reason. I want to see Kenneth More. "You're the one who works in the music industry, am I right?"

I look at my mum, and she looks away. "Not really, no. I own a record shop."

"Oh, well. Same thing, more or less." She laughs again, and though it would be consoling to think that she is drunk, I fear that this is not the case.

"I guess so. And the woman who develops your photos at Boots works in the film industry."

"Would you like my keys, Rob? You can go home and put the kettle on."

"Sure. Heaven forbid that I should be allowed to stay here and have fun."

Yvonne mutters something and glides off. My mum's too pleased to see me to give me a hard time, but even so I feel a bit ashamed of myself.

"Perhaps it's time I had a cup of tea, anyway." She goes over to thank Yvonne, who looks at me, cocks her head on one side, and makes a sad face; Mum's obviously telling her about Laura as an explanation for my rudeness. I don't care. Maybe Yvonne will invite me to the next session.

We go home and watch the rest of *Genevieve.*

My dad comes back maybe an hour later. He's drunk.

"We're all going to the pictures," he says.

This is too much.

"You don't approve of the pictures, Dad."

"I don't approve of the rubbish you go to watch. I approve of nice well-made films. British films."

"What's on?" my mum asks him.

"Howard's End. It's the follow-up to *A Room with a View."*

"Oh, lovely," my mum says. "Is anyone else going from across the road?"

"Only Yvonne and Brian. But get a move on. It starts in half an hour."

"I'd better be going back," I say. I have exchanged hardly a word with either of them all afternoon.

"You're going nowhere," my dad says. "You're coming with us. My treat."

"It's not the money, Dad." It's Merchant and fucking Ivory. "It's the time. I'm working tomorrow."

"Don't be so feeble, man. You'll still be in bed by eleven. It'll do you good. Buck you up. Take your mind off things." This is the first reference to the fact that I have things off which my mind needs taking.

And, anyway, he's wrong. Going to the pictures aged thirty-five with your mum and dad and their insane friends does not take your mind off things, I discover. It very much puts your mind on things. While we're waiting for Yvonne and Brian to purchase the entire contents of the Pick'n'Mix counter, I have a terrible, chilling, bone-shaking experience: the most pathetic man in the world gives me a smile of recognition. The Most Pathetic Man In The World has huge horn-rimmed spectacles and buckteeth; he's wearing a dirty fawn anorak and brown cord trousers which have been rubbed smooth at the knee; he, too, is being taken to see *Howard's End* by his parents, despite the fact that he's in his late twenties. And he gives me this terrible little smile *because he has spotted a kindred spirit.* It disturbs me so much that I can't concentrate on Emma Thompson and Vanessa and the rest, and by the time I rally, it's too late and the story's too far on down the road for me to catch up. In the end, a bookcase falls on someone's head.

I would go so far as to say that TMPMITW's smile has become one of my all-time top-five low points, the other four of which temporarily escape me. I know I'm not as pathetic as the most pathetic man in the world (Did he spend last night in an American recording artist's bed? I very much doubt it.); the point is that the difference between us is not immediately obvious to him, and I can see why. This, really, is the bottom line, the chief attraction of the opposite sex for all of us, old and young, men and women: we need someone to save us from the sympathetic smiles in the Sunday-night cinema queue, someone who can stop us from falling down into the pit where the permanently single live with their mums and dads. I'm not going back there again; I'd rather stay in for the rest of my life than attract that kind of attention.

TWELVE

DURING the week, I think about Marie, and I think about The Most Pathetic Man In The World, and I think, at Barry's command, about my all-time top five episodes of *Cheers:* (1) The one where Cliff found a potato that looked like Richard Nixon. (2) The one where John Cleese offered Sam and Diane counseling sessions. (3) The one where they thought that the chief of staff of the U.S. armed forces—played by the real-life admiral guy—had stolen Rebecca's earrings. (4) The one where Sam got a job as a sports presenter on TV. (5) The one where Woody sang his stupid song about Kelly. (Barry said I was wrong about four of the five, that I had no sense of humor, and that he was going to ask Channel 4 to scramble my reception between nine-thirty and ten every Friday night because I was an undeserving and unappreciative viewer.) But I don't think about anything Laura said that Saturday night until Wednesday, when I come home to find a message from her. It's nothing much, a request for a copy of a bill in our household file, but the sound of her voice makes me realize that there are some things we talked about that should have upset me but somehow didn't.

First of all—actually, first of all and last of all—this business about not sleeping with Ian. How do I know she's telling the truth? She could have been sleeping with him for weeks, *months,* for all I know. And anyway, she only said that she hasn't slept with him *yet,* and she said that on Saturday, five days ago. Five days! She could have slept with him five times since then! (She could have slept with him twenty times since then, but you know what I mean.) And even if she hasn't, she was definitely threatening to. What does "yet" mean, after all? "I haven't seen *Reservoir Dogs* yet." What does that mean? It means you're going to go, doesn't it?

"Barry, if I were to say to you that I haven't seen *Reservoir Dogs* yet, what would that mean?"

Barry looks at me.

"Just . . . come on, what would it mean to you? That sentence? 'I haven't seen *Reservoir Dogs* yet?' "

"To me, it would mean that you're a liar. Either that or you've gone potty. You saw it twice. Once with Laura, once with me and Dick. We had that conversation about who killed Mr. Pink or whatever fucking color he was."

"Yeah, yeah, I know. But say I hadn't seen it and I said to you, 'I haven't seen *Reservoir Dogs* yet,' what would you think?"

"I'd think, you're a sick man. And I'd feel sorry for you."

"No, but would you think, from that one sentence, that I was going to see it?"

"I'd hope you were, yeah, otherwise I would have to say that you're not a friend of mine."

"No, but—"

"I'm sorry, Rob, but I'm struggling here. I don't understand any part of this conversation. You're asking me what I'd think if you told me that you hadn't seen a film that you've seen. What am I supposed to say?"

"Just listen to me. If I said to you—"

—" 'I haven't seen *Reservoir Dogs* yet,' yeah, yeah, I hear you—"

"Would you . . . *would you get the impression that I wanted to see it?*"

"Well . . . you couldn't have been desperate, otherwise you'd have already gone."

"Exactly. We went first night, didn't we?"

"But the word *yet* . . . yeah, I'd get the impression that you wanted to see it. Otherwise you'd say you didn't fancy it much."

"But in your opinion, would I definitely go?"

"How am I supposed to know that? You might get run over by a bus, or go blind, or anything. You might go off the idea. You might be broke. You might just get sick of people telling you you've really got to go."

I don't like the sound of that. "Why would they care?"

"Because it's a brilliant film. It's funny, and violent, and it's got Harvey Keitel and Tim Roth in it, and everything. And a cracking sound track."

Maybe there's no comparison between Ian sleeping with Laura and *Reservoir Dogs* after all. Ian hasn't got Harvey Keitel and Tim Roth in him. And Ian's not funny. Or violent. And he's got a crap sound track, judging from what we used to hear through the ceiling. I've taken this as far as it will go.

But it doesn't stop me worrying about the "yet."

I call Laura at work.

"Oh, hi, Rob," she says, like I'm a friend she's pleased to hear from (1. I'm not a friend. 2. She's not pleased to hear from me. Apart from that . . .) "How's it going?"

I'm not letting her get away with this we-used-to-go-out-but-everything's-OK-now stuff.

"Bad, thanks." She sighs.

"Can we meet? There're some things you said the other night that I wanted to go over."

"I don't want . . . I'm not ready to talk about it all again yet."

"So what am I supposed to do in the meantime?" I know how I'm sounding—whiny, whingey, bitter—but I don't seem to be able to stop myself.

"Just . . . live your life. You can't hang around waiting for me to tell you why I don't want to see you anymore."

"So what happened to us maybe getting back together?"

"I don't know."

"Because the other night you said that might happen." I'm getting nowhere fast here, and I know she's not in the right frame of mind to grant any concessions, but I push it anyway.

"I said nothing of the kind."

"You did! You did! You said there was a chance! That's the same as 'might'!" Jesus. This is truly pitiful.

"Rob, I'm at work. We'll talk when . . ."

"If you don't want me to call you at work, maybe you should give me your home number. I'm sorry, Laura, but I'm not going to put the phone down until you've agreed to meet up for a drink. I don't see why things should be on your terms all the time."

She gives a short, bitter laugh. "OK, OK, OK, OK, OK, OK. Tomorrow night? Come down and get me at the office." She sounds utterly defeated.

"Tomorrow night? Friday? You're not busy? Fine. Great. It'll be nice to see you." But I'm not sure she hears the positive, conciliatory, sincere bit at the end. She's hung up by then.

THIRTEEN

WE'RE messing around at work, the three of us, getting ready to go home and rubbishing each other's five best side one track ones of all time (mine: "Janie Jones," the Clash, from *The Clash;* "Thunder Road," Bruce Springsteen, from *Born to Run;* "Smells Like Teen Spirit," Nirvana, from *Nevermind;* "Let's Get It On," Marvin Gay, from *Let's Get It On;* "Return of the Grievous Angel," Gram Parsons, from *Grievous Angel.* Barry: "Couldn't you make it any more obvious than that? What about the *Beatles?* What about the *Rolling Stones?* What about the fucking. . . fucking. . . *Beethoven?* Track one side one of the Fifth Symphony? You shouldn't be allowed to run a record shop." And then we have the argument about whether he's a snob obscurantist—are the Fire Engines, who appear on Barry's list, really better than Marvin Gaye, who does not?—or whether I'm a boring old middle-of-the-road fart.) And then Dick says, for the first time ever in his Championship Vinyl career, apart from maybe when he's gone somewhere miles away to see some ludicrous band, "I can't make the pub tonight, guys."

There's a mock-stunned silence.

"Don't mess about, Dick," says Barry eventually.

Dick sort of smiles, embarrassed. "No, really. I'm not coming."

"I'm warning you," says Barry. "Unless there's an adequate explanation I shall have to give you the Weedy Wet of the Week award."

Dick doesn't say anything.

"Come on. Who are you going to see?"

He still doesn't say anything.

"Dick, have you pulled?"

Silence.

"I don't believe it," says Barry. "Where is the justice in this world? Where is it? Justice! Where are you? Dick's out on a hot date, Rob's shagging Marie LaSalle, and the best-looking and most intelligent of the lot of them isn't getting anything at all."

He's not just trying it on. There's no little sideways glance to see if he's hit the mark, no hesitation to see if I want to interject; he knows, and I feel both crushed and smug at the same time.

"How did you know about that?"

"Oh, come on, Rob. What do you take us for? I'm more bothered about Dick's date. How did this happen, Dick? What rational explanation can there possibly be? OK, OK. Sunday night you were in, because you made me that Creation B-sides tape. I was with you Monday night and last night, which leaves . . . Tuesday!"

Dick doesn't say anything.

"Where were you Tuesday?"

"Just at a gig with some friends."

Was it that obvious? I guess a bit, on Saturday night, but Barry had no way of knowing that anything had actually happened.

"Well, what sort of gig is it where you just walk in and meet someone?"

"I didn't just walk in and meet her. She came with the friends I met there."

"And you're going to meet her again tonight?"

"Yes."

"Name?"

"Anna."

"Has she only got half a name? Eh? Anna who? Anna Neagle? Anna Green Gables? Anna Conda? Come on."

"Anna Moss."

"Anna Moss. Mossy. The Moss Woman."

I've heard him do this to women before, and I'm not sure why I don't like it. I talked about it to Laura once, because he tried it with her; some stupid pun on her surname, I can't remember what it was now. Lie-down, lied-on, something. And I hated him doing it. I wanted her to be *Laura,* to have a nice, pretty, girl's name that I could dream about when I felt like being dreamy. I didn't want him turning her into a bloke. Laura, of course, thought I was being a bit dodgy, thought I was trying to keep girls fluffy and silly and girly; she said I didn't want to think of them in the same way that I thought about my mates. She was right, of course—I don't. But that's not the point. Barry doesn't do this to strike a blow for equality: he does it because he's being spiteful, because he wants to puncture any sense of romantic well-being that Laura or Anna or whoever might have created in us. He's sharp, Barry. Sharp and nasty. He understands the power that girls' names have, and he doesn't like it.

"Is she all green and furry?"

This started out joky—Barry as demon counsel for the prosecution, Dick as defendant—but now those roles have started to harden. Dick looks guilty as all hell, and all he's done is meet someone.

"Leave it, Barry," I tell him.

"Oh, yeah, you would say that, wouldn't you? You two have got to stick together now. Shaggers United, eh?"

I try to be patient with him. "Are you coming to the pub or what?"

"No. Bollocks."

"Fair enough."

Barry leaves; Dick is now feeling guilty, not because he's met someone, but because I have nobody to drink with.

"I suppose I've got time for a quick one."

"Don't worry about it, Dick. It's not your fault that Barry's a jerk. You have a nice evening."

He flashes me a look of real gratitude, and it breaks your heart.

I feel as though I have been having conversations like this all my life. None of us is young anymore, but what has just taken place could have happened when I was sixteen, or twenty, or twenty-five. We got to adolescence and just stopped dead; we drew up the map then and left the boundaries exactly as they were. And why does it bother Barry so much that Dick is seeing someone? Because he doesn't want a smile from a man with buckteeth and an anorak in the cinema queue, that's why; he's worried about how his life is turning out, and he's lonely, and lonely people are the bitterest of them all.

FOURTEEN

EVER since I've had the shop, we've been trying to flog a record by a group called the Sid James Experience. Usually we get rid of stuff we can't move—reduce it to 10p, or throw it away—but Barry loves this album (he's got two copies of his own, just in case somebody borrows one and fails to return it), and he says it's rare, and that someday we'll make somebody very happy. It's become a bit of a joke, really. Regular customers ask after its health, and give it a friendly pat when they're browsing, and sometimes they bring the sleeve up to the counter as if they're going to buy it, and then say "Just kidding!" and put it back where they found it.

Anyway, on Friday morning, this guy I've never seen before starts flicking through the "British Pop S–Z section," lets out a gasp of amazement and rushes up to the counter, clutching the sleeve to his chest as if he's afraid someone will snatch it from him. And then he gets out his wallet and pays for it, seven quid, just like that, no attempt to haggle, no recognition of the significance of what he is doing. I let Barry serve him—it's his moment—and Dick and I watch every move, holding our breath; it's like someone has walked in, tipped petrol over himself, and produced a box of matches from his pocket. We don't exhale until he's struck the match and set himself alight, and when he's gone we laugh and laugh and laugh. It gives us all strength: if someone can just walk in and buy the Sid James Experience album, then surely anything good can happen at any time.

Laura's changed even since I last saw her. Partly it's the makeup: she's wearing it for work, and it makes her look less stressed-out, less tired, in control. But it's more than that, too. Something else has happened, maybe something real, or maybe something in her head. Whatever it is, you can see that she thinks she's started out on some new stage in her life. She hasn't. I'm not going to let her.

We go to a bar near her work—not a pub, a bar, with pictures of baseball players on the wall, and a food menu chalked up on a noticeboard, and a conspicuous lack of hand-pumps, and people in suits drinking American beer from the bottle. It's not crowded, and we sit in a booth near the back on our own.

And then she's straight in with the "So, how are you?" as if I'm nobody very much. I mumble something, and I know that I'm not going to be able to control it, I'm going to come too quickly: then it's, bang, "Have you slept with him yet?" and it's all over.

"Is that why you wanted to see me?"

"I guess."

"Oh, Rob."

I just want to ask the question again, straightaway; I want an answer, I don't want "Oh, Rob," and a pitying stare.

"What do you want me to say?"

"I want you to say that you haven't, and for your answer to be the truth."

"I can't do that." She can't look at me when she's saying it, either.

She starts to say something else, but I don't hear it; I'm out in the street, pushing through all those suits and raincoats, angry and sick and on my way home to some more loud, angry records that will make me feel better.

The next morning the guy who bought the Sid James Experience album comes in to exchange it. He says it's not what he thought it was.

"What did you think it was?" I ask him.

"I don't know," he says. "Something else." He shrugs, and looks at the three of us in turn. We are all staring at him, crushed, aghast; he looks embarrassed.

"Have you listened to all of it?" Barry asks.

"I took it off halfway through the second side. Didn't like it."

"Go home and try it again," Barry says desperately. "It'll grow on you. It's a grower."

The guy shakes his head helplessly. He's made up his mind. He chooses a secondhand Madness CD, and I put the Sid James Experience back in the rack.

Laura calls in the afternoon.

"You must have known it would happen," she says. "You couldn't have been entirely unprepared. Like you said, I've been living with the guy. We were bound to get around to it sometime." She gives a nervous and, to my way of thinking, highly inappropriate laugh.

"And, anyway, I keep trying to tell you, that's not really the point, is it? The point is, we got ourselves into an awful mess."

I want to hang up, but people only hang up to get called back again, and why should Laura call me back? No reason at all.

"Are you still there? What are you thinking?"

I'm thinking: I've had a bath with this person (just one, years ago, but, you know, a bath's a bath), and I'm already beginning to find it hard to remember what she looks like. I'm thinking: I wish this stage were over, and we could go on to the next stage, the stage where you look in the paper and see that *Scent of a Woman* is on TV, and you say to yourself, Oh, I saw that with Laura. I'm thinking: am I supposed to fight, and what do I fight with, and whom am I fighting?

"Nothing."

"We can meet for another drink if you like. So I can explain better. I owe you that much."

That much.

"How much would be too much?"

"Sorry?"

"Nothing. Look, I've got to go. I work too, you know."

"Will you call me?"

"I haven't got your number."

"You know you can call me at work. And we'll arrange to meet and talk properly."

"OK."

"Promise?"

"Yeah."

"Because I don't want this to be the last conversation we have. I know what you're like."

But she doesn't know what I'm like at all: I call her all the time. I call her later that afternoon, when Barry has gone out to get something to eat and Dick is busy sorting out some mail-order stuff out the back. I call her after six, when Barry and Dick have gone. When I get home, I call Directory Enquiries and get Ian's new number, and I call about seven times, and hang up every time he answers; eventually, Laura guesses what's going on and picks up the phone herself. I call her the following morning, and twice that afternoon, and I call her from the pub that evening. And after the pub I go around to Ian's place, just to see what it looks like from the outside. (It's just another north London three-story house, although I've no idea which story is his, and there are no lights on in any of them, anyway.) I've got nothing else to do. In short, I've lost it again, just like I lost it with Charlie, all those years ago.

. . .

There are men who call, and men who don't call, and I'd much, much rather be one of the latter. They are *proper* men, the sort of men that women have in mind when they moan about us. It's a safe, solid, meaningless stereotype: the man who appears not to give a shit, who gets ditched and maybe sits in the pub on his own for a couple of evenings, and then gets on with things; and though next time around he trusts even less than he did, he hasn't made a fool of himself, or frightened anybody, and this week I've done both of those things. One day Laura's sorry and guilty, and the next she's scared and angry, and I am entirely responsible for the transformation, and it hasn't done me any good at all. I'd stop if I could, but I don't seem to have any choice in the matter: it's all I think about, all the time. "I know what you're like," Laura said, and she does, kind of: she knows that I'm someone who doesn't really bother, who has friends he hasn't seen for years, who no longer speaks to anybody that he has ever slept with. But she doesn't know how you have to work at that.

I want to see them now: Alison Ashworth, who ditched me after three miserable evenings in the park. Penny, who wouldn't let me touch her and who then went straight out and had sex with that bastard Chris Thomson. Jackie, attractive only while she was going out with one of my best friends. Sarah, with whom I formed an alliance against all the dumpers in the world and who then went and dumped me anyway. And Charlie. Especially Charlie, because I have her to thank for everything: my great job, my sexual self-confidence, the works. I want to be a well-rounded human being with none of these knotty lumps of rage and guilt and self-disgust. What do I want to do when I see them? I don't know. Just talk. Ask them how they are and whether they have forgiven me for messing them around, when I have messed them around, and tell them that I have forgiven them for messing me around, when they have messed me around. Wouldn't that be great? If I saw all of them in turn and there were no hard feelings left, just soft, *downy* feelings, Brie rather than old hard Parmesan, I'd feel clean, and calm, and ready to start again.

Bruce Springsteen's always doing it in his songs. Maybe not always, but he's done it. You know that one "Bobby Jean," off *Born in the USA?* Anyway, he phones this girl up but she's left town years before and he's pissed off that he didn't know about it, because he wanted to say good-bye, and tell her that he missed her, and to wish her good luck. And then one of those sax solos comes in, and you get goose pimples, if you like sax solos. And Bruce Springsteen. Well, I'd like my life to be like a Bruce Springsteen song. Just once. I know I'm not born to run, I know that the Seven Sisters' Road is nothing like Thunder Road, but *feelings* can't be so different, can they? I'd like to phone all those people up and say good luck, and good-bye, and then they'd feel good and I'd feel good. We'd all feel good. That would be good. Great, even.

FIFTEEN

I AM introduced to Anna. Dick brings her to the pub on a night when Barry isn't around. She's small, quiet, polite, anxiously friendly, and Dick obviously adores her. He wants my approval and I can give it easily, loads of it. Why would I want Dick to be unhappy? I wouldn't. I want him to be as happy as anybody has ever been. I want him to show the rest of us that it is possible to maintain a relationship and a large record collection simultaneously.

"Has she got a friend for me?" I ask Dick.

Normally, of course, I wouldn't refer to Anna in the third person while she's sitting with us, but I have an excuse: my question is both endorsement and allusion, and Dick smiles happily in recognition.

"Richard Thompson," he explains to Anna. "It's a song off a Richard Thompson album. 'I Want to See the Bright Lights Tonight,' isn't it, Rob?"

"Richard Thompson," Anna repeats, in a voice which suggests that over the last few days she has had to absorb a lot of information very quickly. "Now, which one was he? Dick's been trying to educate me."

"I don't think we've got up to him yet," says Dick. "Anyway, he's a folk/rock singer and England's finest electric guitarist. Would you say that's right, Rob?" He asks the question nervously; if Barry were here, he'd take great pleasure in shooting Dick down at this point.

"That's right, Dick," I reassure him. Dick nods with relief and satisfaction.

"Anna's a Simple Minds fan," Dick confides, emboldened by his Richard Thompson success.

"Oh, right." I don't know what to say. This, in our universe, is a staggering piece of information. We hate Simple Minds. They were number one in our Top Five Bands or Musicians Who Will Have to Be Shot Come the Musical Revolution. (Michael Bolton, U2, Bryan Adams, and, surprise surprise, Genesis were tucked in behind them. Barry wanted to shoot the Beatles, but I pointed out that someone had already done it.) It is as hard for me to understand how he has ended up with a Simple Minds fan as it would be to fathom how he had paired off with one of the royal family, or a member of the shadow cabinet: it's not the attraction that baffles so much as how on earth they got together in the first place.

"But I think she's beginning to understand why she shouldn't be. Aren't you?"

"Maybe. A bit." They smile at each other. It's kind of creepy, if you think about it.

. . .

It's Liz who stops me phoning Laura all the time. She takes me to the Ship and gives me a good talking-to.

"You're really upsetting her," she says. "And him."

"Oh, like I really care about him."

"Well, you should."

"Why?"

"Because . . . because all you're doing is forming a little unit, them against you. Before you started all this, there was no unit. There were just three people in a mess. And now they've got something in common, and you don't want to make it any worse."

"And why are you so bothered? I thought I was an arsehole."

"Yeah, well, so is he. He's an even bigger arsehole, and he hasn't done anything wrong yet."

"Why is he an arsehole?"

"You know why he's an arsehole."

"How do *you* know I know why he's an arsehole?"

"Because Laura told me."

"You had a conversation about what I thought was wrong with her new boyfriend? How did you get onto that?"

"We went the long way round."

"Take me there the quick way."

"You won't like it."

"Come on, Liz."

"OK. She told me that when you used to take the piss out of Ian, when you were living in the flat . . . that was when she decided she was going off you."

"You have to take the piss out of someone like that, don't you? That Leo Sayer haircut and those dungarees, and the stupid laugh and the wanky right-on politics and the . . ."

Liz laughs. "Laura wasn't exaggerating, then. You're not keen, are you?"

"I can't fucking stand the guy."

"No, neither can I. For exactly the same reasons."

"So what's she on about, then?"

"She said that your little Ian outbursts showed her how . . . *sour* was the word she used . . . how *sour* you've become. She said that she loved you for your enthusiasm and your warmth, and it was all draining away. You stopped making her laugh and you started depressing the hell out of her. And now you're scaring her as well. She could call the police, you know, if she wanted."

The police. Jesus. One moment you're dancing round the kitchen to Bob Wills and the Texas Playboys (Hey! I made her laugh then, and that was only a few months ago!), and the next she wants to get you locked up. I don't say anything for ages. I can't think of anything to say that doesn't sound sour. "What have I got to feel warm about?" I want to ask her. "Where's the enthusiasm going to come from? How can you make someone laugh when they want to set the police on you?"

"But why do you keep calling her all the time? Why do you want her back so badly?"

"Why do you think?"

"I don't know. Laura doesn't know either."

"Well, if she doesn't know, what's the point?"

"There's always a point. Even if the point is to avoid this sort of mess next time, that's still a point."

"Next time. You think there'll be a next time?"

"Come on, Rob. Don't be so pathetic. And you've just asked three questions to avoid answering my one."

"Which was the one?"

"Ha, ha. I've seen men like you in Doris Day films, but I never thought they existed in real life." She puts on a dumb, deep, American voice. "The men who can't commit, who can't say 'I love you' even when they want to, who start to cough and splutter and change the subject. But here you are. A living, breathing specimen. Incredible."

I know the films she's talking about, and they're stupid. Those men don't exist. Saying "I love you" is easy, a piece of piss, and more or less every man I know does it all the time. I've *acted* as though I haven't been able to say it a couple of times, although I'm not sure why. Maybe because I wanted to lend the moment that sort of corny Doris Day romance, make it more memorable than it otherwise would have been. You know, you're with someone, and you start to say something, and then you stop, and she goes "What?" and you go "Nothing," and she goes, "Please say it," and you go, "No, it'll sound stupid," and then she makes you spit it out, even though you'd been intending to say it all along, and she thinks it's all the more valuable for being hard-won. Maybe she knew all the time that you were messing about, but she doesn't mind, anyway. It's like a quote: it's the nearest any of us gets to being in the movies, those few days when you decide that you like somebody enough to tell her that you love her, and you don't want to muck it up with a glob of dour, straightforward, no-nonsense sincerity.

But I'm not going to put Liz straight. I'm not going to tell her that all this is a way of regaining control, that I don't know if I love Laura or not but I'm never going to find out while she's living with someone else; I'd rather Liz thought I was one of those anal, tongue-tied, and devoted clichés who eventually sees the light. I guess it won't do me any harm, in the long run.

SIXTEEN

I START at the beginning, with Alison. I ask my mum to look up her parents in the local phone book, and I take it from there.

"Is that Mrs. Ashworth?"

"It is." Mrs. Ashworth and I were never introduced. We never really got to the meet-the-parents stage during our six-hour relationship.

"I'm an old friend of Alison's, and I'd like to get in touch with her again."

"You want her address in Australia?"

"If . . . if that's where she lives, yeah." I won't be forgiving Alison in a hurry. In fact, it will take me weeks: weeks to get around to writing a letter, weeks for a reply.

She gives me her daughter's address, and I ask what Alison's doing out there; it turns out that she's married to someone with a building business, and she's a nurse, and they have two children, both girls, and blah blah. I manage to resist asking whether she ever mentions me at all. You can only take self-absorption so far. And then I ask about David, and he's in London working for a firm of accountants, and he's married, and he's got two girls as well, and can't anybody in the family produce boys? Even Alison's cousin has just had a little girl! I express disbelief in all the right places.

"How did you know Alison?"

"I was her first boyfriend."

There's a silence, and for a moment I worry that for the last twenty years I have been held responsible in the Ashworth house for some sort of sexual crime I did not commit.

"She married her first boyfriend. Kevin. She's Alison Bannister."

She married Kevin Bannister. I was ousted by forces beyond my control. This is tremendous. What chance did I stand against fate? No chance at all. It was nothing to do with me, or any failings on my part, and I can feel the Alison Ashworth scar healing over as we speak.

"If that's what she's saying, she's a liar." This is meant to be a joke, but it comes out all wrong.

"I beg your pardon?"

"No, seriously, joking apart, ha ha, I went out with her before Kevin did. Only for a week or so"—I have to up it a bit, because if I told the truth, she'd think I was mad—"But they all count, don't they? A snog's a snog, after all, ha ha." I'm not going to be written out of history like this. I played my part. I did my bit.

"What did you say your name was?"

"Rob. Bobby. Bob. Robert. Robert Zimmerman." Fucking hell.

"Well, Robert, I'll tell her you called, when I speak to her. But I'm not sure she'll remember you."

She's right, of course. She'll remember the evening she got off with Kevin, but she won't remember the evening before. It's probably only me who remembers the evening before. I guess I should have forgotten about it ages ago, but forgetting isn't something I'm very good at.

This man comes into the shop to buy the Fireball XL_5 theme tune for his wife's birthday (and I've got one, an original, and it's his for a tenner). And he's maybe two or three years younger than me, but he's well-spoken, and he's wearing a suit, and he's dangling his car keys, and for some reason these three things make me feel maybe two decades younger than him, twenty or so to his fortysomething. And I suddenly have this burning desire to find out what he thinks of me. I don't give in to it, of course ("There's your change, there's your record, now come on, be honest, you think I'm a waster, don't you?"), but I think about it for ages afterwards, what I must look like to him.

I mean, he's married, which is a scary thing, and he's got the sort of car keys that you jangle confidently, so he's obviously got, like, a BMW or a Batmobile or something flash, and he does work which requires a suit, and to my untutored eye it looks like an expensive suit. I'm a bit smarter than usual today—I've got my newish black denims on, as opposed to my ancient blue ones, and I'm wearing a long-sleeved polo shirt thing that I actually went to the trouble of ironing—but even so I'm patently not a grown-up man in a grown-up job. Do I want to be like him? Not really, I don't think. But I find myself worrying away at that stuff about pop music again, whether I like it because I'm unhappy, or whether I'm unhappy because I like it. It would help me to know whether this guy has ever taken it seriously, whether he has ever sat surrounded by thousands and thousands of songs about . . . about . . . (say it, man, say it) . . . well, about love. I would guess that he hasn't. I would also guess Prince Philip hasn't, and the guy at the Bank of England hasn't; nor has David Owen or Oliver North or Kate Adie or loads of other famous people that I should be able to name, probably, but can't, because they never played for Booker T. and the MG's. These people look as though they wouldn't have had the time to listen to the first side of *Al Green's Greatest Hits,* let alone all his other stuff (ten albums on the Hi label alone, although only nine of them were produced by Willie Mitchell); they're too busy fixing base rates and trying to bring peace to what was formerly Yugoslavia to listen to "Sha La La (Make Me Happy)."

So they might have the jump on me when it comes to accepted notions of seriousness (although as everyone knows, *Al Green Explores Your Mind* is as serious as life gets), but I ought to have the edge on them when it comes to matters of the heart. "Kate," I should be able to say, "it's all very well dashing off to war zones. But what are you going to do about the only thing that really matters? You *know* what I'm talking about, baby." And then I could give her all the emotional advice I gleaned from the College of Musical Knowledge. It hasn't worked out like that, though. I don't know anything about Kate Adie's love life, but it can't be in a worse state than mine, can it? I've spent nearly thirty years listening to people singing about broken hearts, and has it helped me any? Has it fuck.

So maybe what I said before, about how listening to too many records messes your life up . . . maybe there's something in it after all. David Owen, he's married, right? He's taken care of all that, and now he's a big-shot diplomat. The guy who came into the shop with the suit and the car keys, he's married, too, and now he's, I don't know, a *businessman.* Me, I'm unmarried—at the moment as unmarried as it's possible to be—and I'm the owner of a failing record shop. It seems to me that if you place music (and books, probably, and films, and plays, and anything that makes you *feel*) at the center of your being, then you can't afford to sort out your love life, start to think of it as the finished product. You've got to pick at it, keep it alive and in turmoil, you've got to pick at it and unravel it until it all comes apart and you're compelled to start all over again. Maybe we all live life at too high a pitch, those of us who absorb emotional things all day, and as a consequence we can never feel merely *content:* we have to be unhappy, or ecstatically, head-over-heels happy, and those states are difficult to achieve within a stable, solid relationship. Maybe Al Green is directly responsible for more than I ever realized.

See, records have helped me to fall in love, no question. I hear something new, with a chord change that melts my guts, and before I know it I'm looking for someone, and before I know it I've found her. I fell in love with Rosie the simultaneous orgasm woman after I'd fallen in love with a Cowboy Junkies song: I played it and played it and played it, and it made me dreamy, and I needed someone to dream about, and I found her, and . . . well, there was trouble.

SEVENTEEN

PENNY'S easy. I don't mean, you know, *easy* (if I meant that, I wouldn't have to meet up with her and talk about knobbing and Chris Thomson, because I would have knobbed her first and he wouldn't have been able to shoot his mouth off in the classroom that morning); I mean she's easy to track down. My mum sees her mum quite often, and a while back Mum gave me her phone number and told me to get in touch, and Penny's mum gave her mine, and neither of us did anything about it, but I kept the number anyway. And she's surprised to hear from me—there's a long computer-memory silence while she tries to make sense of the name, and then a little laugh of recognition—but not, I think, displeased, and we arrange to go to a film together, some Chinese thing that she has to see for work, and to eat afterwards.

The film's OK, better than I thought it would be—it's about this woman who's sent off to live with this guy, and he's already got loads of wives, so it's about how he gets on with her rivals, and it all goes horribly wrong. Of course. But Penny's got one of these special film critic pens that have a light in the end of them (even though she's not a film critic, just a BBC radio journalist) and people keep looking round at her and nudging each other, and I feel a bit of a berk sitting there with her. (I have to say, although it is ungallant, that she looks funny, anyway, even without the special film critic pen: she always was a girl for sensible clothes, but what she's wearing tonight—a big floral dress, a beige raincoat—pushes sensible over the edge toward death. "What's that cool guy in the leather jacket doing with Julie Andrews?" the audience is thinking. Probably.)

We go to this Italian place she knows, and they know her, too, and they do vulgar things with the pepper grinder that seem to amuse her. It's often the way that people who take their work seriously laugh at stupid jokes; it's as if they are under-humored and, as a consequence, suffer from premature laugh-ejaculation. But she's OK, really. She's a good sort, a good sport, and it's easy to talk about Chris Thomson and knobbing. I just launch into it, with no real explanation.

I try to tell the story in a lighthearted, self-deprecatory way (it's about me, not him and her), but she's appalled, really disgusted: she puts her knife and fork down and looks away, and I can see that she's close to tears.

"Bastard," she says. "I wish you hadn't told me that."

"I'm sorry. I just thought, you know, long time ago and all that."

"Well, it obviously doesn't seem that long ago to you."

Fair point.

"No. But I just thought I was weird."

"Why this sudden need to tell me about it, anyway?"

I shrug. "Dunno. Just . . ."

And then I show her that, on the contrary, I do know: I tell her about Laura and Ian (although I don't tell her about Marie or money or abortions or pain-in-the-arse Rosie) and about Charlie, maybe more about Charlie than she wants to know; and I try to explain to her that I feel like the Rejection Man, and that Charlie wanted to sleep with Marco and not me, and Laura wanted to sleep with Ian and not me, and Alison Ashworth, even all those years ago, wanted to snog with Kevin Bannister and not me (although I do share with her my recent discovery about the invincibility of fate), and that as she, Penny, wanted to sleep with Chris Thomson and not me, perhaps she would be able to help me understand why it kept happening, why I was apparently doomed to be left.

And she tells me, with great force, with *venom,* frankly speaking, about what she remembers: that she was mad about me, that she wanted to sleep with me, one day, but not when she was sixteen, and that when I packed her in— *"When you packed me in,"* she repeats, furiously, "because I was, to use your charming expression, 'tight,' I cried and cried, and I hated you. And then that little shitbag asked me out, and I was too tired to fight him off, and it wasn't rape, because I said OK, but it wasn't far off. And I didn't have sex with anyone else until after university because I hated it so much. And now you want to have a chat about rejection. Well, fuck you, Rob."

So that's another one I don't have to worry about. I should have done this years ago.

EIGHTEEN

SCOTCH-

taped to the inside of the shop door is a handwritten notice, yellowed and faded with age. It reads as follows:

> HIP YOUNG GUNSLINGERS WANTED (BASS, DRUMS, GUITAR) FOR NEW BAND. MUST BE INTO REM, PRIMAL SCREAM, FANCLUB ETC. CONTACT BARRY IN THE SHOP.

The advertisement used to end with the intimidating postscript "NO SLACKERS PLEASE," but after a disappointing response during the first couple of years of the recruitment drive, Barry decided that slackers were welcome after all, to no noticeable effect; perhaps they couldn't get it together to walk from the door to the counter. A while back, a guy with a set of drums made inquiries, and though this minimalist vocal/drums two-piece did rehearse a few times (no tapes survive, sadly), Barry eventually and perhaps wisely decided that he needed a fuller sound.

Since then, though, nothing . . . until today. Dick sees him first—he nudges me, and we watch fascinated as this guy stares at the notice, although when he turns round to see which of us might be Barry, we quickly get on with what we were doing. He's neither hip, nor young—he looks more like a Status Quo roadie than a *Smash Hits* cover star hopeful. He has long, lank dark hair tied back in a ponytail and a stomach that has wriggled over his belt to give itself a bit more room. Eventually he comes up to the counter and gestures back toward the door.

"Is this Barry geezer around?"

"I'll get him for you."

I go into the stockroom, where Barry is having a lie-down.

"Oi, Barry. There's someone come to see you about your ad."

"What ad?"

"For the band."

He opens his eyes and looks at me. "Fuck off."

"Seriously. He wants to talk to you."

He gets to his feet and walks through to the shop.

"Yeah?"

"You put that ad up?"

"That's right."

"What can you play?"

"Nothing." Barry's all-consuming desire to play at Madison Square Garden has never driven him to do anything as mundane as learn an instrument.

"But you can sing, right?"

"Yeah."

"We're looking for a singer."

"What sort of stuff are you into?"

"Yeah, the kind of stuff you, you know, mentioned. But we want to be a bit more experimental than that. We want to retain our pop sensibilities, but kind of stretch them a bit."

God help us.

"Sounds great."

"We haven't got any gigs or anything. We've only just got together. For a laugh, like. But we'll see how we go, yeah?"

"Fine."

The Quo roadie jots down an address, shakes Barry's hand, and leaves. Dick and I gape at his back view, just in case he self-combusts, or disappears, or sprouts angel's wings; Barry just tucks the address into his jeans pocket and looks for a record to put on, as if what has just happened—a mysterious stranger walking in and granting him one of his dearest wishes—were not the kind of little miracle that most of us wait for in vain.

"What?" he says. "What's up with you two? It's just a poxy little garage band. Nothing special."

Jackie lives in Pinner, not far from where we grew up, with my friend Phil, of course. When I call her, she knows who I am straightaway, presumably because I'm the only Other Man in her whole life, and at first she sounds guarded, suspicious, as if I want to go through the whole thing again. I tell her that my mum and dad are OK, that I have my own shop, that I'm not married and have no children, at which point the suspicion turns to sympathy, and maybe a touch of guilt (Is this my fault? you can hear her thinking. Did his love life just stop dead in 1975, when I got back together with Phil?); she tells me that they have two children and a small house, that they both work, and that she never went to college, just as she feared she wouldn't. To end the brief silence that occurs after this résumé, she invites me to their house for supper, and in the brief silence that ocurs after the invitation, I accept.

Jackie has gray streaks in her hair but otherwise still looks pretty and friendly and sensible and all the other things she used to be; I kiss her and offer Phil my hand. Phil is now a man, with a moustache and shirtsleeves and a bald patch and a loosened tie, but he makes a big show of pausing before he returns the gesture—he wants me to realize that this is a symbolic moment, that he is forgiving me for my misdemeanors of all those years ago. Jesus, I think, it's supposed to be elephants that never forget, not British Telecom customer service people. But then, what am I doing here, if not to meddle around with things that most people would have forgotten about years ago?

Jackie and Phil are the most boring people in the southeast of England, possibly because they've been married too long, and therefore have nothing to talk about, apart from how long they've been married. In the end, I am reduced to asking them, in a joky sort of way, for the secret of their success; I was only saving time, because I think they would have told me anyway.

"If you've found the right person, you've found the right person, it doesn't matter how old you are." (Phil)

"You have to work at relationships. You can't just walk out on them every time something goes wrong." (Jackie)

"That's right. It would have been easy to pack it in and start all over again with someone else who's swept you off your feet, but then you're still going to get to the stage when you're going to have to work at the new one." (Phil)

"There aren't too many candlelit dinners and second honeymoons, I can tell you. We're beyond all that. We're good friends more than anything." (Jackie)

"You can't just jump into bed with the first person you fancy and hope that you don't damage your marriage, no matter what people think." (Phil)

"The trouble with young people today is . . ." No. Just kidding. But they're . . . *evangelical* about what they have, as if I've come up from north London to arrest them for being monogamous. I haven't, but they're right in thinking that it's a crime where I come from: it's against the law because we're all cynics and romantics, sometimes simultaneously, and marriage, with its clichés and its steady low-watt glow, is as unwelcome to us as garlic is to a vampire.

I'm at home, making a tape of some old singles, when the phone goes.

"Hi. Is that Rob?"

I recognize the voice as belonging to someone I don't like, but I don't get any further than that.

"This is Ian. Ray."

I don't say anything.

"I thought maybe we should have a chat? Sort a couple of things out?"

This is . . . *something* . . . gone mad. *Blank* gone mad. You know when people use that expression to communicate the fact that something OK has got right out of control? "This is democracy gone mad." Well, I want to use that expression, but I'm not sure what the something is. North London? Life? The nineties? I don't know. All I do know is that in a decent, sane society, Ian wouldn't be ringing me up to sort a couple of things out. Nor would I be ringing him up to sort a couple of things out. I'd be sorting *him* out, and if he wants to be eating dungarees for a week, he's going the right way about it.

"What needs sorting out?" I'm so angry my voice is shaky, like it used to be when I was on the verge of a fight at school, and consequently I don't sound angry at all: I sound scared.

"Come on, Rob. My relationship with Laura has obviously disturbed you a great deal."

"Funnily enough I haven't been too thrilled about it." Sharp and clear.

"We're not talking joky understatement here, Rob. We're talking harassment. Ten phone calls a night, hanging around outside my house . . ."

Fucking hell. How did he see that?

"Yeah, well, I've stopped all that now." Sharp and clear has gone; now I'm sort of mumbling, like a mad guilty person.

"We've noticed, and we're glad. But, you know . . . how are we going to make the peace here? We want to make things easier for you. What can we do? Obviously I know how special Laura is, and I know things can't be good for you at the moment. I'd hate it if I lost her. But I'd like to think that if she decided she didn't want to see me anymore, I'd respect that decision. D'you see what I'm saying?"

"Yeah."

"Good. So how shall we leave it then?"

"Dunno." And then I put the phone down—not on a smart, crushing one-liner, or after a raging torrent of abuse, but on a "dunno." That's taught him a lesson he won't forget.

HIM: Good. So how shall we leave it then?

ME: I've already left it, you pathetic little twerp. Liz is quite right about you. [*Slams receiver down.*]

HIM: Good. So how shall we leave it then?

ME: We won't leave it, Ian. Or at least, I won't. I'd change your phone number, if I were you. I'd change your address. One day soon you'll look back on one visit to the house and ten phone calls a night as a golden age. Watch your step, boy. [*Slams receiver down.*]

HIM: But I'd like to think that if she decided she didn't want to see me anymore, I'd respect that decision.

ME: If she decided she didn't want to see you anymore, I'd respect that decision. I'd respect her. Her friends would respect her. Everybody would cheer. The world would be a better place.

HIM: This is Ian. Ray.

ME: Fuck off. [*Slams receiver down.*]

Oh, well.

Oh well, nothing. I should have said any of those things. I should have used at least one obscenity. I should certainly have threatened him with violence. I shouldn't have hung up on a "dunno." These things are going to eat away at me and eat away at me and I'm going to drop dead of cancer or heart disease or something. And I shake and shake, and I rewrite the script in my head until it's 100-proof poison, and none of it helps at all.

NINETEEN

SARAH still sends me Christmas cards with her address and phone number on them. (She doesn't write it out: she uses those crappy little stickers.) They never say anything else, apart from "Happy Xmas! Love, Sarah," in her big round schoolteacher's handwriting. I send her equally blank ones back. I noticed a couple of years ago that the address had changed; I also noticed that it had changed from a Whole Number, Something Street to a number with a letter after it, and not even a "b," which can still denote a house, but a "c" or a "d," which can only denote a flat. I didn't think much about it at the time, but now it seems faintly ominous. To me it suggests that the Whole Number, Something Street belonged to Tom, and that Tom isn't around anymore. Smug? Me?

She looks the same—a bit thinner, maybe (Penny was a lot fatter, but then she's doubled her age since I last saw her; Sarah had only gone from thirty to thirty-five, and that's not life's most fattening journey), but she's still peering out from under her bangs. We go out for a pizza, and it's depressing how big a deal this is for her: not the act of eating pizza itself, but the dateness of the evening. Tom *has* gone, and gone in a fairly spectacular fashion. Get this: he told her, not that he was unhappy in the relationship, not that he had met someone else he wanted to see, not that he was seeing someone else, but that he was *getting married* to someone else. Classic, eh? You've got to laugh, really, but I manage not to. It's one of those hard-luck stories that seem to reflect badly on the victims, somehow, so I shake my head at the cruel mysteries of the universe instead.

She looks at her wine. "I can't believe I left you for him," she says. "Mad."

I don't want to hear this. I don't want her rejecting the rejection; I want her to explain it so that I can absolve her.

I shrug. "Probably seemed like a good idea at the time."

"Probably. I can't remember why, though."

I could end up having sex here, and the prospect doesn't appall me. What better way to exorcize rejection demons than to screw the person who rejected you? But you wouldn't just be sleeping with a person: you'd be sleeping with a whole sad single-person culture. If we went to her place there'd be a cat, and the cat would jump on the bed at a crucial point, and we'd have to break off while she shooed it out and shut it in the kitchen. And we'd probably have to listen to her Eurythmics records, and there'd be nothing to drink. And there'd be none of those Marie LaSalle hey-women-can-get-horny-too shrugs; there'd be phone calls and embarrassment and regret. So I'm not going to sleep with Sarah unless at some point during the evening I see quite clearly that it's her or nothing for the rest of my life, and I can't see that sort of vision descending on me tonight: that's how we ended up going out in the first place. That's why she left me for Tom. She made a calculation, worked out the odds, made a solid each-way bet and went. That she wants another go says more about me, and about her, than cash ever can: she's thirty-five, and she's telling herself that life isn't going to offer her any more than what she has here this evening, a pizza and an old boyfriend she didn't like that much in the first place. That's a pretty grim conclusion, but it's not difficult to see how she got there.

Oh, we know, both of us, that it shouldn't matter, that there's more to life than pairing off, that the media is to blame, blah blah blah. But it's hard to see that, sometimes, on a Sunday morning, when you're maybe ten hours from going down to the pub for a drink and the first conversation of the day.

I haven't got the heart for the rejection conversation. There are no hard feelings here, and I'm glad that she ditched me, and not the other way around. I already feel guilty enough as it is. We talk about films, a bit—she loved *Dances with Wolves,* but she didn't like the sound of *Reservoir Dogs*—and work, and a bit more about Tom, and a bit about Laura, although I just tell her that we're going through a rough patch. And she asks me back, but I don't go, and we agree that we've had a nice time, and that we'll do it again soon. There's only Charlie left now.

TWENTY

HOW'S the experimenting going? Are you still stretching your pop sensibilities?"

Barry glowers at me. He hates talking about the band.

"Yeah. Are they really into the same sort of stuff as you, Barry?" asks Dick innocently.

"We're not 'into stuff,' Dick. We play songs. Our songs."

"Right," says Dick. "Sorry."

"Oh, bollocks, Barry," I say. "What do your songs sound like? The Beatles? Nirvana? Papa Abraham and the Smurfs?"

"You probably wouldn't be familiar with our immediate influences," Barry says.

"Try me."

"They're mostly German."

"What, Kraftwerk and that?"

He looks at me pityingly. "Er, hardly."

"Who, then?"

"You wouldn't have heard of them, Rob, so just shut up."

"Just name one."

"No."

"Give us the initial letters, then."

"No."

"You haven't got a fucking clue, have you?"

He stomps out of the shop.

I know this is everybody's answer to everything and I'm sorry, but if ever a chap needed to get laid, it's Barry.

She's still living in London. I get her phone number and address from Directory Enquiries—she lives in Ladbroke Grove, of course. I call, but I hold the receiver about an inch away from the phone, so that I can hang up quick if anyone answers. Someone answers. I hang up. I try again, about five minutes later, although this time I hold the receiver a little nearer to my ear, and I can hear that a machine, not a person, is answering. I still hang up, though. I'm not ready to hear her voice yet. The third time, I listen to her message; the fourth time, I leave one of my own. It's incredible, really, to think that at any time over the last decade I could have done this: she has come to assume such an importance I feel she should be living on Mars, so that attempts to communicate with her would cost millions of pounds and take light-years to reach her. She's an extraterrestrial, a ghost, a myth, not a person with an answering machine and a rusting wok and a two-zone travel pass.

She sounds older, I guess, and a little bit posher—London has sucked the life out of her Bristol burr—but it's obviously her. She doesn't say whether she's living with anyone—not that I was expecting a message giving details of her current romantic situation, but she doesn't say, you know, "Neither Charlie nor Marco can come to the phone right now," or anything like that. Just, "There's no one here, please leave a message after the bleep." I leave my name, including surname, and my phone number, and stuff about long time to see, etc.

I don't hear anything back from her. A couple of days later I try again, and I say the same stuff. Still nothing. Now this is more like it, if you're talking about rejection: someone who won't even return your phone messages a decade after she rejected you.

Marie comes into the shop.

"Hi, guys."

Dick and Barry disappear, conspicuously and embarrassingly.

" 'Bye, guys," she says after they're gone, and shrugs.

She peers at me. "You avoiding me, boy?" she asks, mock-angry.

"No."

She frowns and cocks her head to one side.

"Honest. How could I, when I don't know where you've been the last few days?"

"Well, are you embarrassed, then?"

"Oh, God yes."

She laughs. "No need."

This, it seems, is what you get for sleeping with an American, all this up-front goodwill. You wouldn't catch a decent British woman marching in here after a one-night stand. We understand that these things are, on the whole, best forgotten. But I suppose Marie wants to talk about it, explore what went wrong; there's probably some group-counseling workshop she wants us to go to, with lots of other couples who spent a misguided one-off Saturday night together. We'll probably have to take our clothes off and reenact what happened, and I'll get my sweater stuck round my head.

"I was wondering if you wanted to come see T-Bone play tonight."

Of course I don't. We can't speak anymore, don't you understand, woman? We had sex, and that was the end of it. That's the law in this country. If you don't like it, go back to where you came from.

"Yeah. Great."

"Do you know a place called Stoke Newington? He's playing there. The Weavers Arms?"

"I know it." I could just not turn up, I suppose, but I know I'll be there.

And we have a nice time. She's right to be American about it: just because we've been to bed together doesn't mean we have to hate each other. We enjoy T-Bone's set, and Marie sings with him for his encore (and when she goes up onstage, people look at the place where she was standing, and then they look at the person next to the place where she was standing, and I quite like that). And then the three of us go back to hers for a drink, and we talk about London and

Austin and records, but not about sex in general or the other night in particular, as if it were just something we did, like going to the curry house, which also requires no examination or elaboration. And then I go home, and Marie gives me a nice kiss, and on the way back I feel as though there's one relationship, just one, that is OK really, a little smooth spot I can feel proud of.

Charlie phones, in the end; she's apologetic about not having called sooner, but she's been away, in the States, on business. I try to make out like I know how it is, but I don't, of course—I've been to Brighton on business, and to Redditch, and to Norwich, even, but I've never been to the States.

"So, how are you?" she asks, and for a moment, just a moment but even so, I feel like doing a misery number on her: "Not very good, thanks, Charlie, but don't let that worry you. You just fly out to the States, on business, never mind me." To my eternal credit, however, I restrain myself and pretend that in the twelve years since we last spoke I have managed to live life as a fully functioning human being.

"Fine, thanks."

"Good. I'm glad. You are fine, and you deserve to be fine."

Something's wrong, somewhere, but I can't put my finger on it.

"How are you?"

"Good. Great. Work's good, nice friends, nice flat, you know. College all seems a long time ago, now. You remember when we used to sit in the bar, wondering how life would turn out for us?"

Nope.

"Well . . . I'm really happy with mine, and I'm glad you're happy with yours."

I didn't say I was happy with my life. I said that I was fine, as in no colds, no recent traffic accidents, no suspended prison sentences, but never mind.

"Have you got, you know, kids and stuff, like everybody else?"

"No. I could have had them if I'd wanted them, of course, but I didn't want them. I'm too young, and they're too . . ."

"Young?"

"Well, yes, young, obviously"—she laughs nervously, as if I'm an idiot, which maybe I am, but not in the way she thinks—"but too . . . I don't know, *time-consuming,* I guess is the expression I'm looking for."

I'm not making any of this up. This is how she talks, as if nobody has ever had a conversation about this in the entire history of the world.

"Oh, right. I see what you mean."

I just took the piss out of Charlie. Charlie! Charlie Nicholson! This is weird. Most days, for the last dozen or so years, I have thought about Charlie and attributed to her, or at least to our breakup, most things that have gone wrong for me. Like: I wouldn't have packed in college; I wouldn't have gone to work in Record and Tape; I wouldn't be saddled with this shop; I wouldn't have had an unsatisfactory personal life. This is the woman who broke my heart, ruined my life, this woman is single-handedly responsible for my poverty and directionlessness and failure, the woman I dreamed about regularly for a good five years, and *I'm sending her up.* I've got to admire myself, really. I've got to take my own hat off and say to myself, "Rob, you're one cool character."

"Anyway, are you in or out, Rob?"

"I'm sorry?" It is comforting to hear that she still says things that only she can understand. I used to like it, and to envy it; I could never think of anything to say that sounded remotely strange.

"No, I'm sorry. It's just . . . I find these long-lost boyfriend calls rather unnerving. There's been a spate of them, recently. Do you remember that guy Marco I went out with after you?"

"Um . . . Yeah, I think so." I know what's coming, and I don't believe it. All that painful fantasy, the marriage and the kids, years and years of it, and she probably ended up packing him in six months after I last saw her.

"Well, he called a few months back, and I didn't really know what to say to him. I think he was going through, you know, some kind of what-does-it-all-mean thing, and he wanted to see me, and talk about stuff, and what have you, and I wasn't really up for it. Do all men go through this?"

"I haven't heard of it before."

"It's just the ones I pick, then. I didn't mean . . ."

"No, no, that's OK. It must seem a bit funny, me ringing up out of the blue. I just thought, you know . . ." I don't know, so I don't see why she should. "But what does 'Are you in or out' mean?"

"It means, I don't know, are we pals or aren't we? Because if we are, fine, and if we're not, I don't see the point of messing about on the phone. Do you want to come to dinner Saturday? I'm having some friends over and I need a spare man. Are you a spare man?"

"I . . ." What's the point? "Yes, at the moment."

"So are you in or out?"

"I'm in."

"Good. My friend Clara is coming, and she hasn't got a chap, and she's right up your street. Eight o'clockish?"

And that's it. Now I can put my finger on what's wrong: Charlie is awful. She didn't use to be awful, but something bad has happened to her, and she says terrible, stupid things and has no apparent sense of humor whatsoever. What would Bruce Springsteen make of Charlie?

I tell Liz about Ian phoning me up, and she says it's outrageous, and that Laura will be appalled, which cheers me up no end. And I tell her about Alison and Penny and Sarah and Jackie, and about the stupid little flashlight-pen thing, and about Charlie and how she'd just come back from the States on business, and Liz says that *she's* just about to go to the States on business, and I'm amusingly satirical at her expense, but she doesn't laugh.

"How come you hate women who have better jobs than you, Rob?"

She's like this sometimes, Liz. She's OK, but, you know, she's one of those *paranoid* feminists who see evil in everything you say.

"What are you on about now?"

"You hate this woman who took a little flashlight-pen into the cinema, which seems a perfectly reasonable thing to do if you want to write in the dark. And you hate the fact that . . . Charlie? . . . Charlie went to the States—I mean, maybe she didn't want to go to the States. I know I don't. And you didn't like Laura wearing clothes that she had no choice about wearing when she changed jobs, and now I'm beneath contempt because I've got to fly to Chicago, talk to some men in a hotel conference room for eight hours, and then fly home again . . ."

"Well, I'm sexist, aren't I? Is that the right answer?"

You just have to smile and take it, otherwise it would drive you mad.

TWENTY-ONE

WHEN Charlie opens the door, my heart sinks: she looks beautiful. She still has the short, blond hair, but the cut is a lot more expensive now, and she's aging in a really elegant way—around her eyes there are faint, friendly, sexy crow's-feet which make her look like Sylvia Sims, and she's wearing a self-consciously grown-up black cocktail dress (although it probably only seems self-conscious to me because as far as I'm concerned she's only just stepped out of a pair of baggy jeans and a Television T-shirt). Straightaway I start to worry that I'm going to fall for her again, and I'll make a fool of myself, and it's all going to end in pain, humiliation, and self-loathing, just as it did before. She kisses me, hugs me, tells me I don't look any different and that it's great to see me, and then she points me to a room where I can leave my jacket. It's her bedroom (arty, of course, with a huge abstract painting on one wall and what looks like a rug on another); I have a sudden panic when I'm in there. The other coats on the bed are expensive, and for a moment I entertain the idea of going through the pockets and then doing a runner.

But I want to see Clara, Charlie's friend, who's right up my street. I want to see her because I don't know where my street is; I don't even know which part of town it's in, which *city,* which *country,* so maybe she'll enable me to get my bearings. And it'll be interesting, too, to see what street Charlie thinks I live on, whether it's the Old Kent Road or Park Lane. (Five women who don't live on my street, as far as I know, but would be very welcome if they ever decided to move into the area: the Holly Hunter of *Broadcast News;* the Meg Ryan of *Sleepless in Seattle;* a woman doctor I saw on the telly once, who had lots of long frizzy hair and carved up a Tory MP in a debate about embryos, although I don't know her name and I've never been able to find a pinup of her; Katharine Hepburn in *The Philadelphia Story;* Valerie Harper in the TV series *Rhoda.* These are women who talk back, women with a mind of their own, women with snap and crackle and pop . . . but they are also women who seem to need the love of a good man. I could rescue them. I could redeem them. They could make me laugh, and I could make them laugh, maybe, on a good day, and we could stay in and watch one of their films or TV programs or embryo debates on video and adopt disadvantaged children together and the whole family could play soccer in Central Park.)

. . .

When I walk into the sitting room, I can see immediately that I'm doomed to die a long, slow, suffocating death. There's a man wearing a sort of brick red jacket and another man in a carefully rumpled linen suit and Charlie in her cocktail dress and another woman wearing fluorescent leggings and a dazzling white silk blouse and another woman wearing those trousers that look like a dress but which aren't. Isn't. Whatever. And the moment I see them I want to cry, not only through terror, but through sheer *envy: Why isn't my life like this?*

Both of the women who are not Charlie are beautiful—not pretty, not attractive, not appealing, *beautiful*—and to my panicking, blinking, twitching eye virtually indistinguishable: miles of dark hair, thousands of huge earrings, yards of red lips, hundreds of white teeth. The one wearing the white silk blouse shuffles along Charlie's enormous sofa, which is made of glass, or lead, or gold—some intimidating, unsofa-like material, anyway—and smiles at me; Charlie interrupts the others ("Guys, guys . . .") and introduces me to the rest of the party. Clara's on the sofa with me, as it were, ha ha, Nick's in the brick red jacket, Barney's in the linen suit, Emma's in the trousers that look like a dress. If these people were ever up my street, I'd have to barricade myself inside the flat.

"We were just talking about what we'd call a dog if we had one," says Charlie. "Emma's got a Labrador called Dizzy, after Dizzy Gillespie."

"Oh, right," I say. "I'm not very keen on dogs."

None of them says anything for a while; there's not much they *can* say, really, about my lack of enthusiasm for dogs.

"Is that size of flat, or childhood fear, or the smell, or . . . ?" asks Clara, very sweetly.

"I dunno. I'm just . . ." I shrug hopelessly, "you know, not very keen."

They smile politely.

As it turns out, this is my major contribution to the evening's conversation, and later on I find myself recalling the line wistfully as belonging to a Golden Age of Wit. I'd even use it again if I could, but the rest of the topics for discussion don't give me the chance—I haven't seen the films or the plays they've seen, and I haven't been to the places they've visited. I find out that Clara works in publishing, and Nick's in PR; I find out too that Emma lives in Clapham. Anna finds out that I live in Crouch End, and Clara finds out that I own a record shop. Emma has read *Wild Swans;* Charlie hasn't, but would very much like to, and may even borrow Emma's copy. Barney has been skiing recently. I could probably remember a couple of other things if I had to. For most of the evening, however, I sit there like a pudding, feeling like a child who's been allowed to stay up late for a special treat. We eat stuff I don't know about, and either Nick or Barney comments on each bottle of wine we drink apart from the one I brought.

The difference between these people and me is that they finished college and I didn't (they didn't split up with Charlie and I did); as a consequence, they have smart jobs and I have a scruffy job, they are rich and I am poor, they are self-confident and I am incontinent, they do not smoke and I do, they have opinions and I have lists. Could I tell them anything about which journey is the worst for jet lag? No.

Could they tell me the original lineup of the Wailers? No. They probably couldn't even tell me the lead singer's name.

But they're not bad people. I'm not a class warrior, and anyway, they're not particularly posh—they probably have mothers and fathers just outside Watford or its equivalent, too. Do I want some of what they've got? You bet. I want their opinions, I want their money, I want their clothes, I want their ability to talk about dogs' names without any hint of embarrassment. I want to go back to 1979 and start all over again.

It doesn't help that Charlie talks bollocks all night; she doesn't listen to anyone, she tries too hard to go off at obtuse angles, she puts on all sorts of unrecognizable and inappropriate accents. I would like to say that these are all new mannerisms, but they're not; they were there before, years ago. The not listening I once mistook for strength of character, the obtuseness I misread as mystery, the accents I saw as glamor and drama. How had I managed to edit all this out in the intervening years? How had I managed to turn her into the answer to all the world's problems?

I stick the evening out, even though I'm not worth the sofa space for most of it, and I outstay Clara and Nick and Barney and Emma. When they've gone, I realize that I spent the whole time drinking instead of speaking, and as a consequence I can no longer focus properly.

"I'm right, aren't I?" Charlie asks. "She's just your type."

I shrug. "She's everybody's type." I help myself to some more coffee. I'm drunk, and it seems like a good idea just to launch in. "Charlie, why did you pack me in for Marco?"

She looks at me hard. "I knew it."

"What?"

"You *are* going through one of those what-does-it-all-mean things." She says "what-does-it-all-mean" in an American accent and furrows her brow.

I cannot tell a lie. "I am, actually, yes. Yes, indeed. Very much so."

She laughs—at me, I think, not with me—and then plays with one of her rings.

"You can say what you like," I tell her, generously.

"It's all kind of a bit lost in the . . . in the dense mists of time now." She says "dense mists of time" in an Irish accent, for no apparent reason, and waves her hand around in front of her face, presumably to indicate the density of the mist. "It wasn't that I fancied Marco more, because I used to find you every bit as attractive as him." (Pause.) "It's just that he knew he was nice-looking, and you didn't, and that made a difference, somehow. You used to act as though I was a bit peculiar for wanting to spend time with you, and that got kind of tiring, if you know what I mean. Your self-image started to rub off on me, and *I* ended up thinking I was peculiar. And I knew you were kind, and thoughtful, and you made me laugh, and I loved the way you got consumed by the things you loved, but . . . Marco seemed a bit more, I don't know, glamorous? More sure of himself, more in with the in-crowd?" (Pause.) "Less hard work, 'cause I felt I was dragging you round a bit." (Pause.) "A bit sunnier, and a bit sparkier." (Pause.) "I don't know. You know what people are like at that age. They make very superficial judgments."

Where's the superficial? I was, and therefore am, dim, gloomy, a drag, unfashionable, unfanciable, and awkward.

This doesn't seem like superficial to me. These aren't flesh wounds. These are life-threatening thrusts into the internal organs.

"Do you find that hurtful? He was a wimp, if that's any consolation."

It's not, really, but I didn't want consolation. I wanted the works, and I got it, too. None of Alison Ashworth's fate here; none of Sarah's rewriting of history, and no reminder that I'd got all the rejection stuff the wrong way round, like I did about Penny. Just a perfectly clear explanation of why some people have it and some people don't. Later on, in the back of a minicab, I realize that all Charlie has done is rephrase my own feelings about my genius for being normal; maybe that particular talent—my only one, as it happens—was overrated anyway.

TWENTY-TWO

BARRY'S band is going to play a gig, and he wants to put a poster up in the shop.

"No. Fuck off."

"Thanks for your support, Rob. I really appreciate it."

"I thought we had a rule about posters for crap bands."

"Yeah, for people who come in off the street begging us. All the losers."

"Like . . . let's see. Suede, you turned down. The Auteurs. St. Etienne. Losers like that, you mean?"

"What's all this '*I* turned them down'? It was your rule."

"Yeah, but you loved it, didn't you? It gave you great pleasure to tell all those poor kids to take a running jump."

"Well, I was wrong, wasn't I? Oh, come on, Rob. We need the regulars from here, otherwise there'll be nobody."

"OK, what's the name of the band? If it's any good, you can put a poster up."

He thrusts a poster at me—just the name of the band, with some squiggly design.

" 'Barrytown.' 'Barrytown'? Fucking hell. Is there no end to your arrogance?"

"It's not because of me. It's the Steely Dan song. And it was in *The Commitments.*"

"Yeah, but come on, Barry. You can't be called Barry and sing in a group called Barrytown. It just sounds . . ."

"They were fucking called that before I came along, OK? It wasn't my idea."

"That's why you got the gig, isn't it?"

Barry of Barrytown says nothing.

"Isn't it?"

"That was one of the reasons why they asked me originally, yes. But . . ."

"Brilliant! Fucking brilliant! They only asked you to sing because of your name! Of course you can have a poster up, Barry. I want as many people to know as possible. Not in the window, OK? You can stick it above the browser racks over there."

"How many tickets can I put you down for?"

I hold my sides and laugh mirthlessly. "Ha, ha ha. Ho, ho ho. Stop, Barry, you're killing me."

"You're not even coming?"

"Of course I'm not coming. Do I look like a man who'd want to listen to some terrible experimental racket played in some horrible north London pub? Where is it?" I look at the poster. "The fucking Harry Lauder! Ha!"

"So much for mates, then. You're a bitter bastard, Rob, you know that?"

Sour. Bitter. Everyone seems to agree that I don't taste very nice.

"Bitter? Because I'm not in Barrytown? I hoped it wasn't that obvious. And you've been great to Dick about Anna, haven't you? Really made her feel a part of the Championship Vinyl family."

I'd forgotten that I have been wishing nothing but everlasting happiness to Dick and Anna. How does that fit in with my sourness, eh? What's bitter about that?

"That Anna stuff was just a bit of fun. She's all right. It's just . . . it's not my fault that you're fucking up left, right, and center."

"Oh, and you'd be first in the queue to see me play, wouldn't you?"

"Not first, maybe. But I'd be there."

"Is Dick going?"

" 'Course. And Anna. And Marie and T-Bone."

Is the world really that generous-spirited? I had no idea.

I guess you could see it as bitterness, if you wanted to. I don't think of myself as bitter, but I have disappointed myself; I thought I was going to turn out to be worth a bit more than this, and maybe that disappointment comes out all wrong. It's not just the work; it's not just the thirty-five-and-single thing, although none of this helps. It's . . . oh, I don't know. Have you ever looked at a picture of yourself when you were a kid? Or pictures of famous people when they were kids? It seems to me that they can either make you happy or sad. There's a lovely picture of Paul McCartney as a little boy, and the first time I saw it, it made me feel good: all that talent, all that money, all those years of blissed-out domesticity, a rock-solid marriage and lovely kids, and he doesn't even know it yet. But then there are others—JFK and all the rock deaths and fuckups, people who went mad, people who came off the rails, people who murdered, who made themselves or other people miserable in ways too numerous to mention—and you think, stop right there! This is as good as it gets!

Over the last couple of years, the photos of me when I was a kid, the ones that I never wanted old girlfriends to see . . . well, they've started to give me a little pang of something—not unhappiness, exactly, but some kind of quiet, deep regret. There's one of me in a cowboy hat, pointing a gun at the camera, trying to look like a cowboy but failing, and I can hardly bring myself to look at it now. Laura thought it was sweet (she used that word! Sweet, the opposite of sour!) and pinned it up in the kitchen, but I've put it back in a drawer. I keep wanting to apologize to the little guy: "I'm sorry, I've let you down. I was the person who was supposed to look after you, but I blew it: I made wrong decisions at bad times, and I turned you into me."

See, he would have wanted to see Barry's band; he wouldn't have worried too much about Ian's dungarees or Penny's flashlight-pen (he would have *loved* Penny's flashlight-pen) or Charlie's trips to the States. He wouldn't have understood, in fact, why I was so down on all of them. If he could be here now, if he could jump out of that photo and into this shop, he'd run straight out of the door and back to 1967 as fast as his little legs would carry him.

TWENTY-THREE

FINALLY,

finally, a month or so after she's left, Laura comes to move her stuff out. There's no real argument about what belongs to whom; the good records are mine, the good furniture, most of the cooking stuff, and the hardback books are hers. The only thing I've done is to sort out a whole pile of records and a few CDs I gave her as presents, stuff that I wanted but thought she'd like, and which have somehow ended up being filed away in my collection. I've been really scrupulous about it: she wouldn't have remembered half of these, and I could have got away with it, but I've pulled out every single one.

I was scared she was going to bring Ian round, but she doesn't. In fact, she's obviously uncomfortable about the fact that he rang.

"Forget it."

"He had no right to do that, and I told him so."

"Are you still together?"

She looks at me to see if I'm joking, and then gives a little hard-luck grimace that actually isn't too attractive, if you think about it.

"Going all right?"

"I don't really want to talk about it, to be honest."

"That bad, eh?"

"You know what I mean."

She's borrowed her dad's Volvo Estate for the weekend, and we fill every inch of it; she comes back inside for a cup of tea when we're done.

"It's a dump, isn't it?" I say. I can see her looking round the flat, staring at the dusty, discolored spaces her things have left on the wall, so I feel I have to preempt criticism.

"Please do it up, Rob. It wouldn't cost you much, and it would make you feel better."

"I'll bet you can't remember what you were doing here now, can you?"

"Yes, I can. I was here because I wanted to be with you."

"No, I meant, you know . . . how much are you on now? Forty-five? Fifty? And you lived in this poky little hole in Crouch End."

"You know I didn't mind. And it's not as if Ray's place is any better."

"I'm sorry, but can we get this straight? What is his name, Ian or Ray? What do you call him?"

"Ray. I hate Ian."

"Right. Just so's I know. Anyway, what's Ian's place like?" Childish, but it makes me happy. Laura puts on her pained, stoical face. I've seen that one a few times, I can tell you.

"Small. Smaller than here. But neater, and less cluttered."

"That's 'cause he's only got about ten records. CDs."

"And that makes him an awful person, does it?"

"In my book, yes. Barry, Dick, and I decided that you can't be a serious person if you have—"

"Less than five hundred. Yes, I know. You've told me many, many times before. I disagree. I think it's possible to be a serious person even if you have no records whatsoever."

"Like Kate Adie."

She looks at me, frowns, and opens her mouth, her way of indicating that I'm potty. "Do you know for a fact that Kate Adie's got no records whatsoever?"

"Well, not *none.* She's probably got a couple. Pavarotti and stuff. Maybe some Tracy Chapman, and a copy of *Bob Dylan's Greatest Hits,* and two or three Beatles albums."

She starts to laugh. I wasn't joking, to be honest, but if she thinks I'm funny then I prepared to act like I was.

"And I'll bet she was one of the people at parties who used to go 'Woooh!' to the fade-out of 'Brown Sugar.' "

"There is no greater crime than that, as far as you're concerned, is there?"

"The only thing that runs it close is singing along to the chorus of 'Hi Ho Silver Lining,' at the top of your voice."

"I used to do that."

"You didn't."

The joking has stopped now, and I look at her appalled. She roars.

"You believed me! You believed me! You must think I'm capable of *anything.*" She laughs again, catches herself having a good time, and stops.

I give her the cue. "This is where you're supposed to say that you haven't laughed this much in ages, and then you see the error of your ways."

She makes a so-what face. "You make me laugh much more than Ray does, if that's what you're getting at."

I give a mock-smug smile, but I'm not feeling mock-smug. I'm feeling the real thing.

"But it doesn't make any difference to anything, Rob. Really. We could laugh until I had to be taken away in an ambulance, but it doesn't mean I'm going to unload the car and move all my stuff back in. I already knew you could make me laugh. It's everything else I don't know about."

"Why don't you just admit that Ian's an arsehole and have done with it? It would make you feel better."

"Have you been talking to Liz?"

"Why? Does she think he's an arsehole too? That's interesting."

"Don't spoil it, Rob. We've got on well today. Let's leave it at that."

I pull out the stack of records and CDs that I've sorted out for her. There's *The Nightfly* by Donald Fagen, because she'd never heard it, and some blues compilation samplers I decided she ought to have, and a couple of jazz-dance things I bought for her when she started going to a jazz-dance class, although it turned out to be a different and frankly much crappier form of jazz-dance, and a couple of country things, in my vain attempt to change her mind about country, and . . .

She doesn't want any of it.

"But they're *yours.*"

"They're not really, though, are they? I know you bought them for me, and that was really sweet of you, but that was when you were trying to turn me into you. I can't take them. I know they'd just sit around staring at me, and I'd feel embarrassed by them, and . . . they don't fit in with the rest of what's mine, do you understand? That Sting record you bought me . . . that was a present for *me.* I like Sting and you hate him. But the rest of this stuff . . ." She picks up the blues sampler. "Who the hell's Little Walter? Or Junior Wells? I don't know these people. I . . ."

"OK, OK. I get the picture."

"I'm sorry to go on about it. But, I don't know, there's a lesson in here somewhere, and I want to make sure you get it."

"I get it. You like Sting but you don't like Junior Wells, because you've never heard of him."

"You're being deliberately obtuse."

"I am, actually, yes."

She gets up to go.

"Well, think about it."

And later on, I think, what for? What's the point of thinking about it? If I ever have another relationship, I'll buy her, whoever she is, stuff that she ought to like but doesn't know about; that's what new boyfriends are for. And hopefully I won't borrow money off her, or have an affair, and she won't need to have an abortion, or run away with the neighbors, and then there won't be anything to think about. Laura didn't run off with Ray because I bought her CDs she wasn't that keen on, and to pretend otherwise is just . . . just . . .

psychowank. If she thinks that, then she's missing the Brazilian rain forest for the twigs. If I can't buy specially priced compilation albums for new girlfriends, then I might as well give up, because I'm not sure that I know how to do anything else.

TWENTY-FOUR

I USUALLY enjoy my birthday, but today I don't feel so good about it. Birthdays should be suspended in years like this one: there should be a law, of man if not of nature, that you are only allowed to age when things are ticking along nicely. What do I want to be thirty-six for now? I don't. It's not convenient. Rob Fleming's life is frozen at the moment, and he refuses to get any older. Please retain all cards, cakes, and presents for use on another occasion.

Actually, that seems to be what people have done. Sod's law decrees that my birthday should fall on a Sunday this year, so cards and presents are not forthcoming; I didn't get anything Saturday, either. I wasn't expecting anything from Dick or Barry, although I told them in the pub after work, and they looked guilty, and bought me a drink, and promised me all sorts of things (well, compilation tapes, anyway); but I never remember their birthdays—you don't, do you, unless you are of the female persuasion—so a tantrum would not be particularly appropriate in this case. But Laura? Relatives? Friends? (Nobody you know, but I do have some, and I do see them sometimes, and one or two of them do know when my birthday is.) Godparents? Anyone else at all? I did get a card from my mum and a P.S. from my dad, but parents don't count; if you don't even get a card from your folks, then you're really in trouble.

On the morning of the day itself I spend much too much time fantasizing about some enormous surprise party organized by Laura, maybe, with the help of my mum and dad, who could have provided her with the addresses and phone numbers of some of the people she wouldn't know about; I even find myself irritated by their not having told me about it. Suppose I just took myself off to the pictures for a solitary birthday treat without letting them know? Then where would they be, eh? They'd all be hiding in some cupboard somewhere while I was watching a *Godfather* triple-bill at the Scala. That'd serve them right. I decide not to tell them where I'm going; I'll leave them squashed up in the dark, cramped and ill-tempered. ("I thought *you* were going to ring him?" "I told you I didn't have time," etc.) After a couple of cups of coffee, however, I realize that this sort of thinking is not profitable, that it is, in fact, likely to drive me potty, and I decide to arrange something positive instead.

Like what?

Go to the video shop for a start, and rent loads of things I've been saving up for just such a dismal occasion as this: *Naked Gun 2 ½, Terminator 2, Robocop 2.* And then ring up a couple of people to see if they want a drink tonight. Not Dick and Barry. Marie maybe, or people I haven't seen for a long time. And then watch one or two of the videos, drink some beer, and eat some crisps, maybe even some Kettle Chips. Sounds good. Sounds like the sort of birthday a brand-new thirty-six-year-old should have. (Actually, it is the *only* sort of birthday a brand-new thirty-six-year-old could have—the sort of thirty-six-year-old with no wife, family, girlfriend, or money, anyway. Kettle Chips! Fuck off!)

You thought there was going to be nothing left in the video shop, didn't you? You thought I cut such a tragic figure that I'd be reduced to watching some Whoopi Goldberg comedy-thriller which never got a cinematic release in this country. But no! They're all there, and I walk out with all the rubbish I want tucked under my arm. It's just turned twelve, so I can buy some beer; I go home, pop a can, draw the curtains to keep out the March sunshine, and watch *Naked Gun 2 1/2*, which turns out to be pretty funny.

My mum calls just as I'm putting *Robocop 2* into the machine, and again, I'm disappointed that it isn't someone else. If you can't get a phone call from your mum on your birthday, then you're really in trouble.

She's nice to me, though. She's sympathetic about me spending the day on my own, even though she must be hurt that I'd rather spend the day on my own than spend it with her and Dad. ("D'you want to come to the pictures this evening with your father and Yvonne and Brian?" she asks me. "No," I tell her. That's all. Just "No." Restrained or what?) She can't really think of anything to say after that. It must be hard for parents, I guess, when they see that things aren't working out for their children, but that their children can no longer be reached by the old parental routes, because those roads are now much too long. She starts to talk about other birthdays, birthdays where I was ill because I ate too many nutella sandwiches or drank too many rainbow cocktails, but these were at least pukes conceived in happiness, and her talking about them doesn't cheer me up much, and I stop her. And then she starts on a whiny, how-come-you've-got-yourself-into-this-mess speech, which I know is a result of her powerlessness and panic, but it's my day today, such as it is, and I'm not prepared to listen to that either. She's OK about me shutting her up, though: because she still treats me like a child, birthdays are times when I am allowed to behave like one.

Laura rings in the middle of *Robocop 2, from a callbox.* This is very interesting, but maybe now is not the time to talk about why—not with Laura, anyway. Maybe later, with Liz or someone, but not now. This is obvious to anyone but a complete idiot.

"Why are you ringing from a callbox?"

"Am I?" she says. Not the smoothest answer.

"Did you have to put money or a card into a slot to speak to me? Is there a horrible smell of urine? If the answer to either of these questions is yes, it's a callbox. Why are you ringing from a callbox?"

"To wish you a happy birthday. I'm sorry I forgot to send you a card."

"I didn't mean . . ."

"I was just on my way home, and I . . ."

"Why didn't you wait till you got back?"

"What's the point of me saying anything? You think you know the answer anyway."

"I'd just like it confirmed."

"Are you having a good day?"

"Not bad. *Naked Gun 2 1/2:* very funny. *Robocop 2:* not as good as the first one. So far, anyway."

"You're watching videos?"

"I am."

"On your own?"

"Yep. Want to come round? I've still got *Terminator 2* to see."

"I can't. I've got to get back."

"Right."

"Anyway."

"How's your dad?"

"He's not too bad, at the moment, thanks for asking."

"Good."

"Have a nice day, OK? Do something good with it. Don't waste all day in front of the TV."

"Right."

"Come on, Rob. It's not my fault you're in on your own. I'm not the only person you know. And I am thinking of you, it's not like I've just jumped ship."

"Tell Ian I said hi, OK?"

"Very funny."

"I mean it."

"I know you do. Very funny."

Got her. He doesn't want her to phone, and she's not going to tell him she has. Cool.

I'm at a bit of a loss after *Terminator 2.* It's not four o'clock yet, and even though I've plowed my way through three great crap videos and the best part of a six-pack, I still cannot shake the feeling that I'm not having much of a birthday. There are papers to read, and compilation tapes to make, but, you know. I pick up the phone instead, and start to organize my own surprise party in the pub. I shall gather a few people together, try to forget I called them, take myself off to the Crown or the Queen's Head around eight for a quiet pint, and get my back slapped raw by well-wishers I never expected to see there in a million years.

It's harder than I thought, though. London, eh? You might as well ask people if they'd like to take a year off and travel around the world with you as ask them if they'd like to nip out for a quick drink later on: later on means later on in the month, or the year, or the nineties, but never later on the same day. "Tonight?" they all go, all these people I haven't spoken to for months, ex-colleagues or old college friends, or people I've met through ex-colleagues or old college friends. "Later on *tonight?*" They're aghast, they're baffled, they're kind of amused, but most of all they just can't believe it. Someone's phoning up and suggesting a drink tonight, out of the blue, no Filofax to hand, no lists of alternative dates, no lengthy consultation with a partner? Preposterous.

But a couple of them show signs of weakness, and I exploit that weakness mercilessly. It's not an ooh-I-shouldn't-really-but-I-quite-fancy-a-pint sort of weakness; it's an inability-to-say-no sort of weakness. They don't want to go out tonight, but they can hear the desperation, and they cannot find it in themselves to respond with the necessary firmness.

Dan Maskell (real first name Adrian, but it had to be done) is the first to crack. He's married, with a kid, and he lives in Hounslow, and it's a Sunday night, but I'm not going to let him off the hook.

"Hello, Dan? It's Rob."

"Hello, mate." (Genuine pleasure at this point, which is something, I suppose.)

"How are you?"

So I tell him how I am, and then I explain the sad situation—sorry it's too last-minute, bit of a cock-up on the arrangement front (I manage to resist telling him there's been a bit of a cock-up on the life front generally), be nice to see him anyway, and so on and so forth, and I can hear the hesitation in his voice. And then—Adrian's a big music fan, which is how I met him at college, and why we kept in touch afterwards—I steal a trump card and play it.

"Have you heard of Marie LaSalle? She's a very good folky country kind of singer."

He hasn't, not surprisingly, but I can tell that he's interested.

"Well, anyway, she's a . . . well, a friend, and she'll be

coming along, so . . . she's great, and she's worth meeting, and . . . I don't know if . . ."

It's just about enough. To speak frankly with you, Adrian's a bit of an idiot, which is why I thought Marie might be an enticement. Why do I want to spend my birthday drinking with an idiot? That's a long story, most of which you already know.

Steven Butler lives in north London, doesn't have a wife, and doesn't have that many friends either. So why can't he come out tonight? He's already rented his video, that's why.

"Fucking hell, Steve."

"Well, you should have called me earlier. I've only just come back from the shop."

"Why don't you watch it now?"

"No. I'm a bit funny about watching videos before my tea. It's like you're just watching for the sake of it, do you know what I mean? And every one you watch in the daytime, that's one less you can watch at night."

"How d'you work that out?"

" 'Cause you're wasting them, aren't you?"

"Watch it another time, then."

"Oh, yeah. I've got so much money I can give two pounds to the bloke in the video shop every night."

"I'm not asking you to do it every night. I'm . . . Look, I'll give you the two quid, all right?"

"I dunno. Are you sure?"

I'm sure, and there we have it. Dan Maskell and Steve Butler. They don't know each other, they won't like each other, and they have nothing in common apart from a slight overlap in their record collections (Dan's not very interested in black music, Steve's not very interested in white music, they both have a few jazz albums). And Dan's expecting to see Marie, but Marie's not expecting to see Dan, nor does she even know of his existence. Should be a cracking night out.

Marie's got a phone now, and Barry has her number, and she's happy that I called, and more than happy to come out for a drink, and if she knew it was my birthday she'd probably explode with joy, but for some reason I decide not to tell her. I don't have to sell the evening to her, which is just as well, because I don't think I'd be able to give it away. She's got to do something else first, however, so there's an agonizing hour or so alone with Steve and Dan. I talk to Dan about rock music, while Steve stares at somebody getting lucky on the fruit machine, and I talk to Steve about soul music, while Dan does that trick with a beer mat which only the truly irritating person knows. And then we all talk about jazz, and then there's some pretty desultory what-do-you-do kind of stuff, and then we run out of petrol altogether, and we all watch the guy who's getting lucky on the fruit machine.

Marie and T-Bone and a very blond, very glamorous, and very young woman, also American, finally turn up around quarter to ten, so there's only forty-five minutes of drinking time left. I ask them what they want to drink, but Marie doesn't know, and comes up to the bar with me to have a look at what they've got.

"I see what you mean about T-Bone's sex life," I say as we're waiting.

She raises her eyes to the ceiling. "Isn't she something

else? And you know what? That's the ugliest woman he's ever dated."

"I'm glad you could come."

"The pleasure is ours. Who are those guys?"

"Dan and Steve. I've known them for years. They're a bit dull, I'm afraid, but I have to see them sometimes."

"Duck noires, right?"

"Sorry?"

"I call 'em duck noires. Sort of a mixture of lame duck and *bête noire.* People you don't want to see but kinda feel you should."

Duck noires. Bang on. And I had to fucking beg mine, *pay* mine, to come out for a drink on my birthday.

I never think these things through, ever. "Happy birthday, Rob," says Steve when I put his drink down in front of him. Marie attempts to give me a look—of surprise, I would guess, but also of deepest sympathy and bottomless understanding, but I won't return it.

It's a pretty bad evening. When I was a kid, my granny used to spend Boxing Day afternoon with a friend's granny; my mum and dad would drink with Adrian's mum and dad, and I'd play with Adrian, and the two old codgers would sit in front of the TV exchanging pleasantries. The catch was that they were both deaf, but it didn't really matter: they were happy enough with their version of a conversation, which had the same gaps and nods and smiles as everyone else's conversation, but none of the connections. I haven't thought about that for years, but I remember it tonight.

Steve annoys me throughout: he has this trick of waiting until the conversation is in full flow, and then muttering something in my ear when I'm attempting either to talk or to listen to somebody else. So I can either ignore him and appear rude, or answer him, involve everyone else in what I'm saying, and change their direction entirely. And once he's got everyone talking about soul, or *Star Trek* (he goes to conventions and things), or great bitters of the north of England (he goes to conventions and things), subjects nobody else knows anything about, we go through the whole process all over again. Dan yawns a lot, Marie is patient, T-Bone is tetchy, and his date, Suzie, is positively appalled. What is she doing in a grotty pub with these guys? She has no idea. Neither have I. Maybe Suzie and I should disappear off somewhere more intimate, and leave these losers to get on with it. I could take you through the whole evening, but you wouldn't enjoy it much, so I'll let you off with a dull but entirely representative sample:

MARIE: . . . just unbelievable, I mean, real *animals.* I was singing "Love Hurts" and this guy shouted out, "Not the way I do it, baby," and then he was sick all the way down his T-shirt, and he *didn't move a muscle.* Just stood there shouting at the stage and laughing with his buddies. [*Laughs.*] You were there, weren't you, T-Bone?

T-BONE: I guess.

MARIE: T-Bone *dreams* of fans as suave as that, don't you? The places he plays, you have to . . . [*Inaudible due to interruption from . . .*]

STEVE: [*Whispering in my ear*] They've brought *The Baron* out on video now, you know. Six episodes. D'you remember the theme music?

ME: No. I don't. [*Laughter from Marie, T-Bone, Dan*]

Sorry, Marie, I missed that. You have to do what?

MARIE: I was saying, this place that T-Bone and me . . .

STEVE: It was brilliant. Der-der-DER! Der-der-der DER!

DAN: I recognize that. *Man in a Suitcase?*

STEVE: No. *The Baron.* 'S' out on video.

MARIE: *The Baron?* Who was in that?

DAN: Steve Forrest.

MARIE: I think we used to get that. Was that the one where the guy [*Inaudible due to interruption from* . . .]

STEVE: [*Whispering in my ear*] D'you ever read *Voices from the Shadows?* Soul magazine? Brilliant. Steve Davis owns it, you know. The snooker player. [*Suzie makes a face at T-Bone. T-Bone looks at his watch.*]

Etc.

Never again will this combination of people be seated around a table; it just couldn't possibly happen, and it shows. I thought the numbers would provide a feeling of security and comfort, but they haven't. I don't really know any of these people, not even the one I've slept with, and for the first time since I split up with Laura, I really feel like slumping onto the floor and bawling my eyes out. I'm home-sick.

It's supposed to be women who allow themselves to become isolated by relationships: they end up seeing more of the guy's friends, and doing more of the guy's things (poor

Anna, trying to remember who Richard Thompson is, and being shown the error of her Simple Minded ways), and when they're ditched, or when they ditch, they find they've floated too far away from friends they last saw properly three or four years before. And before Laura, that was what life was like for me and my partners too, most of them.

But Laura . . . I don't know what happened. I liked her crowd, Liz and the others who used to come down to the Groucho. And for some reason—comparative career success, I guess, and the corresponding postponements that brings—her crowd were more single and more flexible than mine. So for the first time ever I played the woman's role, and threw my lot in with the person I was seeing. It wasn't that she didn't like my friends (not friends like Dick and Barry and Steve and Dan, but *proper* friends, the sort of people I have allowed myself to lose). It was just that she liked hers more, and wanted me to like them, and I did. I liked them more than I liked my own and, before I knew it (I never knew it, really, until it was too late), my relationship was what gave me my sense of location. And if you lose your sense of location, you get homesick. Stands to reason.

So now what? It feels as though I've come to the end of the line. I don't mean that in the American rock'n'roll suicide sense; I mean it in the English Thomas the Tank Engine sense. I've run out of puff, and come to a gentle halt in the middle of nowhere.

"These people are your friends?" Marie asks me the next day when she takes me for a post-birthday crispy bacon and avocado sandwich.

"It's not that bad. There were only two of them."

She looks at me to see if I'm joking. When she laughs, it's clear that I am.

"But it was your *birthday.*"

"Well. You know."

"Your *birthday.* And that's the best you can do?"

"Say it was your birthday today, and you wanted to go out for a drink tonight. Who would you invite? Dick and Barry? T-Bone? Me? We're not your bestest friends in the whole world, are we?"

"Come on, Rob. I'm not even in my own *country.* I'm thousands of miles from home."

"My point exactly."

I watch the couples that come into the shop, and the couples I see in pubs, and on buses, and through windows. Some of them, the ones that talk and touch and laugh and inquire a lot, are obviously new, and they don't count: like most people, I'm OK at being half of a new couple. It's the more established, quieter couples, the ones who have started to go through life back-to-back or side-to-side, rather than face-to-face, that interest me.

There's not much you can decipher in their faces, really. There's not much that sets them apart from single people; try dividing people you walk past into one of life's four categories—happily coupled, unhappily coupled, single, and desperate—and you'll find you won't be able to do it. Or rather, you could do it, but you would have no confidence in your choices. This seems incredible to me. The most important thing in life, and you can't tell whether people have it or not. Surely this is wrong? Surely people who are happy should *look* happy, at all times, no matter how much money they have or how uncomfortable their shoes are or how little their child is sleeping; and people who are doing OK but have still not found their soul mate should look, I don't know, well but anxious, like Billy Crystal in *When Harry Met Sally;* and people who are desperate should wear something, a yellow ribbon maybe, which would allow them to be identified by similarly desperate people. When I am no longer desperate, when I have got all this sorted out, I promise you here and now that I will never ever complain again about how the shop is doing, or about the soullessness of modern pop music, or the stingy fillings you get in the sandwich bar up the road (£1.60 for egg mayonnaise and crispy bacon, and none of us have ever had more than four pieces of crispy bacon in a whole round yet) or anything at all. I will beam beatifically at all times, just from sheer *relief.*

Nothing much, by which I mean even less than usual, happens for a couple of weeks. I find a copy of "All Kinds of Everything" in a junk shop near the flat, and buy it for fifteen pence, and give it to Johnny next time I see him, on the proviso that he fuck off and leave us alone forever. He comes in the next day complaining that it's scratched and demanding his money back. Barrytown make a triumphant debut at the Harry Lauder, and rock the place off its foundations, and the buzz is incredible, and there are loads of people there who look like A&R men, and they go absolutely mental, and honestly Rob, you should have been there (Marie just laughs, when I ask her about it, and says that everyone has to start somewhere). Dick tries to get me to make up a foursome with him, Anna, and a friend of Anna's who's twenty-one, but I don't go; we see Marie play at a folk club in Farringdon, and I think about Laura a lot more than I think about Marie during the sad songs, even though Marie dedicates a song to "the guys at Championship Vinyl"; I go for a drink with Liz and she bitches about Ray the whole evening, which is great; and then Laura's dad dies, and everything changes.

TWENTY-FIVE

I HEAR about it on the same morning she does. I ring her number from the shop, intending just to leave a message on her machine; it's easier that way, and I only wanted to tell her about some ex-colleague who left a message for her on our machine. My machine. Her machine, actually, if we're talking legal ownership. Anyway. I wasn't expecting Laura to pick up the phone, but she does, and she sounds as though she's speaking from the bottom of the sea. Her voice is muffled, and low, and flat, and coated from first syllable to last in snot.

"Cor dear oh dear, that's a cold and a half. I hope you're in bed with a hot book and a good water bottle. It's Rob, by the way."

She doesn't say anything.

"Laura? It's Rob."

Still nothing.

"Are you all right?"

And then a terrible moment.

"Pigsty," she says, although the first syllable's just a noise, really, so "pig" is an educated guess.

"Don't worry about that," I say. "Just get into bed and forget about it. Worry about it when you're better."

"Pig's died," she says.

"Who the fuck's Pig?"

This time I can hear her. "My dad's died," she sobs. "My dad, my dad."

And then she hangs up.

I think about people dying all the time, but they're always people connected with me. I've thought about how I would feel if Laura died, and how Laura would feel if I died, and how I'd feel if my mum or dad died, but I never thought about Laura's mum or dad dying. I wouldn't, would I? And even though he was ill for the entire duration of my relationship with Laura, it never really bothered me: it was more like, my dad's got a beard, Laura's dad's got angina. I never thought it would actually *lead* to anything. Now he's gone, of course, I wish . . . what? What do I wish? That I'd been nicer to him? I was perfectly nice to him, the few times we met. That we'd been closer? He was my common-law father-in-law, and we were very different, and he was sick, and . . . we were as close as we needed to be. You're supposed to wish things when people die, to fill yourself full of regrets, to give yourself a hard time for all your mistakes and omissions, and I'm doing all that as best I can. It's just that I can't find any mistakes and omissions. He was my ex-girlfriend's dad, you know? What am I supposed to feel?

"You all right?" says Barry, when he sees me staring into space. "Who were you talking to?"

"Laura. Her dad's died."

"Oh, right. Bad one." And then he wanders off to the post office with a pile of mail orders under his arm. See? From Laura, to me, to Barry: from grief, to confusion, to a fleeting, mild interest. If you want to find a way to extract death's sting, then Barry's your man. For a moment it feels strange that these two people, one who is so maddened by pain that she can hardly speak, the other who can hardly find the curiosity to shrug, should know each other; strange that I'm the link between them, strange that they live in the same place at the same time, even. But Ken was Barry's boss's ex-girlfriend's dad. What is he supposed to feel?

Laura calls back an hour or so later. I wasn't expecting her to.

"I'm sorry," she says. It's still hard to make out what she's saying, what with the snot and the tears and the tone and the volume.

"No, no."

Then she cries for a while. I don't say anything until she's a bit quieter.

"When are you going home?"

"In a minute. When I get it together."

"Can I do anything?"

"No." And then, after a sob, "No" again, as if she's realized properly that there's nothing anybody can do for her, and maybe this is the first time she's ever found herself in that situation. I know I never have. Everything that's ever gone wrong for me could have been rescued by the wave of a bank manager's wand, or by a girlfriend's sudden change of mind, or by some quality—determination, self-awareness, resilience—that I might have found within myself, if I'd looked hard enough. I don't want to have to cope with the sort of unhappiness Laura's feeling, not ever. If people have to die, I don't want them dying near me. My mum and dad won't die near me, I've made bloody sure of that. When they go, I'll hardly feel a thing.

The next day she calls again.

"Mum wants you to come to the funeral."

"Me?"

"My dad liked you. Apparently. And Mum never told him we'd split, because he wasn't up to it and . . . oh, I don't know. I don't really understand it, and I can't be bothered to argue. I think she thinks he'll be able to see what's going on. It's like . . ." She makes a strange noise which I realize is a manic giggle. "Her attitude is that he's been through so much, what with dying and everything, that she doesn't want to upset him any more than she has to."

I knew that Ken liked me, but I could never really work out why, apart from once he was looking for the original London cast recording of *My Fair Lady,* and I saw a copy at a record fair, and sent it to him. See where random acts of kindness get you? To fucking funerals, that's where.

"Do *you* want me there?"

"I don't care. As long as you don't expect me to hold your hand."

"Is Ray going?"

"No, Ray's not going."

"Why not?"

"Because he hasn't been invited, OK?"

"I don't mind, you know, if that's what you want."

"Oh, that's so sweet of you, Rob. It's your day, after all."

Jesus.

"Look, are you coming or not?"

"Yes, of course."

"Liz'll give you a lift. She knows where to go and everything."

"Fine. How are you?"

"I haven't got time to chat, Rob. I've got too much to do."

"Sure. I'll see you Friday." I put the phone down before she can say anything, to let her know I'm hurt, and then I want to phone her back and apologize, but I know I mustn't. It's like you can never do the right thing by someone if you've stopped sleeping with them. You can't see a way back, or through, or round, however hard you try.

There aren't really any pop songs about death—not good ones, anyway. Maybe that's why I like pop music, and why I find classical music a bit creepy. There was that Elton John instrumental, "Song for Guy," but, you know, it was just a plinky-plonky piano thing that would serve you just as well at the airport as at your funeral.

"OK, guys, best five pop songs about death."

"Magic," says Barry. "A Laura's Dad Tribute List. OK, OK. 'Leader of the Pack,' The bloke dies on his motorbike, doesn't he? And then there's 'Dead Man's Curve' by Jan and Dean, and 'Terry,' by Twinkle. Ummm . . . that Bobby Goldsboro one, you know, 'And Honey, I Miss You . . .' " He sings it off-key, even more so than he would have done normally, and Dick laughs. "And what about 'Tell Laura I Love Her.' That'd bring the house down." I'm glad that Laura isn't here to see how much amusement her father's death has afforded us.

"I was trying to think of serious songs. You know, something that shows a bit of respect."

"What, you're doing the DJ-ing at the funeral, are you? Ouch. Bad job. Still, the Bobby Goldsboro could be one of the smoochers. You know, when people need a breather. Laura's mum could sing it." He sings the same line, off-key again, but this time in a falsetto voice to show that the singer is a woman.

"Fuck off, Barry."

"I've already worked out what I'm having at mine. 'One Step Beyond,' by Madness. 'You Can't Always Get What You Want.' "

"Just 'cause it's in *The Big Chill.*"

"I haven't seen *The Big Chill,* have I?"

"You lying bastard. You saw it in a Lawrence Kasdan double bill with *Body Heat.*"

"Oh, yeah. But I'd forgotten about that, honestly. I wasn't just nicking the idea."

"Not much."

And so on.

I try again later.

" 'Abraham, Martin, and John,' " says Dick. "That's quite a nice one."

"What was Laura's dad's name?"

"Ken."

" 'Abraham, Martin, John, and Ken.' Nah, I can't see it."

"Fuck off."

"Black Sabbath? Nirvana? They're all into death."

Thus is Ken's passing mourned at Championship Vinyl.

I have thought about the stuff I want played at my funeral, although I could never list it to anyone, because they'd die laughing. "One Love" by Bob Marley; "Many Rivers to Cross" by Jimmy Cliff; "Angel" by Aretha Franklin. And I've always had this fantasy that someone beautiful and tearful will insist on "You're the Best Thing That Ever Happened to Me" by Gladys Knight, but I can't imagine who that beautiful, tearful person will be. But that's my funeral, as they say, and I can afford to be generous and sentimental about it. It doesn't alter the point that Barry made, even if he didn't know he was making it: we have about seven squillion hours' worth of recorded music in here, and there's hardly a minute of it that describes the way Laura's feeling now.

I've got one suit, dark gray, last worn at a wedding three years ago. It doesn't fit too well now, in all the obvious places, but it'll have to do. I iron my white shirt and find a tie that isn't made of leather and doesn't have saxophones all over it, and wait for Liz to come and pick me up. I haven't got anything to take with me—the cards in the newsagent's were all vile. They looked like the sort of thing the Addams Family would send to each other on their birthdays. I wish I'd been to a funeral before. One of my grandfathers died before I was born, and the other when I was very little; both my grandmothers are still alive, if you can call it that, but I never see them. One lives in a home, the other lives with Aunty Eileen, my dad's sister. And when they do die it will hardly be the end of the world. Just, you know, wow, stop press, extremely ancient person dies. And though I've got friends who have friends who've died—a gay guy that Laura was at college with got AIDS, a mate of my mate Paul was killed in a motorbike crash, and loads of them have lost parents—it's something I've always managed to put off. Now I can see that it's something I'll be doing for the rest of my life. Two grans, Mum and Dad, aunts and uncles, and, unless I'm the first person in my immediate circle to go, loads of people my age, eventually—maybe even sooner than eventually, given that one or two of them are bound to cop it before they're supposed to. Once I start to think about it, it seems terribly oppressive, as though I'll be going to three or four a week for the next forty years, and I won't have the time or the inclination to do anything else. How do people cope? Do you have to go? What happens if you refuse on the grounds of it being just too fucking grim? ("I'm sorry for you and everything, Laura, but it's not really my scene, you know?") I don't think I can bear to get any older than I already am, and I begin to develop a grudging admiration for my parents, just because they've been to scores of funerals and have never really moaned about it, not to me, anyway. Perhaps they just don't have the imagination to see that funerals are actually even more depressing than they look.

. . .

If I'm honest, I'm only going because it might do me some good in the long run. Can you get off with your ex-girlfriend at her father's funeral? I wouldn't have thought so. But you never know.

"So the vicar says nice things, and then, what, we all troop outside and they bury him?"

Liz is talking me through it.

"It's at a crematorium."

"You're having me on."

"Of course I'm not having you on, you fool."

"A crematorium? Jesus."

"What difference does it make?"

"Well, none, but . . . Jesus." I wasn't prepared for this.

"What's the matter?"

"I don't know, but . . . bloody hell."

She sighs. "Do you want me to drop you off at a tube station?"

"No, of course not."

"Shut up, then."

"I just don't want to pass out, that's all. If I pass out because of lack of preparation, it'll be your fault."

"What a pathetic specimen you are. You know that nobody actively enjoys these things, don't you? You know that we're all going to find this morning terribly upsetting? It's not just you. I've been to one cremation in my life and I hated it. And even if I'd been to a hundred it wouldn't be any easier. Stop being such a baby."

"Why isn't Ray going, do you think?"

"Wasn't invited. Nobody in the family knows him. Ken was fond of you, and Jo thinks you're great." Jo is Laura's sister, and I think she's great. She's like Laura to look at, but she hasn't got the sharp suits, or the sharp tongue, or any of the "A" levels and degrees.

"Nothing more than that?"

"Ken didn't die for your benefit, you know. It's like everyone's a supporting actor in the film of your life story."

Of course. Isn't that how it works for everybody?

"Your dad died, didn't he?"

"Yes. A long time ago. When I was eighteen."

"Did it affect you?" Terrible. Stupid. "For ages?" Saved. Just.

"It still does."

"How?"

"I don't know. I still miss him, and think about him. Talk to him, sometimes."

"What do you say?"

"That's between me and him." But she says it gently, with a little smile. "He knows more about me now that he's dead than he ever did when he was alive."

"And whose fault's that?"

"His. He was Stereotype Dad, you know, too busy, too tired. I used to feel bad about it, after he'd gone, but in the end I realized that I was just a little girl, and quite a good little girl, too. It was up to him, not me."

This is great. I'm going to cultivate friendships with people who have dead parents, or dead friends, or dead partners. They're the most interesting people in the world. And they're accessible, too! They're all around us! Even if astronauts or former Beatles or shipwreck survivors did have more to offer—which I doubt—you never get to meet them anyway. People who know dead people, as Barbra Streisand might have sung but didn't, are the luckiest people in the world.

"Was *he* cremated?"

"Why does it matter?"

"I dunno. Just interested. Because you said you'd been to one cremation, and I was wondering, you know . . ."

"I'd give Laura a couple of days before you start pumping her with questions like this. It's not the kind of life experience that lends itself to idle chatter."

"That's your way of telling me to shut up, right?"

"Right."

Fair enough.

The crematorium is in the middle of nowhere, and we leave the car in a huge, almost empty car park and walk over to the buildings, which are new and horrible, too bright, not serious enough. You can't imagine that they're going to burn people in here; you can imagine, however, some iffy happy-clappy new religious group meeting for a sing-song once a week. I wouldn't have my old man buried here. I reckon I'd need some help from the atmosphere to get a really good head of grief going, and I wouldn't get it from all this exposed brickwork and stripped pine.

. . .

It's a three-chapel multiplex. There is even a sign on the wall telling you what's on in each, and at what time:

CHAPEL 1.	11:30	MR. E. BARKER
CHAPEL 2.	12:00	MR. K. LYDON
CHAPEL 3.	12:00	—

Good news in Chapel 3, at least. Cremation canceled. Reports of death exaggerated, ha ha. We sit down in the reception area and wait while the place starts to fill up. Liz nods to a couple of people, but I don't know them; I try to think of men's names beginning with "E." I'm hoping that an old person is getting the treatment in Chapel 1, because if and when we see the mourners come out, I don't want them to be too distressed. Eric. Ernie. Ebenezer. Ethelred. Ezra. We're all right. We're laughing. Well, not laughing, exactly, but whoever it is is at least four hundred years old, and no one will be grieving too much in those circumstances, will they? Ewan. Edmund. Edward. Bollocks. Could be any age.

No one's crying in the reception area yet, but there are a few people on the edge, and you can see they're going to go over it before the morning is over. They are all middle-aged, and they know the ropes. They talk quietly, shake hands, give wan smiles, kiss, sometimes; and then, for no reason I can see, and I feel hopelessly out of my depth, lost, ignorant, they stand, and troop through the door marked CHAPEL 2.

It's dark in there, at least, so it's easier to get into the mood. The coffin is up at the front, slightly raised off the floor, but

I can't work out what it's resting on; Laura, Jo, and Janet Lydon are in the first row, standing very close, with a couple of men I don't know beside them. We sing a hymn, pray, there's a brief and unsatisfactory address from the vicar, some stuff from his book, and another hymn, and then there's this sudden, heart-stopping clanking of machinery and the coffin disappears slowly through the floor. And as it does so, there's a howl from in front of us, a terrible, terrible noise that I don't want to hear: I can only just tell that it's Laura's voice, but I know that it is, and at that moment I want to go to her and offer to become a different person, to remove all trace of what is me, as long as she will let me look after her and try to make her feel better.

When we get out into the light, people crowd around Laura and Jo and Janet, and hug them; I want to do the same, but I don't see how I can. But Laura sees Liz and me hovering on the fringe of the group, and comes to us, and thanks us for coming, and holds us both for a long time, and when she lets go of me I feel that I don't need to offer to become a different person: it has happened already.

TWENTY-SIX

IT'S easier in the house. You can feel that the worst is over, and there's a tired calm in the room, like the tired calm you get in your stomach when you've been sick. You even hear people talking about other stuff, although it's all big stuff—work, children, life. Nobody's talking about their Volvo's fuel consumption, or the names they'd choose for dogs. Liz and I get ourselves a drink and stand with our backs against a bookcase, right in the far corner away from the door, and we talk occasionally, but mostly we watch people.

It feels good to be in this room, even though the reasons for being here aren't so good. The Lydons have a large Victorian house, and it's old and tatty and full of things—furniture, paintings, ornaments, plants—which don't go together but which have obviously been chosen with care and taste. The room we're in has a huge, weird family portrait on the wall above the fireplace, done when the girls were about ten and eight. They are wearing what look like bridesmaids' dresses, standing self-consciously beside Ken; there's a dog, Allegro, Allie, who died before I came along, in front of them and partially obscuring them. He has his paws up on Ken's midriff, and Ken is ruffling the dog's fur and smiling. Janet is standing a little behind and apart from the other three, watching her husband. The whole family are much thinner (and splotchier, but that's the painting for you) than they are in real life. It's modern art, and bright and fun, and obviously done by someone who knew what they were about (Laura told me that the woman who did it has had exhibitions and all sorts), but it has to take its chances with a stuffed otter, which is on the mantelpiece underneath, and the sort of dark old furniture that I hate. Oh, and there's a hammock in one corner, loaded down with cushions, and a huge bank of new black hi-fi stuff in another corner, Ken's most treasured possession, despite the paintings and the antiques. It's all a mess, but you'd have to love the family that lived here, because you'd just know that they were interesting and kind and gentle. I realize now that I enjoyed being a part of this family, and though I used to moan about coming here for weekends or Sunday afternoons, I was never bored once. Jo comes up to us after a few minutes, and kisses both of us, and thanks us for coming.

"How are you?" Liz asks, but it's the "How are you" that has an emphasis on the "are," which makes the question sound meaningful and sympathetic. Jo shrugs.

"I'm all right. I suppose. And Mum's not too bad, but Laura . . . I dunno."

"She's had a pretty rough few weeks already, without this," says Liz, and I feel a little surge of something like pride: That was *me.* I made her feel like that. Me and a couple of others, anyway, including Laura herself, but never mind. I'd forgotten that I could make her feel anything and, anyway, it's odd to be reminded of your emotional power in the middle of a funeral which, in my limited experience, is when you lose sense of it altogether.

"She'll be OK," says Liz decisively. "But it's hard, when you're putting all your effort into one bit of your life, to suddenly find that it's the wrong bit." She glances at me, suddenly embarrassed, or guilty, or something.

"Don't mind me," I tell them. "Really. No problem. Just pretend you're talking about somebody else." I meant it kindly, honest I did. I was simply trying to say that if they wanted to talk about Laura's love life, any aspect of it, then I wouldn't mind, not today, of all days.

Jo smiles, but Liz gives me a look. "We are talking about somebody else. Laura. Laura and Ray, really."

"That's not fair, Liz."

"Oh?" She raises an eyebrow, as if I'm being insubordinate.

"And don't fucking say 'Oh' like that." A couple of people look round when I use the "f"-word, and Jo puts her hand on my arm. I shake it off. Suddenly, I'm raging and I don't know how to calm down. It seems like I've spent the whole of the last few weeks with someone's hand on my arm: I can't speak to Laura because she lives with somebody else and she calls from phone boxes and she pretends she doesn't, and I can't speak to Liz because she knows about the money and the abortion and me seeing someone else, and I can't speak to Barry and Dick because they're Barry and Dick, and I can't speak to my friends because I don't speak to my friends, and I can't speak now because Laura's father has died, and I just have to take it because otherwise I'm a bad guy, with the emphasis on guy, self-centered, blind, and stupid. Well, I'm fucking *not,* not all the time, anyway, and I know this isn't the right place to say so—I'm not that daft—but when am I allowed to?

"I'm sorry, Jo. I'm really sorry." I'm back to the funeral murmur now, even though I feel like screaming. "But you know, Liz . . . I can either stick up for myself sometimes or I can believe anything you say about me and end up hating myself every minute of the day. And maybe you think I should, but it's not much of a life, you know?"

Liz shrugs.

"That's not good enough, Liz. You're dead wrong, and if you don't know it, then you're dimmer than I thought."

She sighs theatrically, and then sees the look on my face.

"Maybe I've been a little unfair. But is this really the time?"

"Only because it's never the time. We can't go on apologizing all our lives, you know."

"If by 'we' you are referring to men, then I have to say that just the once would do."

I'm not going to walk out of Laura's dad's funeral in a sulk. I'm not going to walk out of Laura's dad's funeral in a sulk. I'm just not.

I walk out of Laura's dad's funeral in a sulk.

. . .

The Lydons live a few miles out of the nearest town, which is Amersham, and I don't know which way the nearest town is anyway. I walk round the corner, and round another corner, and come to some kind of main road, and see a bus stop, but it's not the sort of bus stop that fills you with confidence: there's nobody waiting, and nothing much there—a row of large detached houses on one side of the road, a playing field on the other. I wait there for a while, freezing in my suit, but just as I've worked out that it's the sort of bus stop that requires the investment of a few days, rather than a few minutes, I see a familiar green Volkswagen up the road. It's Laura, and she's come looking for me.

Without thinking, I jump over the wall that separates one of the detached houses from the pavement, and lie flat in somebody's flower bed. It's wet. But I'd rather get soaked to the skin than have Laura go mental at me for disappearing, so I stay there for as long as is humanly possible. Every time I think I have got to the bottom, I find a new way to sink even lower, but I know that this is the worst, and that whatever happens to me from now on, however poor or stupid or single I get, these few minutes will remain with me as a shining cautionary beacon. "Is it better than lying face-down in a flower bed after Laura's dad's funeral?" I shall ask myself when the bailiffs come into the shop, or when the next Laura runs off with the next Ray, and the answer will always, always be "Yes."

When I can't take it anymore, when my white shirt is translucent and my jacket streaked with mud and I'm getting stabbing pains—cramps, or rheumatism, or arthritis, who knows?—in my legs, I stand up and brush myself off; and then Laura, who has obviously been sitting in her car by the bus stop all this time, winds down her window and tells me to get in.

What happened to me during the funeral was something like this: I saw, for the first time, how scared I am of dying, and of other people dying, and how this fear has prevented me from doing all sorts of things, like giving up smoking (because if you take death too seriously or not seriously enough, as I have been doing up till now, then what's the point?), and thinking about my life, especially my job, in a way that contains a concept of the future (too scary, because the future ends in death). But most of all it has prevented me from sticking with a relationship, because if you stick with a relationship, and your life becomes dependent on that person's life, and then they die, as they are bound to do, unless there are exceptional circumstances, e.g., they are a character from a science-fiction novel . . . well, you're up the creek without a paddle, aren't you? It's OK if I die first, I guess, but having to die before someone else dies isn't a necessity that cheers me up much: how do I know when she's going to die? Could be run over by a bus tomorrow, as the saying goes, which means I have to throw myself under a bus today. When I saw Janet Lydon's face at the crematorium . . . how can you be that brave? Now what does she do? To me, it makes more sense to hop from woman to woman until you're too old to do it anymore, and then you live alone and die alone and what's so terrible about that, when you look at the alternatives? There were some nights with Laura when I'd kind of nestle into her back in bed when she was asleep, and I'd be filled with this enormous, nameless terror, except now I have a name for it: Brian. Ha, ha. OK, not really a name, but I could see where it came from, and why I wanted to sleep with Rosie the pain-in-the-arse simultaneous orgasm woman, and if that sounds feeble and self-serving at the same time—oh, right! He sleeps with other women because he has a fear of death!—well, I'm sorry, but that's the way things are.

When I nestled into Laura's back in the night, I was afraid because I didn't want to lose her, and we always lose someone, or they lose us, in the end. I'd rather not take the risk. I'd rather not come home from work one day in ten or twenty years' time to be faced with a pale, frightened woman saying that she'd been shitting blood—*I'm sorry, I'm sorry, but this is what happens to people*—and then we go to the doctor and then the doctor says it's inoperable and then . . . I wouldn't have the guts, you know? I'd probably just take off, live in a different city under an assumed name, and Laura would check in to the hospital to die and they'd say, "Isn't your partner coming to visit?" and she'd say, "No, when he found out about the cancer he left me." Great guy! "Cancer? Sorry, that's not for me! I don't like it!" Best not put yourself in that position. Best leave it all alone.

So where does this get me? The logic of it all is that I play a percentage game. I'm thirty-six now, right? And let's say that most fatal diseases—cancer, heart disease, whatever—hit you after the age of fifty. You might be unlucky, and snuff it early, but the fifty-plus age group get more than their fair share of bad stuff happening to them. So to play safe, you stop then: a relationship every couple of years for the next fourteen years, and then get out, stop dead, give it up. It makes sense. Will I explain this to whomever I'm seeing? Maybe. It's fairer, probably. And less emotional, somehow, than the usual mess that ends relationships. "You're going to die, so there's not much point in us carrying on, is there?" It's perfectly acceptable if someone's emigrating, or returning to their own country, to stop a relationship on the grounds that any further involvement would be too painful, so why not death? The separation that death entails has got to be more painful than the separation of emigration, surely? I mean, with emigration, you can always go with her. You can always say to yourself, "Oh, fuck it, I'll pack it all in and go and be a cowboy in Texas/tea-picker in India," etc. You can't do that with the big D, though, can you? Unless you take the Romeo route, and if you think about it . . .

"I thought you were going to lie in that flower bed all afternoon."

"Eh? Oh. Ha ha. No. Ha." Assumed nonchalance is tougher than it looks in this sort of situation, although lying in a stranger's flower bed to hide from your ex-girlfriend on the day that her dad is buried—burned—is probably not a sort, a *genre* of situation at all, more a one-off, nongeneric thing.

"You're soaking."

"Mmm."

"You're also an idiot."

There will be other battles. There's not much point in fighting this one, when all the evidence is conspiring against me.

"I can see why you say that. Look, I'm sorry. I really am. The last thing I wanted was . . . that's why I went, because . . . I lost it, and I didn't want to blow my top in there, and . . . look, Laura, the reason I slept with Rosie and mucked everything up was because I was scared that you'd die. Or I was scared of you dying. Or whatever. And I know what that sounds like, but . . ." It all dries up as easily as it popped out, and I just stare at her with my mouth open.

"Well, I will die. Nothing much has changed on that score."

"No, no, I understand completely, and I'm not expecting you to tell me anything different. I just wanted you to know, that's all."

"Thank you. I appreciate it."

She's making no move to start the car.

"I can't reciprocate."

"How do you mean?"

"I didn't sleep with Ray because I was scared of you dying. I slept with Ray because I was sick of you, and I needed something to get me out of it."

"Oh, sure, no, I understand. Look, I don't want to take up any more of your time. You get back, and I'll wait here for a bus."

"I don't want to go back. I've thrown a wobbler too."

"Oh. Right. Great. I mean, not great, but, you know."

The rain starts again, and she puts the windscreen

wipers on so that we can see not very much out of the window.

"Who upset you?"

"Nobody. I just don't feel old enough. I want someone to look after me because my dad's died, and there's no one there who can, so when Liz told me you'd disappeared, I used it as an excuse to get out."

"We're a right pair, aren't we?"

"Who upset you?"

"Oh. Nobody. Well, Liz. She was . . ." I can't think of the adult expression, so I use the one closest to hand. "She was picking on me."

Laura snorts. "She was picking on you, and you're sneaking out on her."

"That's about the size of it."

She gives a short, mirthless laugh. "It's no wonder we're all in such a mess, is it? We're like Tom Hanks in *Big*. Little boys and girls trapped in adult bodies and forced to get on with it. And it's much worse in a real life, because it's not just snogging and bunk beds, is it? There's all this as well." She gestures through the windscreen at the field and the bus stop and a man walking his dog, but I know what she means. "I'll tell you something, Rob. Walking out of that funeral was the worst thing I've ever done, and also the most exhilarating. I can't tell you how good and bad I felt. Yes I can: I felt like a baked Alaska."

"It's not like you walked out of the funeral, anyway. You walked out of the party thing. That's different."

"But my mum, and Jo, and . . . they'll never forget it. I don't care, though. I've thought so much about him and talked so much about him, and now our house is full of people who want to give me time and opportunity to think and talk about him some more, and I just wanted to scream."

"He'd understand."

"D'you think? I'm not sure I would. I'd want people to stay to the bitter end. That'd be the least they could do."

"Your dad was nicer than you, though."

"He was, wasn't he?"

"About five or six times as nice."

"Don't push your luck."

"Sorry."

We watch a man trying to light a cigarette while holding a dog lead, a newspaper, and an umbrella. It can't be done, but he won't give up.

"When are you going to go back, actually?"

"I don't know. Sometime. Later. Listen, Rob, would you sleep with me?"

"What?"

"I just feel like I want sex. I want to feel something else apart from misery and guilt. It's either that or I go home and put my hand in the fire. Unless you want to stub cigarettes out on my arm."

Laura isn't like this. Laura is a lawyer by profession and a lawyer by nature, and now she's behaving as though she's after a supporting role in a Harvey Keitel movie.

"I've only got a couple left. I'm saving them for later."

"It'll have to be the sex, then."

"But where? And what about Ray? And what about . . ." I want to say "everything." What about everything?

"We'll have to do it in the car. I'll drive us somewhere."

She drives us somewhere.

I know what you're saying: *You're a pathetic fantasist, Fleming, you wish, in your dreams,* etc. But I would never in a million years use anything that has happened to me today as the basis for any kind of sexual fantasy. I'm wet, for a start, and though I appreciate that the state of wetness has any number of sexual connotations, it would be tough for even the most determined pervert to get himself worked up about my sort of wetness, which involves cold, irritation (my suit trousers are unlined, and my legs are being rubbed raw), bad smells (none of the major perfume makers has ever tried to capture the scent of wet trousers, for obvious reasons), and there are bits of foliage hanging off me. And I've never had any ambition to do it in a car (my fantasies have always, always involved beds) and the funeral may have had a funny effect on the daughter of the deceased, but for me it's been a bit of a downer, quite frankly, and I'm not too sure how I feel about sex with Laura when she's living with someone else (is he better is he better is he better?), and anyway . . .

She stops the car, and I realize we've been bumping along for the last minute or two of the journey.

"Dad used to bring us here when we were kids."

We're by the side of a long, rutted dirt road that leads up to a large house. There's a jungle of long grass and bushes on one side of the road, and a row of trees on the other; we're on the tree side, pointing toward the house, tilting into the road.

"It used to be a little private prep school, but they went bust years ago, and it's sat empty ever since."

"What did he bring you here for?"

"Just a walk. In the summer there were blackberries, and in the autumn there were chestnuts. This is a private road, so it made it more exciting."

Jesus. I'm glad I know nothing about psychotherapy, about Jung and Freud and that lot. If I did, I'd probably be extremely frightened by now: the woman who wants to have sex in the place where she used to go for walks with her dead dad is probably very dangerous indeed.

It's stopped raining, but the drips from the trees are bouncing off the roof, and the wind is knocking hell out of the branches, so every now and again large chunks of foliage fall on us as well.

"Do you want to get in the back?" Laura asks, in a flat, distracted voice, as if we're about to pick someone else up.

"I guess so. I guess that would be easier."

She's parked too close to the trees, so she has to clamber out my side.

"Just shift all that stuff on to the back shelf."

There's a big road map, a couple of empty cassette cases, an opened bag of Opal Fruits, and a handful of candy wrappers. I take my time getting them out of the way.

"I knew there was a good reason for putting on a skirt this morning," she says as she gets in. She leans over and kisses me on the mouth, tongues and everything, and I can feel some interest despite myself.

"Just stay there." She makes some adjustments to her dress and sits on top of me. "Hello. It doesn't seem so long ago that I looked at you from here." She smiles at me, kisses me again, reaches underneath her for my fly. And then there's foreplay and stuff, and then—I don't know why—I remember something you're supposed to remember but only rarely do.

"You know with Ray . . ."

"Oh, Rob, we're not going to go through that again."

"No, no. It's not . . . are you still on the pill?"

"Yes, of course. There's nothing to worry about."

"I didn't mean that. I mean . . . was that all you used?"

She doesn't say anything, and then she starts to cry.

"Look, we can do other things," I say. "Or we can go into town and get something."

"I'm not crying because we can't do it," she says. "It's not that. It's just that . . . I lived with you. You were my partner just a few weeks ago. And now you're worried I might kill you, and you're entitled to worry. Isn't that a terrible thing? Isn't that sad?" She shakes her head and sobs, and climbs off me, and we sit there side by side in the backseat saying nothing, just watching the drips crawl down the windows.

Later, I wonder whether I was really worried about where Ray has been. Is he bisexual, or an intravenous drug user? I doubt it. (He wouldn't have the guts for either.) Has he ever slept with an intravenous drug user, or has he ever slept with someone who's slept with a bisexual male? I have no idea, and that ignorance gives me every right to insist on protection. But in truth it was the symbolism that interested me more than the fear. I wanted to hurt her, on this day of all days, just because it's the first time since she left that I've been able to.

. . .

We drive to a pub, a twee little mock-country place that serves nice beer and expensive sandwiches and sit in a corner and talk. I buy some more fags and she smokes half of them or, rather, she lights one, takes a drag or two, grimaces, stubs it out and then five minutes later takes another. She stubs them out with such violence that they cannot be salvaged, and when she does it I can't concentrate on what she's saying, because I'm too busy watching my fags disappear. Eventually she notices and says she'll buy me some more and I feel mean.

We talk about her dad, mostly, or rather, what life will be like without him. And then we talk about what life will be like generally without dads, and whether it's the thing that makes you feel grown-up, finally. (Laura thinks not, on the evidence available to date.) I don't want to talk about this stuff, of course: I want to talk about Ray and me and whether we'll ever come as close to having sex again and whether the warmth and intimacy of this conversation means anything, but I manage to hold myself back.

And then, just as I have begun to accept that none of this is going to be about me me me, she sighs, and slumps back against her chair, and says, half smiling, half despairing, "I'm too tired not to go out with you."

There's a kind of double negative here—"too tired" is a negative because it's not very positive—and it takes me a while to work out what she means.

"So, hold on: if you had a bit more energy, we'd stay split. But as it is, what with you being wiped out, you'd like us to get back together."

She nods. "Everything's too hard. Maybe another time I

would have had the guts to be on my own, but not now I haven't."

"What about Ray?"

"Ray's a disaster. I don't know what that was all about, really, except sometimes you need someone to lob into the middle of a bad relationship like a hand grenade, and blow it all apart."

I'd like to talk, in some detail, about all the ways in which Ray is a disaster; in fact, I'd like to make a list on the back of a beermat and keep it forever. Maybe another time.

"And now you're out of the bad relationship, and you have blown it all apart, you want to be back in it, and put it back together again."

"Yes. I know none of this is very romantic, and there will be romantic bits at some stage, I'm sure. But I need to be with someone, and I need to be with someone I know and get on with OK, and you've made it clear that you want me back, so . . ."

And wouldn't you know it? Suddenly I feel panicky, and sick, and I want to get record label logos painted on my walls and sleep with American recording artists. I take Laura's hand and kiss her on the cheek.

There's a terrible scene back at the house, of course. Mrs. Lydon is in tears, and Jo is angry, and the few guests that are left stare into their drinks and don't say anything. Laura takes her mum through to the kitchen and shuts the door, and I stand in the sitting room with Jo, shrugging my shoulders and shaking my head and raising my eyebrows and shifting from foot to foot and doing anything else I can think of to suggest embarrassment, sympathy, disapproval, and misfortune. When my eyebrows are sore, and I have nearly shaken my head off its hinges, and I have walked the best part of a mile on the spot, Laura emerges from the kitchen in a state and tugs me by the arm.

"We're going home," she says, and that is how our relationship resumes its course.

TWENTY-SEVEN

conversations:

1. (Third day, out for a curry, Laura paying.)

"I'll bet you did. I'll bet you sat there, five minutes after I'd gone, smoking a *fag*"—she always emphasizes the word, to show that she disapproves—"and thinking to yourself, cor, this is all right, I can cope with this. And then you sat and thought up some stupid idea for the flat . . . I know, I know, you were going to get some guy to paint record label logos on the wall before I moved in, weren't you? I'll bet you sat there, smoking a *fag,* and thinking, I wonder if I've still got that guy's phone number?"

I look away so she can't see me smile, but it's no use. "God, I'm so right, aren't I? I'm so right I can't believe it. And then—hold on, hold on—" she puts her fingers to her temples, as if she's receiving the images into her brain—"and then you thought, plenty more fish in the sea, been feeling like a bit of new for ages, and then you stuck something on the hi-fi, and everything was right in your pathetic little world."

"And then what?"

"And then you went to work, and you didn't say anything to Dick or Barry, and you were fine until Liz let the cat out of the bag, and then you became suicidal."

"And then I slept with someone else."

She doesn't hear me.

"When you were fucking around with that prat Ray, I was screwing an American singer-songwriter who looks like Susan Dey out of *L.A. Law.*"

She still doesn't hear me. She just breaks off a bit of papadum and dips it in the mango chutney.

"And I was all right. Not too bad. Quite good, in fact."

No reaction. Maybe I should try again, this time out loud, with my voice instead of the inside of my head.

"You know it all, don't you?"

She shrugs, and smiles, and makes her smug face.

2. (Seventh day, bed, afterward.)

"You don't really expect me to tell you."

"Why not?"

"Because what purpose would it serve? I could describe every second of every time, and there weren't that many of them, and you'd be hurt, but you still wouldn't understand the first thing about anything that mattered."

"I don't care. I just want to know."

"Want to know what?"

"What it was like."

She huffs. "It was like sex. What else could it be like?"

Even this answer I find hurtful. I had hoped it wouldn't be like sex at all; I had hoped that it would be like something much more boring or unpleasant, instead.

"Was it like good sex or was it like bad sex?"

"What's the difference?"

"You know the difference."

"I never asked you how your extracurricular activities went."

"Yes, you did. I remember. 'Have a nice time, dear?' "

"It was a rhetorical question. Look, we're OK now. We've just had a nice time. Let's leave it at that."

"OK, OK. But the nice time we've just had . . . was it nicer, as nice, or less nice than the nice times you were having a couple of weeks ago?"

She doesn't say anything.

"Oh, come on, Laura. Just say anything. Fib, if you want. It'd make me feel better, and it'd stop me asking you questions."

"I was going to fib, and now I can't, because you'd know I was fibbing."

"Why would you want to fib, anyway?"

"To make you feel better."

And so it goes. I want to know (except, of course, I don't want to know) about multiple orgasms and ten times a night and blow jobs and positions that I've never even heard of, but I haven't the courage to ask, and she would never tell me. I know they've done it, and that's bad enough; all I can hope for now is damage limitation. I want her to say that it was dull, that it was bog-standard, lie-back-and-think-of-Rob sort of sex, that Meg Ryan had more fun in the delicatessen than Laura had at Ray's place. Is that too much to ask?

She props herself up on an elbow and kisses me on the chest. "Look, Rob. It happened. It was good that it happened in lots of ways, because we were going nowhere, and now we might be going somewhere. And if great sex was as important as you think it is, and if I'd had great sex, then we wouldn't be lying here now. And that's my last word on the subject, OK?"

"OK." There could have been worse last words, although I know she's not saying anything much.

"I wish your penis was as big as his, though."

This, it would appear, judging from the length and volume of the ensuing snorts, giggles, guffaws, and roars, is the funniest joke Laura has ever made in her life—the funniest joke that anyone has ever made, in fact, in the entire history of the world. It is an example, I presume, of the famous feminist sense of humor. Hilarious or what?

3. (Driving down to her mum's, second weekend, listening to a compilation tape she has made that features Simply Red *and* Genesis *and* Art Garfunkel singing "Bright Eyes.")

"I don't care. You can make all the faces you want. That's one thing that's changing around here. *My* car. *My* car stereo. *My* compilation tape. On the way to see *my* parents."

We let the *s* hang in the air, watch it try to crawl back where it came from, and then forget it. I give it a moment before I return to fight possibly the bitterest of all the bitter battles between men and women.

"How can you like Art Garfunkel *and* Solomon Burke? It's like saying you support the Israelis *and* the Palestinians."

"It's not like saying that at all, actually, Rob. Art Garfunkel and Solomon Burke make pop records, the Israelis and the Palestinians don't. Art Garfunkel and Solomon Burke are not engaged in a bitter territorial dispute, the Israelis and the Palestinians are. Art Garfunkel and Solomon Burke . . ."

"OK, OK. But . . ."

"And who says I like Solomon Burke, anyway?"

This is too much.

"Solomon Burke! 'Got to Get You off My Mind'! That's our song! Solomon Burke is responsible for our entire relationship!"

"Is that right? Do you have his phone number? I'd like a word with him."

"But don't you remember?"

"I remember the song. I just couldn't remember who sang it."

I shake my head in disbelief.

"See, this is the sort of moment when men just want to give up. Can you really not see the difference between 'Bright Eyes' and 'Got to Get You off My Mind'?"

"Yes, of course. One's about rabbits and the other has a brass band playing on it."

"A brass band! A brass band! It's a *horn section*! Fucking hell."

"Whatever. I can see why you prefer Solomon to Art. I understand, really I do. And if I was asked to say which of the two was better, I'd go for Solomon every time. He's authentic, and black, and legendary, and all that sort of thing. But I like 'Bright Eyes.' I think it's got a pretty tune, and beyond that, I don't really care. There are so many other things to worry about. I know I sound like your mum, but they're only pop records, and if one's better than the other, well, who cares, really, apart from you and Barry and Dick? To me, it's like arguing the difference between McDonald's and Burger King. I'm sure there must be one, but who can be bothered to find out what it is?"

The terrible thing is, of course, that I already know the difference, that I have complicated and informed views on the subject. But if I start going on about BK Broilers versus Quarter Pounders with Cheese, we will both feel that I have somehow proved her point, so I don't bother.

But the argument carries on, goes around corners, crosses the road, turns back on itself, and eventually ends up somewhere neither of us has ever been before—at least, not sober, and not during daylight hours.

"You used to care more about things like Solomon Burke than you do now," I tell her. "When I first met you, and I made you that tape, you were really enthused. You said—and I quote—'It was so good that it made you ashamed of your record collection.' "

"Shameless, wasn't I?"

"What does that mean?"

"Well, I fancied you. You were a DJ, and I thought you were groovy, and I didn't have a boyfriend, and I wanted one."

"So you weren't interested in the music at all?"

"Well, yes. A bit. And more so then than I am now. That's life, though, isn't it?"

"But you see . . . *That's all there is of me.* There isn't anything else. If you've lost interest in that, you've lost interest in everything. What's the point of us?"

"You really believe that?"

"Yes. Look at me. Look at the flat. What else has it got, apart from records and CDs and tapes?"

"And do you like it that way?"

I shrug. "Not really."

"That's the point of us. You have potential. I'm here to bring it out."

"Potential as what?"

"As a human being. You have all the basic ingredients. You're really very likable, when you put your mind to it. You make people laugh, when you can be bothered, and you're kind, and when you decide you like someone then that person feels as though she's the center of the whole world, and that's a very sexy feeling. It's just that most of the time you can't be bothered."

"No," is all I can think of to say.

"You just . . . you just don't *do* anything. You get lost in your head, and you sit around thinking instead of getting on with something, and most of the time you think rubbish. You always seem to miss what's really happening."

"This is the second Simply Red song on this tape. One's

unforgivable. Two's a war crime. Can I fast-forward?" I fast-forward without waiting for a reply. I stop on some terrible post-Motown Diana Ross thing, and I groan. Laura plows on regardless.

"Do you know that expression, 'Time on his hands and himself on his mind'? That's you."

"So what should I be doing?"

"I don't know. Something. Working. Seeing people. Running a scout troop, or running a club even. Something more than waiting for life to change and keeping your options open. You'd keep your options open for the rest of your life, if you could. You'll be lying on your deathbed, dying of some smoking-related disease, and you'll be thinking, 'Well, at least I've kept my options open. At least I never ended up doing something I couldn't back out of.' And all the time you're keeping your options open, you're closing them off. You're thirty-six and you don't have children. So when are you going to have them? When you're forty? Fifty? Say you're forty, and say your kid doesn't want kids until *he's* thirty-six. That means you'd have to live much longer than your allotted three-score years and ten just to catch so much as a *glimpse* of your grandchild. See how you're denying yourself things?"

"So it all boils down to that."

"What?"

"Have kids or we split up. The oldest threat in the book."

"Fuck *off,* Rob. That's not what I'm saying to you. I don't care whether you want kids or not. I do, I know that, but I don't know whether I want them with you, and I don't know whether you want them at all. I've got to sort that out for myself. I'm just trying to wake you up. I'm just trying to show you that you've lived half your life, but for all you've got to show for it you might as well be nineteen, and I'm not talking about money or property or furniture."

I know she's not. She's talking about detail, clutter, the stuff that stops you floating away.

"It's easy for you to say that, isn't it, Mzzzz. Hot Shot City Lawyer. It's not my fault that the shop isn't doing very well."

"Jesus Christ." She changes gears with an impressive violence, and doesn't speak to me for a while. I know we nearly got somewhere; I know that if I had any guts I would tell her that she was right, and wise, and that I needed and loved her, and I would have asked her to marry me or something. It's just that, you know, I want to keep my options open, and anyway, there's no time, because she hasn't finished with me yet.

"Do you know what really annoys me?"

"Yeah. All the stuff you just told me. About the way I keep my options open and all that."

"Apart from that."

"Fucking hell."

"I can tell you exactly—exactly—what's wrong with you and what you should be doing about it, and you couldn't even begin to do the same for me. Could you?"

"Yeah."

"Go on, then."

"You're fed up with your job."

"And that's what's wrong with me, is it?"

"More or less."

"See? You haven't got a clue."

"Give me a chance. We've only just started living together again. I'll probably spot something else in a couple of weeks."

"But I'm not even fed up with my job. I quite enjoy it, in fact."

"You're just saying that to make me look stupid."

"No, I'm not. I enjoy my work. It's stimulating, I like the people I work with, I've got used to the money . . . but I don't like liking it. It confuses me. I'm not who I wanted to be when I grew up."

"Who did you want to be?"

"Not some woman in a suit, with a secretary and half an eye on a partnership. I wanted to be a legal-aid lawyer with a DJ boyfriend, and it's all going wrong."

"So find yourself a DJ. What do you want me to do about it?"

"I don't want you to do anything about it. I just want you to see that I'm not entirely defined by my relationship with you. I want you to see that just because we're getting sorted out, it doesn't mean that I'm getting sorted out. I've got other doubts and worries and ambitions. I don't know what kind of life I want, and I don't know what sort of house I want to live in, and the amount of money I'll be making in two or three years frightens me, and . . ."

"Why couldn't you have just come out with it in the first place? How am I supposed to guess? What's the big secret?"

"There's no secret. I'm simply pointing out that what happens to us isn't the whole story. That I continue to exist even when we're not together."

I would have worked that out for myself, in the end. I

would have seen that just because I go all fuzzy around the edges when I don't have a partner, it doesn't mean that everybody else does.

4. (In front of the TV, the following evening.)

". . . somewhere nice. Italy. The States. The West Indies, even."

"Excellent idea. What I'll do is, tomorrow I'll get hold of a box full of mint Elvis Presley 78s on Sun, and I'll pay for it that way." I remember the Wood Green lady with the errant husband and the amazing singles collection, and feel a quick pang of regret.

"I presume that's some kind of sarcastic male record collector joke."

"You know how broke I am."

"You know I'll pay for you. Even though you still owe me money. What's the point of me doing this job if I have to spend my holiday in a tent on the Isle of Wight?"

"Oh yeah, and where am I going to find the money for half a tent?"

We watch Jack Duckworth trying to hide a fifty-pound note he won on the horses from Vera.

"It doesn't matter, you know, about the money. I don't care how little you earn. I'd like you to be happier in your work, but beyond that you can do what you like."

"But it wasn't supposed to be like this. When I met you we were the same people, and now we're not, and . . ."

"How were we the same people?"

"You were the sort of person that came to the Groucho, and I was the sort of person that played the records. You wore leather jackets and T-shirts, and so did I. And I still do, and you don't."

"Because I'm not *allowed* to. I do during the evenings."

I'm trying to find a different way of saying that we're not the same people we used to be, that we've grown apart, blah blah blah, but the effort is beyond me.

" 'We're not the same people we used to be. We've grown apart.' "

"Why are you putting on that silly voice?"

"It's supposed to indicate inverted commas. I was trying to find a new way of saying it. Like you tried to find new way of saying that either we have babies or split up."

"I did *not . . .*"

"Just joking."

"So we should pack it in? Is that what you're arguing? Because if you are, I'm going to run out of patience."

"No, but . . ."

"But what?"

"But why doesn't it matter that we're not the same people we used to be?"

"First, I feel I should point out that you are entirely blameless."

"Thank you."

"You are exactly the same person you used to be. You haven't changed so much as a pair of socks in the years I've known you. If we've grown apart, then I'm the one who's done the growing. And all I've done is changed jobs."

"And hairstyles and clothes and attitude and friends and . . ."

"That's not fair, Rob. You know I couldn't go to work

with my hair all spiked. And I can afford to go out shopping more now. And I've met a couple of people I like over the last year or so. Which leaves attitude."

"You're tougher."

"More confident, maybe."

"Harder."

"Less neurotic. Are you intending to stay the same for the rest of your life? Same friends, or lack of them? Same job? Same attitude?"

"I'm all right."

"Yeah, you're all right. But you're not perfect, and you're certainly not happy. So what happens if you *get* happy, and yes I know that's the title of an Elvis Costello album, I used the reference deliberately to catch your attention, do you take me for a complete idiot? Should we split up then, because I'm used to you being miserable? What happens if you, I don't know, if you start your own record label and it's a success? Time for a new girlfriend?"

"You're being stupid."

"How? Show me the difference between you running a record label and me moving from legal aid to the City."

I can't think of one.

"All I'm saying is that if you believe in a long-term monogamous relationship at all, then you have to allow for things happening to people, and you have to allow for things not happening to people. Otherwise what's the use?"

"No use." I say it mock-meekly, but I am cowed—by her intelligence, and her ferocity, and the way she's always right. Or at least, she's always right enough to shut me up.

. . .

5. (In bed, sort of beforehand and sort of during, if you see what I mean, two nights later.)

"I don't know. I'm sorry. I think it's because I feel insecure."

"I'm sorry, Rob, but I don't believe that for a moment. I think it's because you're half-cut. When we've had this sort of trouble before, it's usually been because of that."

"Not this time. This time is because of insecurity." I have trouble with the word *insecurity,* which in my rendition loses its second *i.* The mispronunciation doesn't strengthen my case.

"What would you say you're insecure about?"

I let out a short, mirthless "Ha!," a textbook demonstration of the art of the hollow laugh.

"I'm still none the wiser."

" 'I'm too tired to split up with you.' All that. And Ray, and you seem . . . *cross* with me all the time. Angry that I'm so hopeless."

"Are we giving up on this?" She's referring to the lovemaking, rather than the conversation or the relationship.

"I s'pose." I roll off her, and lie on the bed with an arm around her, looking at the ceiling.

"I know. I'm sorry, Rob. I haven't been very . . . I haven't really given the impression that this is something I want to do."

"And why's that, do you think?"

"Hold on. I want to try to explain this properly. OK. I thought that we were bound by one simple little cord, our relationship, and if I cut it then that would be that. So I cut it, but that wasn't that. There wasn't just one cord, there were hundreds, thousands, everywhere I turned—Jo going quiet when I said we'd split up, and me feeling funny on your birthday, and me feeling funny . . . not *during* sex with Ray, but afterwards, and I felt sick when I played a tape you'd made me that was in the car, and I kept wondering how you were and . . . oh, millions of things. And then you were more upset than I thought you'd be, and that made it harder . . . and then on the day of the funeral . . . it was me that wanted you to be there, not my mum. I mean, she was quite pleased, I think, but it never occurred to me to ask Ray, and that's when I felt tired. I wasn't prepared to do all that work. It wasn't worth it, just to be shot of you." She laughs a little.

"This is the nice way of saying it?"

"You know I'm not very good at slushy stuff." She kisses me on the shoulder.

You hear that? She's not very good at slushy stuff? That, to me, is a problem, as it would be to any male who heard Dusty Springfield singing "The Look of Love" at an impressionable age. That was what I thought it was all going to be like when I was married (I called it "married" then—I call it "settled" or "sorted" now). I thought there was going to be this sexy woman with a sexy voice and lots of sexy eye makeup whose devotion to me shone from every pore. And there is such a thing as the look of love—Dusty didn't lead us up the garden path entirely—it's just that the look of love isn't what I expected it to be. It's not huge eyes almost bursting with longing situated somewhere in the middle of a double bed with the covers turned down invitingly; it's just as likely to be the look of benevolent indulgence that a mother gives a toddler, or a look of amused exasperation, even a look of pained concern. But the Dusty Springfield look of love? Forget it. As mythical as the exotic underwear.

Women get it wrong when they complain about media images of women. Men understand that not everyone has Bardot's breasts, or Jamie Lee Curtis's neck, or Cindy Crawford's bottom, and we don't mind at all. Obviously we'd take Kim Basinger over Phyllis Diller, just as women would take Keanu Reeves over Sergeant Bilko, but it's not the body that's important, it's the level of abasement. We worked out very quickly that Bond girls were out of our league, but the realization that women don't ever look at us the way Ursula Andress looked at Sean Connery, or even in the way that Doris Day looked at Rock Hudson, was much slower to arrive, for most of us. In my case, I'm not at all sure that it ever did.

I'm beginning to get used to the idea that Laura might be the person I spend my life with, I think (or at least, I'm beginning to get used to the idea that I'm so miserable without her that it's not worth thinking about alternatives). But it's much harder to get used to the idea that my little-boy notion of romance, of negliges and candlelit dinners at home and long, smoldering glances, had no basis in reality at all. That's what women ought to get all steamed up about; that's why we can't function properly in a relationship. It's not the cellulite or the crow's feet. It's the . . . the . . . the *disrespect.*

TWENTY-EIGHT

ABOUT two weeks in, after a lot of talking and a lot of sex and a tolerable amount of arguing, we go for dinner with Laura's friends Paul and Miranda. This might not sound very exciting to you, but it's a really big deal to me: it's a vote of confidence, an endorsement, a sign to the world that I'm going to be around for a few months at least. Laura and I have never seen eye-to-eye about Paul and Miranda, not that I've ever met either of them. Laura and Paul joined the law firm around the same time, and they got on well, so when she (and I) were asked round, I refused to go. I didn't like the sound of him, or Laura's enthusiasm for him, although when I heard that there was a Miranda I could see I was being stupid, so I made up a load of other stuff. I said that he sounded typical of the sort of people she was going to be meeting all the time now that she had this flash new job, and I was being left behind, and she got cross, so I upped the ante and prefaced his name with the words "this" and "wanker" whenever I mentioned him, and I attributed to him a hoity-toity voice and a whole set of interests and attitudes he probably hasn't got, and then Laura got *really* cross and went on her own. And having called him a wanker so many times, I felt that Paul and I had got off on the wrong foot, and when Laura invited them round to ours I went out until two in the morning just to make sure I didn't bump into them, even though they've got a kid and I knew they'd be gone by half-past eleven. So when Laura said we'd been invited again, I knew it was a big deal, not only because she was prepared to give it another go, but because it meant she'd been saying stuff about our living together again, and the stuff she'd been saying couldn't have been all bad.

As we stand on the doorstep of their house (nothing swanky, a three-bedroom terraced in Kensal Green), I fiddle with the fly button on my 501s, a nervous habit that Laura strongly disapproves of, for perhaps understandable reasons. But tonight she looks at me and smiles, and gives my hand (my other hand, the one that isn't scrabbling frantically at my groin) a quick squeeze, and before I know it we're in the house amid a flurry of smiles and kisses and introductions.

Paul is tall and good-looking, with long (untrendy, can't-be-bothered-to-have-it-cut, computer-nerdy long, as opposed to hairdressery long) dark hair and a shadow that's nearer six-thirty than five o'clock. He's wearing a pair of old brown cords and a Body Shop T-shirt depicting something green, a lizard or a tree or a vegetable or something. I wish a few of the buttons on my fly were undone, just so I wouldn't feel overdressed. Miranda, like Laura, is wearing a baggy jumper and leggings, and a pair of pretty cool rimless specs, and she's blond and round and pretty, not quite Roseanne Barr round, but round enough for you to notice straightaway. So I'm not intimidated by the clothes, or by the house, or the people, and anyway, the people are so nice to me that for a moment I almost feel a bit weepy: it's obvious to even the most insecure that Paul and Miranda are delighted that I am here, either because they have decided that I am a Good Thing, or because Laura has told them that she is happy with the way things are (and if I've got it all wrong, and they're just acting, then who cares anyway, when the actors are this good?).

There isn't any what-would-you-call-your-dog stuff, partly because everyone knows what everyone does (Miranda is an English lecturer at a community college), and partly because the evening isn't like that for a moment. They ask about Laura's dad, and Laura tells them about the funeral, or at least some of it, and also some stuff I didn't know—like, she says she felt a little thrill, momentarily, before all the pain and the grief and everything hit her—"Like, God, this is the most grown-up thing that's ever happened to me."

And Miranda talks a bit about her mum dying, and Paul and I ask questions about that, and Paul and Miranda ask questions about my mum and dad, and then it all somehow moves on from there to aspirations, and what we want, and what we're not happy about, and . . . I don't know. It sounds stupid to say it, but despite what we're talking about, I really enjoy myself—I don't feel afraid of anybody, and whatever I say people take seriously, and I catch Laura looking fondly at me from time to time, which helps morale. It's not like anyone says any one thing that's memorable, or wise, or acute; it's more a mood thing. For the first time in my life I felt as though I'm in an episode of *thirtysomething* rather than an episode of . . . of . . . of some sitcom that hasn't been made yet about three guys who work in a record shop and talk about sandwich fillings and sax solos all day, and I love it. And I know *thirtysomething* is soppy and clichéd and American and naff, I can see that. But when you're sitting in a one-bedroom flat in Crouch End and your business is going down the toilet and your girlfriend's gone off with the guy from the flat upstairs, a starring role in a real-life episode of *thirtysomething,* with all the kids and marriages and jobs and barbecues and k.d. lang CDs that this implies, seems more than one could possibly ask of life.

The first time I had a crush on anyone was four or five years before Alison Ashworth came along. We were on holiday in Cornwall, and a couple of honeymooners had the next breakfast table to us, and we got talking to them, and I fell in love with both of them. It wasn't one or the other—it was the unit. (And now that I come to think about it, it was maybe these two as much as Dusty Springfield that gave me unrealistic expectations about relationships.) I think that each was trying, as newlyweds sometimes do, to show that they were brilliant with kids, that he'd make a brilliant dad and she'd make a fantastic mum, and I got the benefit of it: they took me swimming and rock-pooling, and they bought me Sky Rays, and when they left I was heartbroken.

It's kind of like that tonight, with Paul and Miranda. I

fall in love with both of them—with what they have, and the way they treat each other, and the way they make me feel as if I am the new center of their world. I think they're great, and I want to see them twice a week every week for the rest of my life.

Only right at the end of the evening do I realize that I've been set up. Miranda's upstairs with their little boy; Paul's gone to see whether there's any ropy holiday liqueurs moldering in the back of a cupboard anywhere, so that we can stoke up the log-fire glow we all have in our stomachs.

"Go and look at their records," says Laura.

"I don't have to. I am capable of surviving without turning my nose up at other people's record collections, you know."

"Please. I want you to."

So I wander over to the shelf, and turn my head to one side and squint, and sure enough, it's a disaster area, the sort of CD collection that is so poisonously awful that it should be put in a steel case and shipped off to some Third World waste dump. They're all there: Tina Turner, Billy Joel, Kate Bush, Pink Floyd, Simply Red, the Beatles, of course, Mike Oldfield (*Tubular Bells I* and *II*), Meat Loaf . . . I don't have much time to examine the vinyl, but I see a couple of Eagles records, and I catch a glimpse of what looks suspiciously like a Barbara Dickson album.

Paul comes back into the room.

"I shouldn't think you approve of many of those, do you?"

"Oh, I don't know. They were a good band, the Beatles."

He laughs. "We're not very up on things, I'm afraid.

We'll have to come into the shop, and you can put us right."

"Each to his own, I say."

Laura looks at me. "I've never heard you say it before. I thought 'each to his own' was the kind of sentiment that'd be enough to get you hung in the brave new Fleming world."

I manage a crooked smile, and hold out my brandy glass for some ancient Drambuie out of a sticky bottle.

"You did that deliberately," I say to her on the way home. "You knew all along I'd like them. It was a trick."

"Yeah. I tricked you into meeting some people you'd think were great. I conned you into having a nice evening."

"You know what I mean."

"Everybody's faith needs testing from time to time. I thought it would be amusing to introduce you to someone with a Tina Turner album, and then see whether you still felt the same."

I'm sure I do. Or at least, I'm sure I will. But tonight, I have to confess (but only to myself, obviously) that maybe, given the right set of peculiar, freakish, probably unrepeatable circumstances, it's not what you like but what you're like that's important. I'm not going to be the one who explains to Barry how this might happen, though.

TWENTY-NINE

I TAKE Laura to see Marie; she loves her.

"But she's brilliant!" she says. "Why don't more people know about her? Why isn't the pub packed?"

I find this pretty ironic, as I've spent our entire relationship trying to make her listen to people who should be famous but aren't, though I don't bother pointing this out.

"You need pretty good taste to see how great she is, I suppose, and most people haven't got that."

"And she's been to the shop?"

Yeah. I slept with her. Pretty cool, eh?

"Yeah. I served her in the shop. Pretty cool, eh?"

"Starfucker." She claps the back of the hand that's holding the half of Guinness when Marie finishes a song. "Why don't you get her to play in the shop? A personal appearance? You've never done one of those before."

"I haven't been in a position to before."

"Why not? It would be fun. She probably wouldn't even need a mike."

"If she needed a mike in Championship Vinyl, she'd have some kind of major vocal cord disorder."

"And you'd probably sell a few of her tapes, and probably a couple of extra things besides. And you could get it put into the *Time Out* gigs list."

"Ooer, Lady Macbeth. Calm down and listen to the music." Marie's singing a ballad about some uncle who died, and one or two of the people look round when Laura's excitement gets the better of her.

But I like the sound of it. A personal appearance! Like at HMV! (Do people sign cassettes? I suppose they must do.) And maybe if the Marie one goes well, then other people would want to do it—bands maybe, and if it's true about Bob Dylan buying a house in north London . . . well, why not? I know that pop superstars don't often do in-store appearances to help flog secondhand copies of their back-catalogue, but if I could get a shot of that mono copy of *Blonde on Blonde* at an inflated price, I'd go halves with him. Maybe even sixty-forty, if he threw in a signature.

And from a small, one-off acoustic event like Bob Dylan at Championship Vinyl (with a limited-edition live album, maybe? Could be some tricky contractual stuff to deal with, but nothing impossible, I wouldn't have thought), it's easy to see bigger, better, brighter days ahead. Maybe I could reopen the Rainbow? It's only down the road, and nobody else wants it. And I could launch it with a charity one-off, maybe a reenactment of Eric Clapton's Rainbow Concert . . .

We go to see Marie in the interval, when she's selling her tapes.

"Oh, hiii! I saw Rob out there with someone, and I hoped it might be you," she says to Laura, with a big smile.

I was so busy with all the promotion stuff going on in my head that I forgot to be nervous about Laura and Marie face to face (Two Women. One Man. Any fool could see there was going to be trouble, etc.), and already I have some explaining to do. I served Marie in the shop a couple of times, according to me. On what basis, then, was Marie hoping that Laura is Laura? ("That'll be five pounds ninety-nine, please. Oh, my girlfriend's got a wallet like that. My ex-girlfriend, actually. I'd really like you to meet her, but we've split up.")

Laura looks suitably mystified, but plows on.

"I love your songs. And the way you sing them." She colors slightly, and shakes her head impatiently.

"I'm glad you did. Rob was right. You *are* special." ("There's four pounds and a penny change. My ex-girlfriend's special.")

"I didn't realize you two were such pals," says Laura, with more acidity than is good for my stomach.

"Oh, Rob's been a good friend to me since I've been here. And Dick and Barry. They've made me feel real welcome."

"We'd better let Marie sell her tapes, Laura."

"Marie, will you do a PA in Rob's shop?"

Marie laughs. She laughs, and doesn't reply. We stand there foolishly.

"You're kidding me, right?"

"Not really. On a Saturday afternoon, when the shop's busy. You could stand on the counter." This last embellishment is Laura's own, and I stare at her.

Marie shrugs. "OK. But I get to keep any money I make from the tapes."

"Sure." Laura again. I'm still staring at her from before, so I have to content myself with staring at her even harder.

"Thanks, it was nice to meet you."

We go back to where we were standing.

"See?" she says. "Easy."

Occasionally, during the first few weeks of Laura's return, I try to work out what life is like now: whether it's better or worse, how my feelings for Laura have changed, if they have, whether I'm happier than I was, how near I am to getting itchy feet again, whether Laura's any different, what it's like living with her. The answers are easy—better, kind of, yes, not very near, not really, quite nice—but also unsatisfying, because I know they're not answers that come from down deep. But somehow, there's less time to think since she came back. We're too busy talking, or working, or having sex (there's a lot of sex at the moment, much of it initiated by me as a way of banishing insecurity), or eating, or going to the pictures. Maybe I should stop doing these things, so as I can work it all out properly, because I know these are important times. But then again, maybe I shouldn't; maybe this is how it's done. Maybe this is how people manage to have relationships.

. . .

"Oh, great. You never asked us to play here, did you?"

Barry. Idiot. I might have known he'd find something in Marie's imminent in-store performance to moan about.

"Didn't I? I thought I did, and you said no."

"How are we ever going to get going if even our friends won't give us a break."

"Rob let you put the poster up, Barry. Be fair." This is quite assertive for Dick, but there is something in him that doesn't like the idea of Barry's band anyway. For him, I think, a band is too much like action, and not enough like fandom.

"Oh, fucking great. Big fucking deal. A poster."

"How would a band fit in here? I'd have to buy the shop next door, and I'm not prepared to do that just so's you can make a terrible racket one Saturday afternoon."

"We could have done an acoustic set."

"Oh, right. Kraftwerk unplugged. That'd be nice."

This gets a laugh from Dick, and Barry looks round at him angrily.

"Shut up, jerk. I told you, we're not doing the German stuff anymore."

"What would be the point? What do you have to sell? Have you ever made a record? No? Well, there you are, then."

So forceful is my logic that Barry has to content himself with stomping around for five minutes, and then sitting on the counter with his head buried in an old copy of *Hot Press.* Every now and again he says something feeble—"Just because you've shagged her," for example, and, "How can you run a record shop when you have no interest in music at all?" But mostly he's quiet, lost in contemplation of what might have been had I given Barrytown the opportunity to play live in Championship Vinyl.

It's a stupid little thing, this gig. All it will be, after all, is half a dozen songs played on an acoustic guitar in front of half a dozen people. What depresses me is how much I'm looking forward to it, and how much I've enjoyed the pitiful amount of preparation (a few posters, a couple of phone calls to try and get hold of some tapes) it has involved. What if I'm about to become dissatisfied with my lot? What do I do then? The notion that the amount of . . . of *life* I have on my plate won't be enough to fill me up alarms me. I thought we were supposed to ditch anything superfluous and get by on the rest, and that doesn't appear to be the case at all.

The big day itself goes by in a blur, like it must have done for Bob Geldof at Live Aid. Marie turns up, and loads of people turn up to watch her (the shop's packed, and though she doesn't stand on the counter to play, she does have to stand behind it, on a couple of crates we found for her), and they clap, and at the end, some of them buy tapes and a few of them buy other stuff they see in the shop; my expenses came to about ten pounds, and I sell thirty or forty quid's worth of stock, so I'm laughing. Chuckling. Smiling broadly, anyway.

Marie flogs the stuff for me. She plays about a dozen songs, only half of which are her own; before she starts, she spends some time rummaging through the browsing racks checking that I've got all the cover versions she was intending to play, and writing down the names and the prices of the albums they come from. If I haven't got it, she crosses the song off her set list and chooses one I do have.

"This is a song by Emmylou Harris called 'Boulder to Birmingham,' " she announces. "It's on the album *Pieces of the Sky,* which Rob is selling this afternoon for the unbelievable price of five pounds and ninety-nine pence, and you can find it right over there in the 'Country Artists (Female)' section.' This is a song by Butch Hancock called . . ." And at the end, when people want to buy the songs but have forgotten the names, Marie is there to help them out. She's great, and when she sings, I wish that I weren't living with Laura, and that my night with Marie had gone better than it did. Maybe next time, if there is a next time, I won't feel so miserable about Laura going, and then things might be different with Marie, and . . . but I'm always going to feel miserable about Laura going. That's what I've learned. So I should be happy that she's staying, right? That's how it should work, right? And that's how it does work. Kind of. When I don't think about it too hard.

It could be argued that my little event is, on its own terms, more successful than Live Aid, at least from the technical point of view. There are no glitches, no technical fuck-ups (although admittedly it would be hard to see what could go wrong, apart from a broken guitar string, or Marie falling over), and only one untoward incident: two songs in, a familiar voice emerges from the back of the shop, right next to the door.

"Will you play 'All Kinds of Everything'?"

"I don't know that," says Marie sweetly. "But if I did, I'd sing it for you."

"You don't know it?"

"Nope."

"You don't know it?"

"Nope again."

"Jesus, woman, it won the Eurovision Song Contest."

"Then I guess I'm pretty ignorant, huh? I promise that the next time I play live here, I'll have learned it."

"I should fockin' hope so."

And then I push through to the door, and Johnny and I do our little dance, and I shove him out. But it's not like Paul McCartney's microphone conking out during "Let It Be," is it?

"I had a terrific time," says Marie afterwards. "I didn't think it would work, but it did. And we all made money! That always makes me feel good."

I don't feel good, not now that it's all over. For an afternoon I was working in a place that other people wanted to come to, and that made a difference to me—I felt, I felt, I felt, go on say it, *more of a man,* a feeling both shocking and comforting.

Men don't work in quiet, deserted side streets in Holloway: they work in the City or the West End, or in factories, or down mines, or in stations or airports or offices. They work in places where other people work, and they have to fight to get there, and perhaps as a consequence they do not get the feeling that real life is going on elsewhere. I don't even feel as if I'm the center of my own world, so how am I supposed to feel as though I'm the center of anyone else's? When the last person has been ushered out of this place, and I lock the door behind him, I suddenly feel panicky. I know I'm going to have to do something about the shop—let it go, burn it down, whatever—and find myself a career.

THIRTY

BUT

look:

My five dream jobs

1. *New Musical Express*
   journalist, 1976–1979
   Get to meet the Clash,
   Sex Pistols, Chrissie
   Hynde, Danny Baker,
   etc. Get loads of free
   records—good ones, too.
   Go on to host my own
   quiz show or something.
2. Producer, Atlantic
   Records, 1964–1971
   (approx.)

Get to meet Aretha, Wilson Pickett, Solomon Burke, etc. Get loads of free records (probably)—good ones, too. Make piles of money.

3. Any kind of musician (apart from classical or rap)
   Speaks for itself. But I'd have settled just for being one of the Memphis Horns—I'm not asking to be Hendrix or Jagger or Otis Redding.
4. Film director
   Again, any kind, although preferably not German or silent.
5. Architect
   A surprise entry at number 5, I know, but I used to be quite good at technical drawing at school.

And that's it. It's not even as though this list is my *top* five, either: there isn't a number six or seven that I had to omit because of the limitations of the exercise. To be honest, I'm not even that bothered about being an architect—I just thought that if I failed to come up with five, it would look a bit feeble.

It was Laura's idea for me to make a list, and I couldn't think of a sensible one, so I made a stupid one. I wasn't going to show it to her, but something got to me—self-pity, envy, something—and I do anyway.

She doesn't react.

"It's got to be architecture, then, hasn't it?"

"I guess."

"Seven years' training."

I shrug.

"Are you prepared for that?"

"Not really."

"No, I didn't think so."

"I'm not sure I really want to be an architect."

"So you've got a list here of five things you'd do if qualifications and time and history and salary were no object, and one of them you're not bothered about."

"Well, I did put it at number five."

"You'd really rather have been a journalist for the *New Musical Express,* than, say, a sixteenth-century explorer, or king of France?"

"God, yes."

She shakes her head.

"What would you put down, then?"

"Hundreds of things. A playwright. A ballet dancer. A musician, yes, but also a painter or a university don or a novelist or a great chef."

"A chef?"

"Yes. I'd love to have that sort of talent. Wouldn't you?"

"Wouldn't mind. I wouldn't want to work evenings, though." I wouldn't, either.

"Then you might just as well stay at the shop."

"How d'you work that out?"

"Wouldn't you rather do that than be an architect?"

"I suppose."

"Well, there you are then. It comes in at number five in your list of dream jobs, and as the other four are entirely impractical, you're better off where you are."

I don't tell Dick and Barry that I'm thinking of packing it in. But I do ask them for their five dream jobs.

"Are you allowed to subdivide?" Barry asks.

"How d'you mean?"

"Like, does saxophonist and pianist count as two jobs?"

"I should think so."

There's silence in the shop; for a few moments it has become a primary school classroom during a quiet drawing period. Bics are sucked, crossings out are made, brows are furrowed, and I look over shoulders.

"And what about bass guitarist and lead guitarist?"

"I don't know. Just the one, I should think."

"What, so Keith Richards had the same job as Bill Wyman, according to you?"

"I didn't say they've got . . ."

"Someone should have told them that. One of them could have saved himself a lot of trouble."

"What about, say, film reviewer and album reviewer?" says Dick.

"One job."

"Brilliant. That frees me up for other things."

"Oh yeah? Like?"

"Pianist and saxophonist, for a start. And I've still got two places left."

And so on, and on. But the point is, my own list wasn't

freakish. It could have been made by anybody. Just about anybody. Anybody who works here, anyway. Nobody asks how to spell "solicitor." Nobody wants to know whether "vet" and "doctor" count as two choices. Both of them are lost, away, off in recording studios and dressing rooms and Holiday Inn bars.

THIRTY-ONE

LAURA and I go to see my mum and dad, and it feels sort of official, like we're announcing something. I think that feeling comes from them rather than from us. My mum's wearing a dress, and my dad doesn't buzz around doing things to his stupid and vile homemade wine, and nor does he reach for the TV remote control; he sits down in a chair and listens and asks questions, and in a dim light he would resemble an ordinary human being having a conversation with guests.

It's easier to have parents if you've got a girlfriend. I don't know why this is true, but it is. My mum and dad like me more when I have someone, and they seem more comfortable; it's as if Laura becomes a sort of human microphone, somebody we speak into to make ourselves heard.

"Have you been watching *Inspector Morse?*" Laura asks, apropos of nothing.

"No," says my dad. "They're repeats, aren't they? We've got them on video from the first time around." See, this is typical of my dad. It's not enough for him to say that he never watches repeats, that he's the first on the block; he has to add an unnecessary and mendacious embellishment.

"You didn't have a VCR the first time around," I point out, not unreasonably. My dad pretends he hasn't heard.

"What did you say that for?" I ask him. He winks at Laura, as if she's in on a particularly impenetrable family joke. She smiles back. Whose family is it, anyway?

"You can buy them in the shops," he says. "Ready-made ones."

"I know that. But you haven't got any, have you?"

My dad pretends he hasn't heard and, at this point, if it had been just the three of us, we would have had a row. I would have told him that he was mental and/or a liar; my mother would have told me not to make mountains out of molehills, etc., and I would have asked her whether she had to listen to this stuff all day, and we would have taken it on from there.

When Laura's here, though . . . I wouldn't go so far as to say she actively likes my parents, but she certainly thinks that parents generally are a good thing, and that therefore their little quirks and idiocies are there to be loved, not exposed. She treats my father's fibs and boasts and non sequiturs as waves, giant breakers, and she surfs over them with skill and pleasure.

"They're really expensive, though, aren't they, those ready-made ones?" she says. "I bought Rob a couple of things on video for his birthday a few years ago, and they came to nearly twenty-five pounds!"

This is shameless stuff. She doesn't think twenty-five pounds is a lot of money, but she knows they will, and my mum duly gives a loud, terrified, twenty-five-quid shriek. And then we're off onto the prices of things—chocolates, houses, anything we can think of, really—and my dad's outrageous lies are forgotten.

And while we're washing up, more or less the same thing happens with my mum.

"I'm glad you're back to sort him out," she says. "God knows what the flat would look like if he had to look after himself."

This really fucks me off, a) because I'd told her not to mention Laura's recent absence, b) because you don't tell any woman, but especially not Laura, that one of her major talents is looking after me, and c) I'm the tidier one of the two of us, and the flat was actually cleaner during her absence.

"I didn't know you'd been letting yourself in to examine the state of our kitchen, Mum."

"I don't need to, thanks all the same. I know what you're like."

"You knew what I was like when I was eighteen. You don't know what I'm like now, bad luck." Where did that "bad luck"—childish, taunting, petulant—come from? Oh, I know where, really. It came from straight out of 1973.

"He's much tidier than me," says Laura, simply and gravely. I've heard this sentence about ten times, with exactly the same intonation, ever since I was forced to bring Laura here for the first time.

"Oh, he's a good lad, really. I just wish he'd sort himself out."

"He will." And they both look at me fondly. So, yes, I've

been rubbished and patronized and worried over, but there's a glow in the kitchen now, genuine three-way affection, where previously there might have been simply mutual antagonism, ending with my mum's tears and me slamming the door. I do prefer it this way, really; I'm happy Laura's here.

TWENTY-TWO

FLY posters. I'm for them. The only creative idea I have ever had in my life was for an exhibition of fly poster photographs. It would take two or three decades to get enough stuff, but it would look really good when it was finished. There are important historical documents on the window of the boarded-up shop opposite mine: posters advertising a Frank Bruno fight, and an Anti-Nazi rally, and the new Prince single, and a West Indian comedian, and loads of gigs, and in a couple of weeks they will be gone, covered over by the shifting sands of time—or at least, an advert for the new U2 album. You get a sense of the spirit of the age, right? (I'll let you into a secret: I actually started on the project. In 1988 I took about three pictures on my Instamatic of an empty shop on the Holloway Road, but then they let the shop, and I kind of lost enthusiasm. The photos came out OK—OKish, anyway—but no one's going to let you exhibit three photos, are they?)

Anyway, every now and then I test myself: I stare at the shopfront to make sure that I've heard of the bands with gigs coming up, but the sad truth is that I'm losing touch. I used to know everyone, every single name, however stupid, whatever the size of the venue the band was playing. And then, three or four years ago, when I stopped devouring every single word in the music papers, I began to notice that I no longer recognized the names playing some of the pubs and smaller clubs; last year, there were a couple of bands playing at the Forum who meant absolutely nothing to me. The Forum! A fifteen-hundred-capacity venue! One thousand five hundred people going to see a band I'd never heard of! The first time it happened I was depressed for the entire evening, probably because I made the mistake of confessing my ignorance to Dick and Barry. (Barry almost exploded with derision; Dick stared into his drink, too embarrassed for me even to meet my eye.)

Anyway, again. I'm doing my spot-check (Prince is there, at least, so I don't score *nul points*—one day I'm going to score *nul points,* and then I'll hang myself) and I notice a familiar-looking poster. "BY POPULAR DEMAND!" it says. "THE RETURN OF THE GROUCHO CLUB!" And then, underneath, "EVERY FRIDAY FROM 20TH JULY, THE DOG AND PHEASANT." I stand there looking at it for ages, with my mouth open. It's the same size and color as ours used to be, and they've even had the cheek to copy our design and our logo—the Groucho Marx glasses and moustache in the second "o" of "Groucho," and the cigar coming out of the bumcrack (that's probably not the correct technical term, but that's what we used to call it) in the "b" at the end of "club."

On our old posters, there used to be a line at the bottom listing the type of music I played; I used to stick the name of the brilliant, gifted DJ at the end, in the doomed hope of creating a cult following for him. You can't see the bottom of this one because some band has plastered a load of little flyers over it; so I peel them off, and there it is: "STAX ATLANTIC MOTOWN R&B SKA MERSEYBEAT AND THE OCCASIONAL MADONNA SINGLE—DANCE MUSIC FOR OLD PEOPLE—DJ ROB FLEMING." It's nice to see I'm still doing it after all these years.

What's going on? There are only three possibilities, really: (a) this poster has been there since 1986, and fly poster archaeologists have just discovered it; (b) I decided to restart the club, got the posters done, put them up, and then suffered a pretty comprehensive attack of amnesia; (c) someone else has decided to restart the club for me. I reckon that explanation "c" is the best bet, and go home to wait for Laura.

"It's a late birthday present. I had the idea when I was living with Ray, and it was such a good one that I was really annoyed that we weren't together anymore. Maybe that's why I came back. Are you pleased?" she says. She's been out with a couple of people for a drink after work, and she's a bit squiffy.

I hadn't thought about it before, but I am pleased. Nervous and daunted—all those records to dig out, all that equipment to get hold of—but pleased. Thrilled, really.

"You had no right," I tell her. "Supposing . . ." What?

"Supposing I was doing something that couldn't be canceled?"

"What do you ever do that can't be canceled?"

"That's not the point." I don't know why I have to be like this, all stern and sulky and what-business-is-it-of-yours. I should be bursting into tears of love and gratitude, not sulking.

She sighs, slumps back on the sofa, and kicks her shoes off.

"Well, tough. You're doing it."

"Maybe."

One day, when something like this happens, I'm just going to go, thanks, that's great, how thoughtful, I'm really looking forward to it. Not yet, though.

"You know we're doing a set in the middle?" says Barry.

"Like fuck you are."

"Laura said we could. If I helped out with the posters and all that."

"Jesus. You're not going to take her up on it?"

" 'Course we are."

"I'll give you ten percent of the door if you don't play."

"We're getting that anyway."

"What's she fucking playing at? OK, twenty percent."

"No. We need the gig."

"One hundred and ten percent. That's my final offer."

He laughs.

"I'm not kidding. If we get one hundred people paying a

fiver a throw, I'll give you five hundred and fifty pounds. That's how much it means to me not to hear you play."

"We're not as bad as you think, Rob."

"You couldn't be. Look, Barry. There's going to be people from Laura's work there, people who own dogs and babies and Tina Turner albums. How are you going to cope with them?"

"How are they going to cope with us, more like. We're not called Barrytown anymore, by the way. They got sick of the Barry/Barrytown thing. We're called SDM. Sonic Death Monkey."

" 'Sonic Death Monkey.' "

"What do you think? Dick likes it."

"Barry, you're over thirty years old. You owe it to yourself and to your friends and to your mum and dad not to sing in a group called Sonic Death Monkey."

"I owe it to myself to go out on the edge, Rob, and this group really does go out on the edge. Over it, in fact."

"You'll be going fucking right over it if you come anywhere near me next Friday night."

"That's what we want. Reaction. And if Laura's bourgeois lawyer friends can't take it, then fuck 'em. Let 'em riot, we can handle it. We'll be ready." He gives what he fondly imagines to be a demonic, drug-crazed chuckle.

Some people would relish all this. They'd make an anecdote out of it, they'd be getting the phrasing right in their heads even as the pub was being torn apart, even as weeping lawyers with bleeding eardrums were heading for the exits. I am not one of those people. I just gather it all up into a hard ball of nervous anxiety and put it in my gut, somewhere between the belly button and the arsehole, for safe keeping. Even Laura doesn't seem to be that worried.

"It's only the first one. And I've told them they can't go on for longer than half an hour. And OK, you might lose a couple of my friends, but they won't be able to get baby-sitters every week, anyway."

"I've got to pay a deposit, you know. As well as the rental on the room."

"That's all taken care of."

And just that one little sentence sets something off in me. I suddenly feel choked up. It's not the money, it's the way she's thought of everything: one morning I woke up to find her going through my singles, pulling out things that she remembered me playing and putting them into the little carrying cases that I used to use and put away in a cupboard somewhere years ago. She knew I needed a kick up the backside. She also knew how happy I was when I used to do this; and from whichever angle I examine it, it still looks as though she's done it because she loves me.

I cave in to something that has been eating away at me for a while, and put my arms around her.

"I'm sorry I've been a bit of a jerk. I do appreciate what you've done for me, and I know you've done it for the best possible reasons, and I do love you, even though I act as though I don't."

"That's OK. You seem so cross all the time, though."

"I know. I don't get myself."

But if I had to take a wild guess, I'd say that I'm cross

because I know I'm stuck, and I don't like it. It would be nicer, in some ways, if I wasn't so bound to her; it would be nicer if those sweet possibilities, that dreamy anticipation you have when you're fifteen or twenty or twenty-five, even, and you know that the most perfect person in the world might walk into your shop or office or friend's party at any moment . . . it would be nicer if all that were still around somewhere, in a back pocket or a bottom drawer. But it's all gone, I think, and that's enough to make anyone cross. Laura is who I am now, and it's no good pretending otherwise.

THIRTY-THREE

I MEET Caroline when she comes to interview me for her newspaper, and I fall for her straightaway, no messing, while she's at the bar in the pub waiting to buy me a drink. It's a hot day, the first of the year—we go and sit at a trestle table outside and watch the traffic—and she's pink cheeked and wearing a sleeveless, shapeless summer dress with clumpy boots, and for some reason the outfit looks really good on her. But I think I would have gone for anyone today. The weather makes me feel as though I've lost all the dead nerve-ends that were stopping me from feeling and, anyway, how can you fail to fall in love with someone who wants to interview you for a newspaper?

She writes for the *Tufnell Parker,* one of those free magazines full of advertisements that people shove through your door and you shove into the rubbish bin. Actually, she's a student—she's doing a journalism course, and she's on work experience. And, actually, she says her editor isn't sure whether he'll want the piece, because he's never heard of the shop or the club, and Holloway is right on the borderline of his parish, or constituency, or catchment area, or whatever it is. But Caroline used to come to the club in the old days, and loved it, and wanted to give us a plug.

"I shouldn't have let you in," I say. "You must only have been about sixteen."

"Dear me," she says, and I can't see why until I think about what I've just said. I didn't mean it as a pathetic chat-up line, or indeed any sort of a chat-up line; I just meant that if she's a student now, she must have been at school then, even though she looks as though she's in her late twenties or early thirties. When I find out that she's a mature student and she worked as a secretary for some left-wing publishing company, I try to correct the impression I must have given without whiting it out altogether, if you see what I mean, and I make a bit of a hash of it.

"When I said that thing about not letting you in, I didn't mean you look young. You don't." Jesus. "You don't look old, either. You just look as old as you are." Fucking hell. What if she's forty-five? "Well, you do. A bit younger, maybe, but not a lot. Not too much. Just right. I'd forgotten about mature students, you see." I'd rather be a smoothy slimeball than a blundering, semi-coherent, gushing twit any day of the week.

Within minutes, however, I'm looking back fondly on those gushing twit days; they seem infinitely preferable to my next incarnation, Sleaze Man.

"You must have an enormous record collection," Caroline says.

"Yeah," I say. "Do you want to come round and see it?"

I meant it! I meant it! I thought maybe they'd want a picture of me standing by it or something! But when Caroline looks at me over the top of her sunglasses, I rewind and listen to what I said, and let out an audible groan of despair. At least that makes her laugh.

"I'm not usually like this, honest."

"Don't worry. I don't think he'll let me do one of those *Guardian*-type profiles, anyway."

"That wasn't why I was worried."

"It's OK, really."

It's all forgotten, though, with her next question. All my life I have been waiting for this moment, and when it comes I can hardly believe it: I feel unprepared, caught short.

"What are your five favorite records of all time?" she says.

"Pardon?"

"What are your all-time top five records? Your desert island discs, minus—how many? Three?"

"Minus three what?"

"It's eight on *Desert Island Discs,* isn't it? So eight minus five is three, right?"

"Yeah. Plus three, though. Not minus three."

"No, I just said . . . anyway. Your all-time top five records."

"What, in the club, or at home?"

"Is there a difference?"

"OF COURSE . . ." Too shrill. I pretend I've got something in my throat, clear it, and start again. "Well, yeah, a bit. There's my top five dance records of all time, and then there's my top five records of all time. See, one of my favorite-ever records is 'Sin City' by the Flying Burrito Brothers, but I wouldn't play that at the club. It's a country-rock ballad. Everyone would go home."

"Never mind. Any five. So four more."

"What d'you mean, four more?"

"Well, if one of them is this 'Sin City' thing, that leaves four more."

"NO!" This time I make no attempt to disguise the panic. "I didn't say it was in my top five! I just said it was one of my favorites! It might turn out to be number six or seven!"

I'm making a bit of a fool of myself, but I can't help it: this is too important, and I've waited for it too long. But where have they gone, all these records I've had in my head for years, just in case Roy Plomley or Michael Parkinson or Sue Lawley or whoever used to do *My Top Twelve* on Radio One contacted me and asked me in as a late and admittedly unknown replacement for someone famous? For some reason I can think of hardly any record at all apart from "Respect," and that's definitely not my favorite Aretha song.

"Can I go home and work it out and let you know? In a week or so?"

"Look, if you can't think of anything, it doesn't matter. I'll do one. My five favorites from the old Groucho Club or something."

She'll do one! She'll rob me of my one and only chance to make a list for publication in a magazine! I don't think so!

"Oh, I'm sure I can manage something."

"A Horse with No Name." "Beep Beep." "Ma Baker." "My Boomerang Won't Come Back." My head is suddenly flooded with the titles of terrible records, and I'm almost hyperventilating.

"OK, put 'Sin City' down." There must be one other good record in the entire history of pop.

" 'Baby Let's Play House'!"

"Who's that by?"

"Elvis Presley."

"Oh. Of course."

"And . . ." Aretha. Think Aretha.

" 'Think' by Aretha. Franklin."

Boring, but it'll do. Three down. Two left. Come *on,* Rob.

" 'Louie, Louie' by the Kingsmen. 'Little Red Corvette' by Prince."

"Fine. That's great."

"Is that it?"

"Well, I wouldn't mind a quick chat, if you've got time."

"Sure. But is that it for the list?"

"That's five. Do you want to change anything?"

"Did I say 'Stir It Up'? Bob Marley?"

"No."

"I'd better have that in."

"What do you want to leave out?"

"Prince."

"No problem."

"And I'll have 'Angel' instead of 'Think.' "

"Right." She looks at her watch. "I'd better ask you a

couple of questions before I get back. Why did you want to start it up again?"

"It was a friend's idea really." A friend. Pathetic. "She organized it without telling me, as a sort of birthday present. I'd better have a James Brown in there, too, I think. 'Papa's Got a Brand New Bag.' Instead of the Elvis."

I watch her carefully while she does the necessary crossing out and writing in.

"Nice friend."

"Yeah."

"What's her name?"

"Umm . . . Laura."

"Surname?

"Just . . . Lydon."

"And that motto, 'Dance Music for Old People.' Is that yours?"

"Laura's."

"What does it mean?"

"Look, I'm sorry about this, but I'd like 'Family Affair' by Sly and the Family Stone in there. Instead of 'Sin City.' "

She crosses out and scribbles again.

" 'Dance Music for Old People'?"

"Oh, you know . . . a lot of people aren't too old for clubs, but they're too old for acid jazz and garage and ambient and all that. They want to hear a bit of Motown and vintage funk and Stax and a bit of new stuff and so on all jumbled together, and there's nowhere for them."

"Fair enough. That'll do me, I think." She drains her orange juice. "Cheers. I'm looking forward to next Friday. I used to love the music you played."

"I'll make you a tape, if you want."

"Would you? Really? I could have my own Groucho Club at home."

"No problem. I love making tapes."

I know that I'll do it, tonight, probably, and I also know that when I'm peeling the wrapper off the cassette box and press the pause button, it will feel like a betrayal.

"I don't believe it," says Laura when I tell her about Caroline. "How could you?"

"What?"

"Ever since I've known you you've told me that 'Let's Get It On' by Marvin Gaye was the greatest record of all time, and now it doesn't even make your top five."

"Shit. Fuck. Bollocks. I knew I'd . . ."

"And what happened to Al Green? And the Clash? And Chuck Berry? And that man we had the argument about? Solomon somebody?"

Jesus.

I call Caroline the next morning. She's not there. I leave a message. She doesn't call back. I ring again. I leave another message. It's getting kind of embarrassing, but there's no way "Let's Get It On" isn't going in that top five. The third time I try I get through to her, and she sounds embarrassed but apologetic, and when she realizes that I'm only calling to change the list she relaxes.

"OK. Definitive top five. Number one, 'Let's Get It On,'

by Marvin Gaye. Number two, 'This Is the House That Jack Built,' by Aretha Franklin. Number three, 'Back in the USA,' by Chuck Berry. Number four, 'White Man in the Hammersmith Palais,' by the Clash. And the last one, last but not least, ha ha, 'So Tired of Being Alone,' by Al Green."

"I can't change it again, you know. That's it."

"Fine."

"But I was thinking that maybe it would make sense to do your five favorite club records. The editor likes the story, by the way, the Laura stuff."

"Oh."

"Is it possible to get a quick list of floor-fillers off you, or is that too much to ask?"

"No. I know what they are." I spell it all out for her (although when the article appears it says *"In* the Ghetto," like the Elvis song, a mistake that Barry pretends is due to my ignorance).

"I've nearly finished your tape."

"Have you? That's really sweet of you."

"Shall I send it to you? Or do you fancy a drink?"

"Umm . . . A drink would be great. I'd like to buy you one to thank you."

"Great."

Tapes, eh? They work every time.

"Who's it for?" Laura asks when she sees me fiddling around with fades and running orders and levels.

"Oh, just that woman who interviewed me for the free paper. Carol? Caroline? Something like that. She said it would be easier, you know, if she had a feel for the kind of music we play." But I can't say it without blushing and staring intently at the cassette deck, and I know she doesn't really believe me. She of all people knows what compilation tapes represent.

The day before I'm supposed to be meeting Caroline for a drink, I develop all the textbook symptoms of a crush: nervous stomach, long periods spent daydreaming, an inability to remember what she looks like. I can bring back the dress and the boots, and I can see her bangs, but her face is a blank, and I fill it in with some anonymous rent-a-cracker details—pouty red lips, even though it was her well-scrubbed English clever-girl look that attracted me to her in the first place; almond-shaped eyes, even though she was wearing sunglasses most of the time; pale, perfect skin, even though I know she's quite freckly. When I meet her I know there'll be an initial twinge of disappointment—*this* is what all that internal fuss was about?—and then I'll find something to get excited about again: the fact that she's turned up at all, a sexy voice, intelligence, wit, something. And between the second and the third meeting a whole new set of myths will be born.

This time, something different happens, though. It's the daydreaming that does it. I'm doing the usual thing—imagining in tiny detail the entire course of the relationship, from first kiss, to bed, to moving in together, to getting married (in the past I have even organized the track listing of the party tapes), to how pretty she'll look when she's pregnant, to names of children—until suddenly I realize that there's nothing left to actually, like, *happen.* I've done it all, lived through the whole relationship in my head. I've watched the film on fast-forward; I know the whole plot, the ending, all the good bit. Now I've got to rewind and watch it all over again in real time, and where's the fun in that?

And fucking . . . when's it all going to fucking stop? I'm going to jump from rock to rock for the rest of my life until there aren't any rocks left? I'm going to run each time I get itchy feet? Because I get them about once a quarter, along with the utilities bills. More than that, even, during British Summer Time. I've been thinking with my guts since I was fourteen years old, and frankly speaking, between you and me, I have come to the conclusion that my guts have shit for brains.

I know what's wrong with Laura. What's wrong with Laura is that I'll never see her for the first or second or third time again. I'll never spend two or three days in a sweat trying to remember what she looks like, never again will I get to a pub half an hour early to meet her, staring at the same article in a magazine and looking at my watch every thirty seconds, never again will thinking about her set something off in me like "Let's Get It On" sets something off in me. And sure, I love her and like her and have good conversations, nice sex and intense rows with her, and she looks after me and worries about me and arranges the Groucho for me, but what does all that count for, when someone with bare arms, a nice smile, and a pair of Doc Martens comes into the shop and says she wants to interview me? Nothing, that's what, but maybe it should count for a bit more.

Fuck it. I'll post the fucking tape. Probably.

THIRTY-FOUR

SHE'S quarter of an hour late, which means I've been in the pub staring at the same article in a magazine for forty-five minutes. She's apologetic, although not *enthusiastically* apologetic, considering; but I don't say anything to her about it. Today's not the right day.

"Cheers," she says, and clinks her spritzer against my bottle of Sol. Some of her makeup has sweated off in the heat of the day, and her cheeks are pink; she looks lovely. "This is a nice surprise."

I don't say anything. I'm too nervous.

"Are you worried about tomorrow night?"

"Not really." I concentrate on shoving the bit of lime down the neck of the bottle.

"Are you going to talk to me, or shall I get my paper out?"

"I'm going to talk to you."

"Right."

I swish the beer around so it'll get really limey.

"What are you going to talk to me about?"

"I'm going to talk to you about whether you want to get married or not. To me."

She laughs a lot. "Ha ha ha. Hoo hoo hoo."

"I mean it."

"I know."

"Oh, well thanks a fucking bunch."

"Oh, I'm sorry. But two days ago you were in love with that woman who interviewed you for the local paper, weren't you?"

"Not in *love* exactly, but . . ."

"Well, forgive me if I don't feel that you're the world's safest bet."

"Would you marry me if I was?"

"No, I shouldn't think so."

"Right. OK, then. Shall we go home?"

"Don't sulk. What's brought all this on?"

"I don't know."

"Very persuasive."

"Are you persuadable?"

"No. I don't think so. I'm just curious about how one goes from making tapes for one person to marriage proposals to another in two days. Fair enough?"

"Fair enough."

"So?"

"I'm just sick of thinking about it all the time."

"All what?"

"This stuff. Love and marriage. I want to think about something else."

"I've changed my mind. That's the most romantic thing I've ever heard. I do. I will."

"Shut up. I'm only trying to explain."

"Sorry. Carry on."

"See, I've always been afraid of marriage because of, you know, ball and chain, I want my freedom, all that. But when I was thinking about that stupid girl I suddenly saw it was the opposite: that if you got married to someone you know you love, and you sort yourself out, it frees you up for other things. I know you don't know how you feel about me, but I do know how I feel about you. I know I want to stay with you and I keep pretending otherwise, to myself and you, and we just limp on and on. It's like we sign a new contract every few weeks or so, and I don't want that anymore. And I know that if we got married I'd take it seriously, and I wouldn't want to mess about."

"And you can make a decision about it just like that, can you? In cold blood, bang bang, if I do that, then this will happen? I'm not sure that it works like that."

"But it *does,* you see. Just because it's a relationship, and it's based on soppy stuff, it doesn't mean you can't make intellectual decisions about it. Sometimes you just have to, otherwise you'll never get anywhere. That's where I've been going wrong. I've been letting the weather and my stomach muscles and a great chord change in a Pretenders single make up my mind for me, and I want to do it for myself."

"Maybe."

"What d'you mean, maybe?"

"I mean, maybe you're right. But that doesn't help me, does it? You're always like this. You work something out and everyone else has to fall into line. Were you really expecting me to say yes?"

"Dunno. Didn't think about it, really. It was the asking that was the important thing."

"Well, you've asked." But she says it sweetly, as if she knows that what I've asked is a nice thing, that it has some sort of meaning, even though she's not interested. "Thank you."

THIRTY-FIVE

BEFORE the band comes on, everything's brilliant. It used to take a bit of time to warm people up, but tonight they're up for it straightaway. This is partly because most of the crowd here tonight are a few years older than they were a few years ago, if you see what I mean —in other words, this is exactly the same lot, not their 1994 equivalents—and they don't want to wait until half-twelve or one before they get going: they're too tired for that now, and anyway, some of them have to go home to relieve baby-sitters. But mostly it's because there's a real party atmosphere, a genuine make-hay-while-the-sun-shines air of celebration, as though this were a wedding reception or a birthday party, rather than a club that will be here next week and maybe even the week after that.

But I have to say that I'm fucking good, that I haven't lost any of the old magic. One sequence—the

O'Jays ("Back Stabbers"), Harold Melvin and the Bluenotes ("Satisfaction Guaranteed"), Madonna ("Holiday"), "The Ghetto" (which gets a cheer, as if it's my song rather than Donny Hathaway's) and "Nelson Mandela" by the Specials—has them begging for mercy. And then it's time for the band.

I've been told to introduce them; Barry has even written down what I'm supposed to say: "Ladies and gentlemen, be afraid. Be very afraid. Here comes . . . SONIC DEATH MONKEY!" But bollocks to that, and in the end I just sort of mumble the name of the group into the microphone.

They're wearing suits and skinny ties, and when they plug in there's a terrible feedback whine which for a moment I fear is their opening number. But Sonic Death Monkey are no longer what they once were. They are no longer, in fact, Sonic Death Monkey.

"We're not called Sonic Death Monkey anymore," Barry says when he gets to the mike. "We might be on the verge of becoming the Futuristics, but we haven't decided yet. Tonight, though, we're Backbeat. One two three . . . WELL SHAKE IT UP BABY . . ." And they launch into "Twist and Shout," note perfect, and everyone in the place goes mad.

And Barry can sing.

They play "Route 66" and "Long Tall Sally" and "Money" and "Do You Love Me?" and they encore with "In the Midnight Hour" and "La Bamba." Every song, in short, is naff and recognizable, and guaranteed to please a crowd of thirty-somethings who think that hip-hop is something their children do in music-and-movement classes. The crowd is so pleased, in fact, that they sit out the songs I have lined up to get them going again after Sonic Death Monkey has frightened and confused them.

"What was all that about?" I ask Barry when he comes up to the deck, sweaty and half dead and pleased with himself.

"Was that all right?"

"It was better than what I was expecting."

"Laura said we could only play if we learned some proper songs for the evening. But we loved it. The boys are talking about packing up the pop star thing and playing at silver wedding anniversaries."

"How d'you feel about that?"

"All right, yeah. I was beginning to wonder about our musical direction, anyway. I'd rather see people dancing to 'Long Tall Sally' than running for the exit with their hands over their ears."

"You enjoying the club?"

"It's OK. Bit, you know, populist for my taste," he says. He's not joking.

The rest of the evening is like the end of a film. The entire cast is dancing: Dick with Anna (he's sort of standing still and shuffling, Anna is holding his hands and attempting to get him to let go a bit), Marie with T-Bone (Marie is drunk, T-Bone's looking over her shoulder at someone—Caroline!—that he's obviously interested in), Laura with Liz (who's talking animatedly and apparently angrily about something).

I play "Got to Get You off My Mind" by Solomon Burke, and everyone has a go, just out of duty, even though only the best dancers would be able to make something of it, and nobody in the room could claim to be among the best dancers, or even among the most average. When Laura hears the opening bars she spins round and grins and makes several thumbs-up signs, and I start to compile in my head a compilation tape for her, something that's full of stuff she's heard of, and full of stuff she'd play. Tonight, for the first time ever, I can sort of see how it's done.